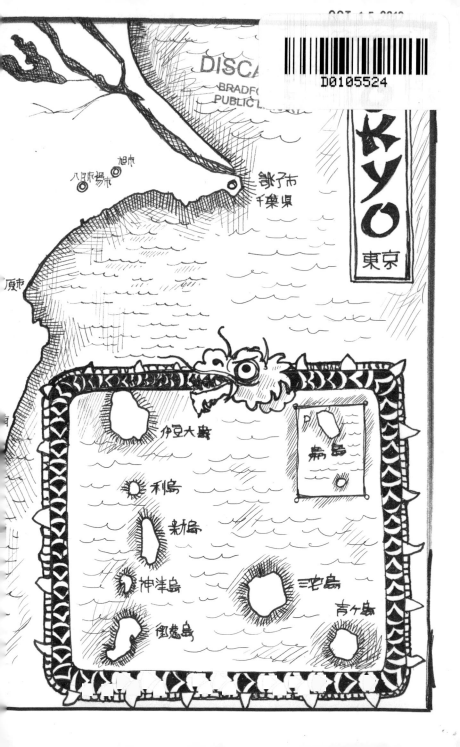

Neil Flambé
AND THE
TOKYO TREASURE

Neil Flambé
AND THE
TOKYO TREASURE

KEVIN SYLVESTER

SIMON & SCHUSTER BOOKS FOR YOUNG READERS
New York London Toronto Sydney New Delhi

SIMON & SCHUSTER BOOKS FOR YOUNG READERS

An imprint of Simon & Schuster Children's Publishing Division

1230 Avenue of the Americas, New York, New York 10020

This book is a work of fiction. Any references to historical events, real people,

or real locales are used fictitiously. Other names, characters, places, and incidents are products of the author's imagination, and any resemblance to actual events

or locales or persons, living or dead, is entirely coincidental.

Copyright © 2012 by Kevin Sylvester

All rights reserved, including the right of reproduction in whole or in part in any form.

SIMON & SCHUSTER BOOKS FOR YOUNG READERS is a trademark of Simon & Schuster, Inc.

For information about special discounts for bulk purchases, please contact Simon &

Schuster Special Sales at 1-866-506-1949 or business@simonandschuster.com.

The Simon & Schuster Speakers Bureau can bring authors to your live event. For more

information or to book an event, contact the Simon & Schuster Speakers Bureau

at 1-866-248-3049 or visit our website at www.simonspeakers.com.

Book design by Laurent Linn.

The text for this book is set in Goudy Old Style.

The illustrations for this book are rendered in pen and ink.

Manufactured in the United States of America

0912 FFG

10 9 8 7 6 5 4 3 2 1

CIP data for this book is available from the Library of Congress.

ISBN 978-1-4424-4288-7

ISBN 978-1-4424-4298-6 (eBook)

FIRST
EDITION

To all the people of Japan

Neil Flambé
AND THE
TOKYO TREASURE

6

Chapter One

Manga Mania

Neil Flambé leaned back in his chair and watched the final panel of *The Chef* fade to black on the laptop screen. His arms hung limply at his sides and his jaw was practically touching his chest. A thousand thoughts were going through his head. Some of them weren't about food, which was unusual. Neil was possibly the best chef in the world, and he was certainly the best teenage chef in the world. Food was his oxygen and it took a lot to distract him.

"What the heck *was* that . . . ?" he said under his breath. He gave his head a shake.

Neil's cousin Larry peeked over the top of the laptop and smiled. "So, waddya think of my manga?"

There was always a little risk in asking Neil what he thought, because he was never shy about answering the question honestly, and loudly. That was one of the many reasons why he had so many enemies.

But this time, Neil wasn't sure *what* he thought about Larry's latest, and possibly craziest, project, his online manga comic, *The Chef*.

"Well?" Larry said, wiggling his eyebrows hopefully. At least that's what Neil thought he was doing. It was hard to see anything under Larry's shaggy hair.

Larry was Neil's older cousin and also his sous-chef, and Neil knew all too well that "crazy projects" and Larry went together like chocolate and chilies. Larry had recently made a foray into the fashion world with his line of me-shirts—T-shirts with messages printed on the inside, so only the person wearing it had any idea what it said. He was always studying some foreign language or trying out some new art project—usually in an effort to impress a pretty face.

Neil could never quite figure out how Larry ever slept. Then again, considering how much coffee Larry consumed—maybe he didn't sleep at all.

Now Larry was trying to get Neil's opinion of *The Chef*, and Neil was searching for an answer.

Neil's immediate reaction was at least partly annoyance. He was a little unhappy that the main character bore a striking, and *unauthorized*, resemblance to a certain teenage wonder chef. And the young woman looked like their friend Isabella Tortellini, but in a skimpy Japanese schoolgirl costume.

Neil wondered if Isabella had seen the comic. He assumed not, since Larry was still alive.

"Let me guess. It's SO good that you're at a loss for words," Larry said with a satisfied grin. "The words you're looking for, by the way, are 'amazing', 'cool', and 'wow.' Feel free to use them."

The words Neil was coming up with, though, were slightly different—"annoyed" and maybe "confused." Did he like the story? Did he hate it? Was it any good? He didn't know. He couldn't concentrate on much past his shock at the whole situation. After all, Neil had only found out about the comic *yesterday*. Larry had dumped the news of its existence on him like a bomb-shell along with other, even more explosive, news— Larry was leaving.

Apparently, Larry and his collaborator Hiro Takoyaki had been posting an online version of *The Chef* for months. Larry wrote the story. Hiro did the pictures. *The Chef* had become a viral sensation and now a Japanese book company was offering them a book deal, but the editors wanted the manuscript ASAP—and suddenly Larry had himself a one-way ticket to Tokyo, courtesy of his partner.

Neil had not looked or sounded happy about this unexpected news. On the other hand, as Larry pointed out, Neil rarely looked or sounded happy.

"Yes, real amazing literature that will soon be a real book." Larry beamed, more than happy to fill the void left by Neil's silence. "And to think it all started with a chance meeting at a comic book convention. Hiro, an illustrator in search of a poet, and me, a poet in search of an illustrator. A match made in manga heaven. But don't worry—I'll try to remember you little people when I'm at the Hollywood premiere of the film version of *The Chef*."

Neil hated to admit it, but he was going to miss Larry. A lot. The pair had just returned from a trip to Paris where they'd been seconds away from dying together on top of a crazy woman's skyscraper. (The woman, Jeanne Valette, had been part of an elaborate thousand-year-old plot against the Flambé family—a plot foiled by Neil and his friends.) With that now in the past, Neil had hoped he and Larry could return to their restaurant forever.

That was also part of his hesitation in giving Larry an answer. If Neil said he liked it, would that encourage Larry to leave? But if he said he hated it, would that convince Larry to stay? Not likely. Neil changed the subject. "Explain, again, why can't you keep writing this comic from here?"

"It'll be way faster if Hiro and I are working together side by side. The publisher wants original stories and artwork by the end of next month, so with time zones and e-mail and stuff it's just way easier to do it in person. He lives right on the coast south of Tokyo. It's beautiful." Larry sighed.

Neil nodded slowly. "Ah . . . cute sister?"

Larry's grin grew improbably bigger. "Her name's Koko. But HE sent me the ticket, remember."

"Why do the characters look so, shall we say, familiar? I've never met this Hiro guy."

Larry shrugged. "You think the Chef looks like you?"

Neil arched an eyebrow. "Is that a joke?"

Larry smiled. "I showed Hiro some pictures of all of us. I guess he liked the way we looked. I know *I'm* handsome."

"For a sheepdog, maybe."

"Woof. And anyway, that's still not an answer. What do you think of the manga?"

Neil stalled for more time while he marshaled his thoughts. An ornate wooden clock above the door chimed two o'clock. Two tiny chefs came out of little doorways and began tenderizing a carved side of beef with tiny mallets. Larry had made the clock in wood shop. He wasn't technically in the class, but the teacher, Caroline Dubois, had been giving him private lessons.

"Um, it's time to prep for dinner," Neil mumbled, standing up.

Larry didn't budge.

"Hey, Gary's on it," Larry said, wagging his thumb over his shoulder toward the kitchen. Gary was the bike courier/drifter that Larry had hired as his own replacement at Chez Flambé. Neil thought Gary looked like a shabbier version of Larry (if that was even possible).

Neil could hear Gary humming away, occasionally washing some vegetable or other and even chopping a few onions. Maybe it was a good thing Neil couldn't see him. He had a sneaking suspicion Gary's so-called "experience" with cooking was limited to shoplifting candy bars and beef jerky.

"Fine. If you say so," Neil said, sitting back down with a thump. Neil had no patience to train another sous-chef. He was sure he'd have to fire Gary sooner rather than later, and searching for a better assistant was going to take him time he didn't have. But he was going to have to make it work for now—he desperately needed to reopen and start making money. Fighting Valette had not been cheap. She'd even arranged for a fake food poisoning scandal and bad reviews—a possibly lethal combination for a restaurant. And Neil had to admit, to himself, that Gary's presence was one more concrete sign that Larry was, in fact, leaving.

Larry snapped his fingers in front of Neil's face. "Hey, chef-boy, wake up. What do you think of *The Chef*?"

"I think . . ." Neil slipped back into silence for a few more seconds.

He wanted to say he hated it, that it was all a stupid idea, and that Larry should stick to cooking, with Neil, in Chez Flambé.

But it didn't stink. In fact, it was pretty good. Praise was never an easy thing for Neil to dole out. So when he did open his mouth, it wasn't praise that came out.

"Avocado," Neil said, finally.

Larry rolled his eyes. "I think you meant awesome. It's pronounced AWE-SOME," Larry said with a smile, shutting the lid of the laptop with a flourish.

"No, I meant avocado."

"Av-o-ca-do," Larry repeated slowly. "Sorry, don't get it."

Neil sighed. "What I mean is, why does the Chef have an exploding avocado?"

"Duh, because it's *cool*."

Neil shook his head and leaned forward in his chair. "No. It's wrong. A pomegranate would make more sense. It's got a harder shell and would make a way better explosive."

"Um, okay." Larry looked skeptical.

"The way Hiro draws the chef's grenade doesn't even make sense."

"How do you mean?"

"He's got the thing exploding all over the place, but an avocado just has one big seed." Neil grew more animated. "Think of all the pips inside a really ripe pomegranate, not one of those stringy things you get at the market, but a really good one from Iran. If I grabbed an avocado the way the Chef is holding the one in the comic, I'd end up with instant guacamole running through my fingers. You should replace the avocado with a pomegranate."

Larry rubbed his stubbly chin and considered. "Naw. I still think the avocado sounds better. 'I will attack you with my atomic avocado' is way better than 'pelt you with my potent pomegranate.'"

"Ax the avocado." Neil stood up suddenly, sniffing the air.

Larry seemed surprised. "What? That's it?"

"Um, no . . . the manga . . . it's not bad," Neil said, walking past Larry toward the doorway.

"Ooooh," Larry said. "Maybe the publisher will let me put that on the cover. 'Celebrity Chef Neil Flambé says it's not bad'! A blurb like that could sell tens of copies."

But Neil ignored his cousin. Something was distracting him—a smell from the kitchen. A smell that, like Larry's web comic, unexpectedly *didn't* stink.

Chapter Two

Gary's Secret . . . Recipe

Neil? What is it?" Larry said. Neil seemed to be in a trance. Larry knew there were only two things that had that effect on his cousin—Isabella Tortellini and gourmet food. He didn't hear Isabella or her giant bodyguard, Jones, come in, so presumably there was a delectable dish being served somewhere. "C'mon, snap out of it, chef-boy," Larry said, snapping his fingers in Neil's ear.

Neil continued to ignore him. He walked out of the office and into the kitchen . . . where Gary was hovering over the farthest stove, humming and stirring something on the burner in front of him.

The powerful aroma filled Neil's nose.

"What are you doing?" Neil asked slowly.

Gary spun around with a surprised look on his face. He had been so engrossed that he hadn't heard Neil and Larry walk up behind him. He dropped the spoon. It clattered to the floor.

"Hey, dude, you, like, scared me. Don't mess with my head like that, okay?"

"What are you doing?" Neil repeated.

"I'm just making a snack. I get hungry being around all this food."

Neil walked past him and stood over the pot Gary had been stirring so meticulously. The aroma hit him like a ton of bricks—bricks of glorious fresh seafood. Gary was making a bouillabaisse—a simple fish stew, but it smelled amazing.

The distinct aroma reminded Neil of something. It was the smell of a longhouse ceremony, when he'd been eleven. He'd been invited as a special guest by the great aboriginal chef Joe Chinook after Neil had helped Chinook recover a stolen stash of incredibly valuable spiny scallops.

No one could stumble upon a mixture like this by chance.

He turned on Gary with a furious look. "Where did you learn to make this? Who are you?" Neil glared.

Gary looked scared. He'd only known Neil for a few hours but had already heard him shatter glass with his voice. "Gary, man. Just Gary."

Neil grabbed a ladleful of stew and held it accusingly in front of Gary. "Okay, just Gary . . . where did

you learn to make just THIS? Living under the Burrard Street Bridge?"

"Why? You like it? It's pretty good, isn't it?" Gary relaxed and even grinned. "I make it for the other guys in the village. . . . Well, not a village, really . . . You know, the park where we pitch our tents. Well, I don't make it often, only when we can get the right ingredients."

This was the exact phrase Neil was waiting for. "That's what I mean, Gary. These ingredients are all local and *regulated*! It's illegal to buy and sell them! You're a criminal!"

"No, I'm not," Gary said nervously.

"Then I guess you won't mind if I give my friend Inspector Sean Nakamura a call?" Neil pulled out his cell phone and flipped it open.

"NO!" Gary said. "Don't. I don't need him digging around, you know?"

Neil stopped dialing. "Then tell me where you got these ingredients. Salmon roe, sturgeon, angelwing clams . . ."

"Okay, let me explain. I'm not a criminal. At least, I didn't steal any fish, okay?"

"Okay . . . OKAY?!" Neil said, raising his eyebrow and his voice. Larry, from experience, stuck his fingers in his ears. "WHAT DOES THAT MEAN?"

Gary waited for the pots to stop clanking and continued. "Well, you see . . . it's a bit complicated. I'm not stealing the fish. Well, I sort of stole the clams, but not really, because they were on the shore next to my uncle's boat. But don't call the cops because, well, because there are some people looking for me. Um, not because of the clams, unless Uncle Fred called the cops. I guess he might have, but probably not. We keep the locations of our fishing grounds *really* secret. Anyway, don't call the cops, because . . . where was I? Oh yeah, I didn't steal any fish. . . ."

Neil turned toward Larry. "This replacement souschef you found makes *you* sound coherent."

Larry just shrugged and smiled. "But boy, can he cook! I picked a winner and you know it."

"How did that 'picking a winner' happen again?"

"Well, I said, 'Gary, how would you like to get paid next to nothing and get yelled at by a cocky teenager?' He said, 'sure.' I said, 'When can you start?' Simple."

"Yes, you are," Neil gave an annoyed sigh and turned his attention back to Gary, who was still talking.

" . . . You see, then when I was in Europe, well, not just Europe, anyway I learned some really good recipes and just kind of brought them home with me. . . . Well, I did steal a few of the recipes from the General. Boy, was that a bad few months. . . ."

"STOP!" Neil yelled. The pans over the stove rattled again. Neil rubbed his temples. Gary was rambling and Neil wasn't getting any real information. "Let's try this a different way."

Gary nodded silently.

"Gary. Where did you get the fish?"

"My family."

"Are they fish poachers?"

"Um, no. They're part of one of the coastal first nations bands. We've got the right to fish these species, and we are VERY careful."

A lightbulb went off over Neil's head. Of course! Gary was aboriginal. He was using traditional ingredients his people had been using for centuries. They had the right to fish for personal use. Okay, answer to question number one made sense. Now to the other questions swirling around Neil's head.

"Okay, but this is bouillabaisse, NOT a traditional coastal dish, the last time I checked. It's French. Gary, where did you learn to cook French food?"

"I just told you: I was in Europe, and Asia, and lots of places. I just wasn't supposed to be . . . I was kind of hanging around."

Neil grabbed Gary by his shoulders and stared at him. "How does one 'hang around' Europe? Were you there or weren't you?"

"Yes . . ."

"When?"

"After I bolted the army."

"Wait, what?" Neil was struggling to keep track.

Larry was finding the whole thing kind of funny and was chuckling away behind Neil.

Gary let out a deep sigh. "Okay, man, here's the whole story. I was in the army. You know, young guy, got into a little trouble. I thought some discipline would be good for me. I was always pretty good with food, especially fish. . . ."

Neil could tell this was true. The fish stew was obviously amazing, and he hadn't even tasted it yet.

". . . So they made me a cook. It was kind of funny, really. The food they had was awful, all canned fish, milk, even the herbs. But, I don't know, somehow I could kind of tell what spices to throw in to make it taste okay. Eventually this visiting general came through the mess hall one day. He was from some little country I'd never even heard of, but he was working with us on some battle or something. I dunno, I didn't see much fighting from the mess hall. Anyway, this visiting general tried the food I was making. It was a really interesting lamb kebab, made with canned yogurt sauce and some quinoa and—"

"FOCUS!" Larry yelled from the back of the kitchen, grinning. Neil was constantly yelling this at Larry. Larry chuckled. "Hey, it's way more fun to say that than to hear it!"

Neil rolled his eyes but had to agree Gary was losing the thread, and dinner service was inching closer. "Gary, is there a shorter version of this story?"

"Long story short. The general scooped me up as his personal chef. I'm not even sure how that happened: He was from a completely different army but my superior said I'd been seconded, or transferred. He was wearing a really nice new gold watch, now that I think of it. Anyway, I got sent to work for the general and ended up traveling all over the place meeting interesting people, learning new recipes."

"So that explains the bouillabaisse. Why didn't you just tell me all this five minutes ago?"

"Well, the general, it turns out, was a real . . . dictator. And I mean that literally. He was bad news. After touring around Europe, we stopped off in his own country. He had this compound that was packed with stuff—gold and weapons. It turned out he was stealing stuff from our army and selling it to pay for his own. He had these really scary bodyguards. Those guys were roughing up the locals, shaking down people for money they didn't have. Not my scene, if you follow. So as soon as I could, I bolted."

"You resigned?"

"I wish! Nah, I went AWOL, absent without official leave. If the army ever finds me, they'll throw me in the clink."

"Why didn't you tell them about this general?"

"I tried to, but let's just say a guy like me doesn't have a lot of . . . credibility in the army. So, rather than keep working for the guy, I jumped a wall and wandered around. I'd made a lot of friends in the cooking world so they just hid me until I could smuggle myself on a boat back home."

Neil considered the story. He wasn't sure what to do. He was tempted to fire Gary on the spot, for any number of reasons—lying, going AWOL, stealing clams.

There was one huge reason not to fire him—Gary could cook. Neil leaned against the counter and pondered his options.

Just then there was a loud bang as the kitchen doors swung open violently. The Soba twins, Chez Flambé's waitstaff, came rushing into the kitchen. "Neil!" Zoe huffed and puffed. "That rock band is on the way here, like NOW."

Neil stood bolt upright. "I thought that party was next week!"

"I just checked the messages. They called this morning and changed it to today." Outside, Neil could hear the sound of the tour buses pulling up. The band "The Tintinitus Orchestra" was a thirty-member thrash metal and Italian Opera ensemble. They were also incredibly demanding gourmands who were notorious for searching out the best pre-gig meal in every city. Fans who couldn't stand their music would still follow them on tour to see where they ate. Just a rumor that they'd dined in your restaurant could justify raising prices for a year.

Not only that, but Neil had already been paid up front for the food. There was no getting out of this now. In about two minutes there would be thirty tattooed, pierced, and leather-clad violent violinists sitting in his dining room.

"Gary, I'm not sure what to do with you tomorrow, but tonight you're working, and working a LOT."

"Okay, chef," Gary said.

"Can you make more of that bouillabaisse in the next thirty minutes?"

Gary nodded. "You got any more fish?"

Neil was about to launch into a tirade about how a restaurant works, but Larry (sensing the urgency of the situation) headed him off.

"There's plenty in the fridge," Larry said, leading Gary over to the gleaming steel doors. "And it's all legal."

Neil heard them chatter as he started prepping the grill.

"Wow, ditching the general . . . Big step, Gary!" Larry said, slapping him on the back. "And you gave up months of army pay!"

"Well, not really. I only had one day left before they were going to discharge me."

Larry gave out a huge laugh. "Cool! One day! There's gotta be a medal for that!"

Neil fired up the burners and shook his head. "You are such an idiot," he said under his breath. He didn't specify whether he was talking about Larry, Gary . . . or himself.

Chapter Three

Soy Long Sous-chef

Neil strummed his fingers along the top of the stainless steel counters. The kitchen was eerily quiet and felt empty. No, Neil thought, it *was* empty. Larry was gone. The surest sign of that was the coffee machine that sat cold and silent on the far end of the counter. Neil could still smell the traces of the cup of expensive "bird poo" coffee Larry had gleefully made the night before, after cleaning the kitchen.

"It's from the Jacu bird. Eats the beans, poops 'em out. Farmers collect them, clean them, roast them . . . and I drink them! I'm not sure how many beans to grind. I guess I'll just *wing* it!"

"Don't you have to pack?" Neil had found himself both urging Larry to go and dreading his departure.

"Already done. I've got my pens, paper, a couple of pairs of underwear—what else could I need?"

"Can you pack someone who's not a total idiot?"

"Sorry. Don't know anyone like that." Larry had practically beamed as Neil glared at him.

Now Larry's bad puns were gone along with the Jacu bird coffee beans. Neil couldn't even join him on the drive to the airport. He couldn't afford to close the restaurant. It was finally starting to make some money again after two horrible weeks of bad reviews, near explosions, and fake health warnings.

Larry had driven off on his motorcycle, waving and calling back, "I'll see you before you know it!" How comforting, Neil thought, given Larry's incredibly BAD habit of saying exactly the opposite of what ended up happening.

Police Inspector Sean Nakamura had offered to pick Larry up at home and drop him off at the airport. "I can give him some last-minute tourist advice while we drive," Nakamura had said. "After all, I was born there." Nakamura and Neil and Larry had worked on a number of cases together, ranging from forged coffee beans to the Marco Polo murders. At this point, he was more than just an acquaintance. He was a friend.

Neil looked at the clock. The flight would be boarding soon. Larry had sent a text an hour before to say everything was going fine, then said he needed to save his battery power for playing video games on the flight.

Neil sighed. He decided he might as well keep prepping for dinner. The feast for the band had gone extremely well, and Neil had Gary to thank for that. His bouillabaisse had been a huge hit, and he'd followed it up with equally succulent salmon and oysters. None of them were the protected varieties, of course. Neil was no fan of cooking endangered species, and anyway Gary refused to break the law by selling them.

But Gary had a knack for finding amazing salmon and oysters and clams—and for cooking them too. There was no doubt about that.

There was a light knock at the back door. Without looking up, Neil sniffed the air; scented perfume wafted through the screen door. "Nice perfume, *bella*. It smells a little like Thai basil."

Isabella Tortellini chuckled as she opened the door and walked in. Neil and Isabella had grown even closer since they'd returned from Paris. She, too, had been there for the final battle with Valette, and it was her wits that had stopped the building from self-destructing. "Beautiful basil" was Neil's way of complimenting her. To be compared with food in Neil Flambé's eyes was no insult.

"Where's Jones?" Neil said, a bit surprised that Isabella's family friend/bodyguard/human tank wasn't trailing her like a menacing shadow. "Not far," she said cryptically. "But I thought you might need a visit from a friend today. Maybe just to *parlare*? To talk?"

"I don't need to talk." Neil turned his attention back to dinner prep, trying his best to sound nonchalant. "The 'coffee must go on' as Larry would say."

Isabella came up behind him and gently placed a hand on his shoulder. She knew Neil well enough to know when he was upset. Neil was always tough, in control . . . or trying to be.

"So what's on the menu?" she asked lightly.

Neil actually chuckled. "Fish. Larry hates seafood, so while he's gone I'm going to make this place look and smell like the Vancouver Fish Market."

"Then you can *scale it* back when he comes home." She laughed at her own pun.

Neil groaned. "You should scale back hanging around with Larry. His so-called 'sense of humor' is clearly contagious."

"He is a bit of a *scampi*," she said, chuckling again.

"Making a fish pun in Italian doesn't make it batter. Ugh, I mean better," Neil said. Isabella almost doubled over with laughter.

"And you call Larry's puns bad?" she said, laughing.

"I also said they were contagious, like the flu." Neil couldn't help it; looking at Isabella laughing broke down his defenses and he started laughing too.

They finally calmed down, and Neil prepped a quick snack of tuna ceviche. They sat next to each other on stools and ate and talked.

"I'm a bit worried about him, of course," Neil said, lifting the lime-splashed fish to his mouth with a fork.

"You Flambés do have a bit of a habit of getting into trouble," Isabella agreed.

Neil chewed lightly, letting the complex flavors hit his taste buds one by one. He swallowed and sighed. "What do we really know about this Hiro guy anyway?" Neil had done some online searching but all the pages had been in Japanese.

Isabella grinned and winked at Neil. "Well, Jones and Nakamura had the same question, apparently, and got together last night to do a little *indagine*, investigation." Neil guessed that it was Isabella who'd had the same question but kept his opinion to himself. "He says there are some interesting things here, but nothing criminal." She placed a thin file folder on the counter and the two began sifting through the pages.

"Hiro is a fairly well-known manga illustrator. 'Manga moron' was the term Jones used." Isabella ran her finger down the point-form notes Nakamura had left them. "He draws all the time. He's gone on lots of tours for his artwork, mostly comic book conventions, that sort of thing."

"Larry said he'd met him at a convention a year or so ago." Neil scanned the notes. "He lives on the east coast of the main island, not far south of Tokyo."

Isabella arched her eyebrow. "This is interesting. His family is descended from royalty. They can trace their history all the way back to the shogun dynasties. But there seems to have been a falling-out, about a hundred and fifty years ago. There's no reason given, but they were stripped of all their belongings and exiled."

Neil felt a twinge of sympathy for the Takoyakis. Being exiled was no fun. Neil had recently learned that his own family had been exiled for standing up to a particularly ruthless order of knights during the Crusades.

"You said they lost their money. Are they poor?"

Isabella read on. "No . . . but not rich, either. The father is a mathematician."

"Ugh," Neil said. "The only math I like is measured in teaspoons." He thought of the small pile of unfinished math assignments that was even now sitting on his desk back home.

Isabella ignored him. "The mother, Machiko Takoyaki, is a famous architect. Nakamura wrote, 'She specializes in green technology.'"

Neil noticed that Nakamura had drawn a star next to this tidbit and a small note in the margin that read, "Looks like she's been in trouble with the authorities a few times." The next page was a newspaper clipping; Nakamura had translated the text: "Machiko Takoyaki has been arrested again for her part in a showdown with a fishing boat. The fishers had been illegally trolling for tuna, killing hundreds of other fish in the process."

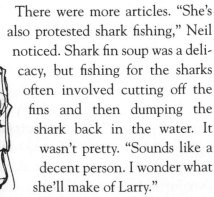

There were more articles. "She's also protested shark fishing," Neil noticed. Shark fin soup was a delicacy, but fishing for the sharks often involved cutting off the fins and then dumping the shark back in the water. It wasn't pretty. "Sounds like a decent person. I wonder what she'll make of Larry."

"Oh," Isabella said, catching her breath as she turned to the next clipping. "She and her husband died a year ago. Their boat sank after getting rammed by a fishing trawler."

Neil saw the picture that accompanied the story. It showed Hiro at the burial ceremony. Nakamura had written "Buried in Taku, Saga Prefecture" in the margin. "That's the name of the boat in the manga—Takusaga. Maybe that's a nod to his parents' memory."

Isabella nodded. "That makes sense. You know, I haven't seen the manga yet. Is it good?"

Neil hesitated, remembering the Isabella character's outfit. "I don't think it's really your, um, kind of thing."

Isabella didn't seem to notice the hesitation in his voice and continued reading. "The rest of the articles seem to be about Hiro's artwork." She closed the folder. "Hiro is what you call a . . . nerd?"

Neil chuckled. The word seemed very strange coming from Isabella, but he nodded.

"Yes. 'Comic-book geek' would also work."

Isabella smiled. "So, he's probably harmless. It's just Larry we have to worry about."

"Like always." Neil sighed. "Anything in those notes about the sister? I don't see her in the picture from the funeral or anything."

Isabella looked back at the notes. "She seems to be a marine biologist, but there's not a lot of info about her."

Just then the back door swung open and Gary walked in carrying a cooler. The lid was opened a crack and Neil caught a hint of the freshest clams he'd ever smelled.

"Hey, gang. I just paid another visit to my uncle's dock. These aren't endangered clams, don't worry. But my uncle is an amazing fisherman and he knows all the best places."

Neil looked at Gary and smiled. "Shall we add pasta alle vongole to the menu?"

Gary nodded. "My idea exactly, Mr. Super-chef. Pasta with claws!" Then he made his way to the sink to soak the wonderful bivalves in fresh water. "Just let me get rid of the salt and sand and these babies will taste awesome!"

Neil had still been debating the "Gary problem." Was he harboring a fugitive? Gary opened the cooler and the full aroma of the still breathing clams wafted over to Neil's nose.

He turned to Isabella. "You know what? I'm missing Larry less and less every minute."

Chapter Four

Life Is Good. . . .

It was time to prep for dinner. Neil walked into the kitchen and got to work organizing all the ingredients he'd need for his new seafood-heavy menu. He smiled.

The days since Larry's departure had passed pretty well, all things considered. Gary and Neil had already found a kind of rhythm in the kitchen. Neil concentrated on the meat and vegetarian dishes, and let Gary go crazy with the fish. Gary wasn't the most inventive of chefs—Neil had already cornered the market on that title, of course. But when it came to the basics – steaming, smoking, grilling, poaching—Gary was a pro. The twins were happy as well, now that the tips were starting to climb back to pre-Crusader's curse levels.

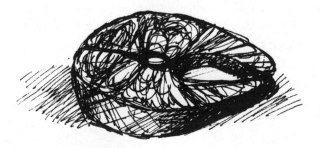

They'd even initiated Gary into the "make fun of Neil" kitchen banter. On Gary's second night in the kitchen, Neil got mad at Zoe for leaving a dish of steamed mussels on the kitchen counter for five seconds too long.

"Did you ever notice that 'Zoe' and 'ZONED OUT' start with the same letter?" Neil had barked.

Zoe feigned a look of shocked surprise. "Wow, Neil. Did you figure that out all by yourself?"

Then Amber walked through the doors to grab her plates of risotto, adding, "Hey, that's just like 'Neil' and 'Noodlehead.'" The twins proceeded to add a new word to the list every time they entered or left the kitchen.

"Nimrod!"

"Nincompoop!"

"Needlenose."

"Nerdlinger."

Finally Gary added, almost under his breath, "Hey, dudettes, don't forget 'nitwit.'" Then he showed amazing physical agility by dodging the whisk Neil flung at him.

The twins immediately raised Gary on their shoulders, shouting "Go, Gary, Go!" "He's officially a Team Flambé member!" "There's no getting rid of him now!", along with a few hip-hip-hoorays and pats on the back.

"Get back to work!" Neil had yelled, but he had to admit that Gary wasn't going anywhere anytime soon.

Neil looked up at the clock. Gary would be by in an hour or so. He was still doing side work as a bike courier and said he had a few deliveries to make first.

Neil was not normally in favor of part-time work. He worked *more* than full-time. But he owed Gary. Just the night before, Gary had saved Neil's bacon, so to speak.

Near the end of the evening, a table of latecomers had ordered three salmon dinners—the reputation of Chez Flambé as a fish lover's destination was growing—and Neil had only one salmon fillet left.

Neil had peeked into the dining room and noticed that the three people who'd asked for the salmon were not just any regulars—they were food critics. *Why do they always show up at the worst time?* he thought. Giving only one of them a salmon dinner and offering steak to the others was not going to be good enough. What was Neil going to do? Cut the salmon filet into thirds? He could just imagine the headline in the paper: "Chez Flambé cuts corners, cheats customers.

He turned back to the kitchen, scrambling for a plan. Gary was gone. Neil ran over to the back door, which was still creaking on its rusty hinges.

"AWOL!" Neil had shouted, scaring two of the more agile cats that had gathered outside his restaurant. They retreated behind the Dumpster and meowed huffily. Neil could feel the sweat beading on his forehead. What was he going to do?

Neil stalled the critics with a series of scallop and whitefish appetizers, when Gary reappeared suddenly, breathing hard and holding a very fresh, beautiful, and dripping-wet salmon.

"It's straight from the dock," he said, handing Neil the fish. The smell was amazing. Neil had paid top dollar to the best fish mongers in the city, but he'd never had a salmon this good in his kitchen before.

"Where is this dock exactly?"

"Sorry, boss, that's a secret. But it's a bit of a ways away. . . . Let's leave it at that."

"How did you get there and back so fast?"

"Hey, man, I'm a bike courier. . . . You don't really want to know."

Neil just nodded, and began to expertly clean the wonderful salmon. The critics had been wowed and the reviews were certainly going to be as wonderful as the fish. If they kept this up, the restaurant might actually start making money.

Neil gave a sigh as he chopped some shallots.

Neil's parents were constantly asking him when he was going to start turning a profit. They were both very successful businesspeople. Neil tried to explain that the restaurant business was tough and he needed to constantly reinvest any money he made in better stoves, ingredients, chairs . . . the list never ended. He tried *not* to tell them about all the destruction that had been caused by the recent spate of duels he'd fought against crazed Crusaders, computers, Aztecs, and rival chefs.

Luckily, Neil was getting a bit of a breather from his parents, who had joined Larry's parents on a vacation in Spain. (Technically it was a business trip for a new anti-bacterial cream they were hoping to develop, although the sales conference *was* near a beach.) But the important part was that Neil's parents had let him stay home on his own, on the condition that Neil checked in with Angel regularly. Angel Jícama was Neil's mentor, hero, and friend. A great chef, who was constantly warning Neil about the dangers of the life of haute cuisine. Neil rarely listened.

Even school didn't stink. Neil had handed in two math worksheets in a row. It didn't hurt that the questions had all been about heat conduction and how long to cook a proper soufflé. It looked like he might actually pass his least favorite subject. Plus, Billy Berger had finally transferred schools, so that was one fewer arch-enemy to worry about.

Neil's sideline as a human bloodhound was also good. He and Sean Nakamura had solved a minor food crime—smelling out a shipload of illegal chocolate bars. He'd left Gary in charge of dinner prep while they'd run out to gather evidence, and Neil had returned to a counter full of nearly perfect diced onions and chopped herbs.

And his red hair was starting to reemerge from his recent blond dye job.

Yes, Neil Flambé's life was going well.

Neil had even found time to steal a few glances at

the ongoing adventures of *The Chef*. Vegemight had been inching closer and closer to the Chef's secret kitchen hideout, as the Chef began to nurture himself back to health. Clearly, a huge showdown was looming. In the latest installment, Vegemight landed his ship on the island and walked right to the Chef's door—a cliff-hanger, to say the least. But there hadn't been a new comic in days.

Neil assumed the manga was on hiatus while Larry and Hiro got down to the business of writing their book. He didn't actually know, because Larry had also stopped texting him updates on his trip. Neil shook his head. Larry was always immersing himself in his various projects.

Neil understood that. It was the way he felt every time he walked into his kitchen. He grabbed some onions and started chopping them into quarters, getting them ready for the salsa he planned to serve with his grilled arctic char.

"Angel," Zoe said, entering the kitchen.

Neil stole a look at the clock. Oops. He was supposed to check in with Angel hours ago. "Is he on the phone?"

Zoe shook her head. "Angel is here to see you." She paused. "Nakamura is with him."

"Um, okay. Tell them to come in."

Angel and Nakamura showing up to talk to Neil at the same time wasn't that unusual, but they almost always gave him advance warning by loudly arguing about some food bylaw. Showing up together silently— that was odd. Neil felt his knees start to quiver.

The look on Angel's face as he slowly swung open

the kitchen doors confirmed Neil's worst fears. Had Angel been crying? Nakamura followed him and put his hand gently on Neil's shoulder. His voice cracked as he said, "Neil, I think you should sit down. I'm afraid I've got . . . horrible news."

Chapter Five

Sayonara

There were no survivors." The words had hit Neil in the gut, like a boxer's best punch. He couldn't breathe. He couldn't think. His head spun. Sean Nakamura kept talking, but Neil couldn't hear him anymore. He looked to Angel for some kind of assurance, some sign that this wasn't happening, but Angel had taken Neil's hand and was patting it gently.

At some point Neil must have gotten up and walked away. Hours later, it seemed, he noticed he was lying on the pull-out mattress he kept in his office. He had no idea how he'd gotten there. He was alone. The door was locked and there were no lights on in the kitchen beyond. It was dark outside.

Had he fallen asleep at all? Neil wasn't sure. His head hurt. His stomach lurched. He brought his hand to his eyes. They were dry. He was surprised to find he was too numb to cry. He realized there was a sound in his ear. No, not in his ear, exactly, but in his head. It was Nakamura's voice, coming back to him in snippets.

. . . *they went on a boating trip* . . .

. . . *two days ago* . . .

. . . *Hiro and Larry* . . .

. . . *storm came up suddenly* . . .

. . . *huge waves* . . .

. . . *battered the boat into pieces* . . .

. . . *no bodies recovered* . . .

. . . *found a shirt with writing on the inside. It said "puts the man in manga"* . . .

. . . *Japanese police say there was no chance of survival* . . .

. . . *Larry's parents have decided to have a memorial service right away. . . . They are coming back tomorrow night. . . . They asked me to tell you in person* . . .

. . . *a service for Hiro a few days from now in Japan* . . .

. . . *I'm really sorry* . . . .

Neil now remembered. That's when he'd gotten up, let Angel's hand fall to his side, and had walked into his office, almost robotically grabbing his mattress from under his desk and lying down. He didn't even know if the twins or Gary had served the last few customers, or cleaned up. He didn't care.

Neil closed his eyes. He wanted to moan, but he felt completely drained. His hand flopped against something on the floor. There was a whirring noise and

Neil could see a soft red glow inside his eyelids.

He opened his eyes and found himself staring at his open laptop. The screen shimmered with the last Web page he had been looking at: the latest—and now, last—installment of *The Chef*. There was Vegemight closing in on the Chef's lair with his evil boat. The Chef was grabbing his atomic avocados in anticipation of the coming fight. A fight, Neil realized, that would never come. Larry would never finish the stupid manga. Neil reached over to close the laptop and found he couldn't. Somehow, turning off the screen felt like closing off his last connection with his cousin.

Tears welled in his eyes. Every time the screen went dark he would reach over to wake it up. He felt like a little boy asking his big brother to read his favorite bedtime story over and over again. Neil had spent most of his life desperately trying to not be a little boy. Now that Larry was gone, he felt everything collapsing around him. He tried to call his parents but there was no answer. They must have boarded their flight home.

Finally, Neil curled up with his knees held tight against his chest and fell into a deep, and thankfully dreamless, sleep. The screen finally went dark and the laptop turned off.

Chapter Six

The Coffee Goes On

Neil woke to the shuffling of feet outside his office. Someone was walking
up to the door. There was a light
tap on the frosted glass. He
could smell lavender. "Neil,
it's me, Isabella. I am so . . .
sorry." Neil said nothing. He closed his eyes tightly and
stayed curled up.

Isabella leaned close to the door. "Please just let me
know you are okay. *Bene.* I can hear you breathing. I will
not leave. You come out when you are ready." She paused.
"We all loved Larry. We all love you, Neil." He heard her
sniffle and then quickly walk through, across the kitchen
floor to the stools that were set up near the counter.

Neil reached over and tapped the computer key-
board. *The Chef* illuminated once again, exactly the
same panels as the night before. Vegemight's ship docked
on the cake-shaped island and the evil king of frozen
fish stood at the locked door of the kitchen cavern. Neil
stared blankly at the interrupted story. The last line

filled the last frame: "Knock knock, Chef. Lettuce in!"

Larry's final words were a pun. How fitting. Neil wondered if the puns worked the same in translation. He let out a sigh and continued staring. What would Larry have written next?

Angel, the twins, Isabella, Nakamura, and even Jones had tried to cajole him from the office floor. Neil could hear them all gathered in the kitchen, and then the dining room, chatting . . . sometimes even laughing at some memory of Larry.

Neil's parents had called him in the middle of the night as they waited for one of their many connecting

flights home. The phone call had been short, with Neil mostly moaning and his parents telling him they'd see him soon but that the flight from Germany had been delayed and it now looked like they'd arrive just in time for the memorial.

"Larry's parents say Father Costello has already been working on the details so there's no reason to delay," his dad had said, in his grown-up ad executive voice. That was the Flambés, all business and details. "Make sure you check in with Angel," his mom added.

"I miss him," Neil squeaked in reply. There was a long pause.

"We love you, son," his mom and dad had said together.

"You too," Neil croaked between tears. Then they'd gone to figure out their flights and Neil had fallen back to sleep.

Finally, it was Gary, of all people, who spoke the magic words that roused Neil. "Hey, boss. I know I'm no replacement for Larry the Loafer. That's what we always called him when we played soccer. No offense intended. He said it was a baking pun. He even called our team the Early Risers. I think that was supposed to be funny too. I never saw Larry before noon. But I do know one thing Larry would say. Well, he'd say it if he were here, which he's not. Oh, man, sorry . . . no offense intended. It's just that it's like I can hear his voice when I read this note he left. Well, it's not a note, really . . ."

Gary, like his precious bike, only had two speeds. Stop and goooooooooo. He was quiet until you got him started talking—then he could talk your ear off.

". . . Well, I guess it is a note. It's on paper. He left it for me, but he told me to give it to you. Well, not right away. He said only to give it to you if things got a little, you know, tough around here. I'm not totally convinced that he was sure you and I would get along, to be honest. We do get along, but I think this is a good time, I mean a bad time, I mean an appropriate *tough* time—"

"GARY! WHAT NOTE?" Neil yelled, all of a sudden and so loudly that he surprised himself.

Gary didn't say anything but Neil heard the sound of paper sliding under the door. Neil crawled over. There was an envelope. It smelled like coffee. He picked it up slowly. On the outside, in Larry's handwriting, was a short note. *Don't worry, chef boy . . . just hurry and curry!* Neil turned the envelope over.

Open me, mon captiaine! ☺ was written on the back flap. Neil stood up and walked over to his desk. He opened the drawer and grabbed a knife. He slit the envelope open. Out dropped a small vacuum-packed envelope of a brilliant red spice. Neil recognized it instantly. It was Sargol saffron—picked from the crocus fields of Iran. The most expensive, most aromatic, most wonderful spice in the world, costing more per pound than gold—and worth every penny in the right chef's hands. Those hands now used the knife to split the package open. The smell escaped and hit Neil's nose. It was . . . perfect.

Larry had known Neil would eventually need a pick-me-up. He always had, and Larry usually provided one with a well-timed joke or story. There's no way Larry could have guessed how awful things would get, but he'd left him a gift that only Neil would fully understand. Neil was instantly transported back to a conversation they'd had on the plane back from Paris, several hours after narrowly escaping the explosions that had rocked the office tower they had been standing on.

"Wow, that was a blast!" Larry had said. . . . One more bad pun.

Neil had shaken his head. "I'm looking forward to getting back to a safe, sound kitchen. No more brushes with death for this chef."

Larry had smiled. "I hope death and I dance a few

more times. It's like being in a really good mosh pit. Exciting and possibly dangerous. Life presents opportunities when you least expect them. Grab 'em or spend your life watching other people living."

Neil had responded that he thought Larry did a little too much life-grabbing—speeding around on his Harley, sacrificing sleep for who knows what, jumping into dangerous situations, drinking enough coffee to wake a corpse—and sometimes hanging around with people who *looked* like corpses.

Larry had just chuckled. "I'm happy. And for my next risky move, I will order the pork stew that lovely flight attendant is about to bring down the aisle. If the plane crashes, at least I'll join the heavenly choir with a full stomach."

"I've heard you sing. I think the *other* choir might be a better fit. And eating too much airplane food might get you there quicker than a crash."

"Ha, ha." Larry had spent the rest of the flight chatting up the attendant and scoring three extra servings of stew and her phone number on the back of an airsickness bag.

Another whiff of the saffron knocked Neil back into the present. He held the package to his chest and dried his eyes. Neil would never know how Larry planned to finish *The Chef*, but he knew what Larry would say to him right now: *Life doesn't come with guarantees. LIVE.*

For Neil *live* and *cook* were the same. Larry knew that, and that's why he'd left Neil the precious saffron—delicate, fragile, and not to be wasted. Neil took a deep breath. He stood up straight, walked to the door, and unlocked it. Gary was sitting on the floor outside the door. Neil almost tripped over him as he turned the handle and made his way into the kitchen.

"Gary. Thank you," Neil said, in a hoarse whisper as he stepped around him and made his way to the counter. Gary just nodded.

Isabella, hearing the office door open, was the first into the kitchen. She ran up to Neil and was about to hug him when she saw the look on his face. Instead, she kissed him on the cheek and gave him a tender smile. "Are you okay?"

Neil just nodded and grabbed a chopping block and some onions. He instinctively reached for his best knife, but paused as his fingers felt the handle. Larry's knife, a present from Neil, hung on the magnetic rack  right next to Neil's. Neil grabbed it instead and began to slice the onions. Angel, Nakamura, Jones, and the twins all came in to see him. Neil stopped them with a wave of his hand and shook his head. They backed away.

Neil started to tear up again, despite his best efforts to stay calm. He pointed at the onions by way of explanation.

"Neil, did you want to close for a few days?" Amber said, walking toward him slowly.

Neil shook his head again. In what was barely a

whisper he said, "I need you to rewrite the menu . . . please. No seafood, just for tonight. Instead it's all meat, pasta, and everyone gets free coffee and a serving of *risotto alla Milanese*."

He held the saffron up to the light and watched the beautiful red gift dance before his watery eyes. "Made with saffron à la Larry the Loafer."

Chapter Seven

Fire and Fury

Neil lost himself in his art. He cooked with a silent ferocity that turned his always fabulous food into fiery works of art. For the next two days everything Neil cooked seemed to be on fire. He served flaming *steak Diane*, blazing *baked Alaska*, burning *Lobster Fra Diavolo*. His choice of spices was equally hot and a steady stream of curries, chilies, and spicy Asian soups flowed from his hands to the waiting diners.

Neil was cooking, but he didn't speak, or even yell. Neil *would* call out instructions to Gary and occasionally nod to show he'd received an order from the twins. But that was it. He'd even stopped his habit of walking through the din-ing room to fish for compliments.

At night he would retreat back into his office and

lock the door. Only a faint blue electric light gave any indication he was in there.

Isabella tried to lure him out, to go to a movie, to shop for spices, to smell new scents . . . but he would just shake his head and go back to work. Neil's parents had checked in but continued to face delays in their attempt to get home. Neil assured them he was working hard and that he was checking in with Angel. He lied about the Angel part.

Isabella decided she needed to call in the heavy artillery. The night before Larry's memorial, she went to visit Angel.

"You have to do something," Isabella said to Angel, as they stood in his living room. Jones eyed the various drying herbs with suspicion. "If he goes on like this, he will . . . how do you say, be *consumare*."

"Burn himself out, yes, I agree," Angel said.

"Then you'll go talk to him tonight? I'm worried that after the memorial tomorrow he will get worse, not better."

Angel considered. "He doesn't want to talk. He is not ready. We just have to be here when he needs us. But we cannot force him to that moment. He is stubborn."

"Like all the chefs I have ever met," Jones added, casting a sideways glance at the various bylaw infraction notices Angel kept tacked up next to his stove. Sean Nakamura was constantly giving him tickets for running an urban farm in his apartment building. Every once in a while, Angel would use a ticket to light the charcoal grill he kept on his balcony.

Angel gave a deep sigh. "Neil feels powerless, as we all do when we grow up. Food is what he can control, what we chefs can always control, even when our lives are crumbling. I will leave him to that, even though it hurts us to see him go through this pain. But he will speak to us when he is ready."

Isabella stood up quickly. "Then we agree."

"Agree on what, exactly?" Angel said, not moving from his chair.

"We agree that Neil needs us near him. You are going to him now and you are going to speak to him now. Then he'll realize that he needs to snap out of his shock now."

"I'm not sure that's exactly what I was saying. Tomorrow might be bett—"

"You either stand up now or Jones can personally escort you to our car." Isabella crossed her arms and tapped her foot.

Jones stood up and cracked his knuckles. The sound frightened a flock of sparrows four blocks away.

Angel stood up. He allowed himself a tiny smile. Isabella was a force of nature. Larry's death had affected all of them, but Isabella never lost her will, what the Italians call her *forte volonta*. He hoped Neil recognized how great his friend really was.

Thirty minutes later Angel walked quietly through the back door of Chez Flambé.

Neil was hunched over the kitchen counter,

furiously chopping up some poblano chili peppers. Angel stopped and smelled. Neil was making chicken in a rich *mole* sauce and Angel knew why. It was a meal Larry had devoured like candy on their recent trip to Mexico City.

"It smells wonderful," Angel said, walking up to the counter next to Neil.

Neil just nodded and slid the peppers into a large skillet, along with cumin, garlic, tomatillos, and other spices.

"I do wonder if it might be a touch spicy." To Angel's surprise, Neil didn't scowl or frown or throw anything. He stopped chopping, took a deep breath through his nose . . . and shook his head. Then he turned his attention to cutting some onions.

"Hey, Angel! How goes the battle, old man?" Gary yelled, walking into the kitchen carrying a large basket of fresh coriander, lettuce, and radicchio. "You here to lend a hand?"

"Larry—I mean, Gary, please stop. . . ." Neil whipped his head around and glared at Gary who immediately stopped talking. Neil pointed to the sink with his knife, making a stabbing motion in the air.

"That's unsettling," Gary said sheepishly.

"I think he wants you to rinse the herbs," Angel said. "Silently."

Gary smiled and waved at Angel, then he turned on the tap and began rinsing, humming along to some tune in his head.

Neil turned back to the onions. Angel knew Neil wasn't angry with Gary for talking. He was angry that

Gary sounded so much like Larry. As long as Gary stayed quiet and cooked, Neil was able to keep it together. Angel, not for the first time in his life or the last, felt sad for his troubled young protégé.

"Neil, I just want you to know that we are all here when you are ready to talk," Angel said softly. Then he did the only thing he could think of to help: He grabbed a handful of garlic cloves and began peeling off their delicate skin.

Neil didn't say a word. He began cutting the lemongrass, the cool steel of his knife resting gently but safely against his knuckles, slicing the grass into delicate disks.

Maybe Neil's parents had had the secret all along—lose yourself in work. The world was too painful, too complicated, too dangerous. Keep family and friends far away—the closer you let them get, the more pain you could suffer. You could have disappointment in a career, but never the type of pain Neil was dealing with now.

Neil had a horrible thought. There were billions of things happening in the world, right now, every second . . . any one of which could leap from the dark and destroy a life. He couldn't stop them. He didn't even know what they were, what was going on a million miles away, but they were heading invisibly for him as he worked away in his kitchen . . . just like Larry didn't know about the freak storm that was brewing off the Japanese coast the day he went on a boating trip.

Neil pushed the thought out of his mind by grabbing a chicken breast and his meat tenderizer. He pounded and pounded until the meat was flattened, then he pounded some more.

Chapter Eight

Putting the Fun in Funeral

Neil woke up groggy. The laptop continued to glow on the floor next to his pillow, but in the glare of the morning sunlight it was impossible to make out the manga on the screen.

"Get up, you lazy chef," Larry's voice called out from Neil's phone. Larry had helpfully recorded his own voice as Neil's phone alarm, then promptly neglected to tell Neil how to change it to something else.

"Get up, you lazy chef."

Neil reached over and clicked the alarm off. He saw that there were three text messages waiting in his inbox. One from Nakamura saying that he and Angel were picking up the elder Flambés at the airport and would meet Neil at the church.

The second message was from Neil's school, asking him if he had dropped out.

Then there was a third message, also from

Nakamura, saying they had arrived at the church early, and that Neil might want to brace himself—the service was "all Larry".

"Brace myself? What does that mean?" Neil said. He stood up slowly and made his way to the kitchen sink. He turned on the tap and then cupped his hands to accept the cold, clear water. He splashed his face and ran wet fingers through his hair. "Brace myself," Neil said. "Brace myself for what?"

Neil walked back into the office and put on his best suit; actually, his only suit. He'd grown since its purchase, and the arms of the suit didn't quite reach his wrists. And the new shirt he was wearing had cuffs that extended down to his knuckles. Neil knew he looked comical, but he had a sneaking suspicion that it might be just the right look for a funeral that was "all Larry."

Neil reached down and picked up his laptop. He put it on the desktop and took one final look at *The Chef*. "I guess this is really good-bye, cousin," Neil said, reaching across to close the laptop.

He stopped.

Something wasn't right. Neil leaned in and peered closely at the final panel of the manga. Something was *definitely* not right. In fact, something was distinctly . . . *different*.

Neil had seen the panel so many times in the past few days that he had memorized every line, every curve, every detail. What had changed? The Chef stood at the ready, poised to defend his kitchen cave and his best friend. His legs were wide apart, his teeth were gritted, his hands . . . his HANDS!

Neil stared so hard at the hands he thought he might burn a hole in the screen.

In his hands, the Chef was clutching two perfectly ripe pomegranates.

The tiny church of St. Lawrence—the patron saint of cooks—stood on a small hill not far from Chez Flambé. Parishioners climbed a flight of thirty steps before entering the weathered cedar doors.

Decades before, when the neighborhood wasn't quite so run-down, a wealthy chef had paid for an enormous marble statue of the saint to stand at the base of the stairs. Years of rain and seagull poop had covered the statue with a thick mossy patina—not unlike a bear's fur coat, if bears were green.

As Neil pedaled up to the church, he saw that the fuzzy saint was wearing a sombrero. A sash with the words Viva Zapata ran over his shoulder, a souvenir of their trip to Mexico. Neil started to realize what Nakamura had meant by "brace yourself" and "all Larry."

Neil just shook his head and ditched his bike at the saint's feet. He was bursting with his news. Larry had left him a clue. Larry was alive. Neil was sure of it. He'd never been so happy to see pomegranates.

Neil practically flew up the stairs and into the back of the church. He had to pull up short to avoid colliding with Father Costello. The small, round man stood in the entranceway, a confused look on his face. He was holding a pen above what appeared to be a ringed notebook.

"Ah, Neil," Father Costello said, looking over the tops of his round glasses. "I need a noun."

"Um . . . a what?" Neil said.

"I need a noun."

The sheer weirdness of the request left Neil stunned.

Father Costello looked back down at his notes. "I also need an adjective. . . ."

A thought struck Neil. Larry must have written his own eulogy, sort of. "Let me guess. Mad Libs?"

"Larry always worried that he'd die young. He told me exactly how he wanted his funeral to 'go down.' It's very unusual, and not strictly according to church rules, but your cousin was very persuasive. Some of it is very . . . Larry."

Neil craned his neck to see past the priest. But there was a large curtain covering the archway. Neil noticed it was emblazoned with the words EARLY RISERS FOOTBALL CLUB. THE YEAST AMONG US SHALL RISE! It was Larry's favorite color, coffee brown.

Neil realized with a sniff that Larry had actually dyed the fabric himself, with cheap instant coffee. "Never drink the stuff. Life's too short," Larry often said if someone offered him a cup. Just a few minutes before, that memory would have made Neil cry. Now he actually chuckled.

"For a noun, how about 'pomegranate'? And 'alive' is probably a good adjective." He stepped past the priest. "And if you need another noun, try 'instant coffee.'"

Father Costello scribbled down the words. "Alive? Instant coffee?" he asked, but Neil had already gone through the curtain.

Neil opened his mouth to tell everyone his news, but he saw the bowed heads and stopped. Was he right? Was he one hundred percent sure Larry was alive? He hadn't seen or heard from Larry directly. Could he prove Larry had made the change in the manga? Neil was convinced— at least ninety-five percent convinced—but yelling the news to a few hundred mourners might not be . . . appropriate? Sensitive? This was a funeral, after all.

Maybe telling his family and friends first would make sense. Neil looked around the church. What he saw was more clear evidence of Larry's peculiar instructions. In lieu of a coffin there was a giant papier-mâché bust of Larry's head in the middle of the nave. The grin was huge. The hair and scruffy beard were made from what appeared to be spaghetti noodles. The eyes were hand-painted bowls.

Neil recognized them as the expensive crème brulée ramekins he'd been looking for a couple of weeks before.

The whole goofy-looking mess sat on the handlebars of Larry's beloved motorcycle. Neil assumed the giant Larry head was from his recent night-school course with the famous papier-mâché artist Louise Bond.

Neil heard the sound of a sobbing woman to his left. Actually, it was too loud, he realized, for just one person. *I wonder if Louise is here?* Neil thought, glancing over. The entire left side of the church was packed with black-clad mourners. They all appeared to be female.

Most had their faces buried in handkerchiefs. No. Neil looked more closely. They weren't handkerchiefs but leftover me-shirts. A woman Neil recognized as the actress Ellen Sage wiped her eyes on the words *I'm with Cupid.* Most of the wailing girlfriends were entirely new to Neil. Many of them seemed surprised to see so many other girlfriends. Neil spied more than a few shaking fists peeking out from behind the shirts.

Neil shook his head in wonder and walked to the front of the church. Isabella, Jones, Angel, and Nakamura were sitting a few rows from the front and Neil signaled that he'd be back.

His parents and Larry's were seated together in the front row. They were leaning over, praying, although from habit Neil double-checked that they weren't actually just checking their e-mails.

Neil wanted to rush right up to them, to tell them that Larry was alive . . . but he paused. He could see that Larry's parents looked exhausted and sad. Neil reminded himself that he needed to be one hundred percent sure he was right before he got their hopes up, and even hinting at his thoughts might be too much of a shock. If he tried to explain the clue in the Chef's hand, would they even understand?

Instead he sat down behind them and ran his hand gently over his uncle's back. Neil's parents turned and hugged him. They looked exhausted too. Neil felt the tears well up again in his eyes, and was confused. If he thought Larry was alive, then why was he crying?

"I'm going to say hi to my friends," he said. "I'll be back in a minute."

Neil walked back to the pew where his friends were busy wiping their eyes.

"Where have you been?" Isabella said. "You're late."

Neil saw that her eyes were red. Neil realized that he could tell Isabella his news about Larry. She'd understand. She'd be happy.

Neil smiled and opened his mouth just as the organ interrupted with a loud blast, sort of like an explosion but less musical. For a moment Neil thought the motorcycle had somehow started. Then he realized the organist was actually launching into one of the punk anthems Larry used to blare from his radio—usually a few seconds before getting a ticket for noise violations.

Neil leaned in close to Isabella. "You won't believe it," he said, so excited with his news that he spoke louder than he'd expected. That and the organ's growing whine approximated the relative volume of a jumbo jet. Angel, Nakamura, and Jones stared over at him with angry looks.

"Shhh," Isabella said.

"But I have news!" Neil said.

"Shhhh," said two hundred women behind him.

"Show some respect," Jones added, poking a muscular finger at Neil. He seemed to bruise the air.

Neil sat back in his seat and decided he'd better just go along for the ride until the end of the service. "Okay, but I highly doubt *respect* is going to be a big part of any funeral scripted by Larry."

"Shhh . . ." Isabella said again.

Now the organ was in full punk rock mode, and Neil watched as cracks started to appear in the plaster ceiling of the church. He stared up at the organ loft. He could just make out the neon red spiked hair of Larry's friend Emily Ivy peeking out from over the railing. He started to get up to rejoin his parents but spied Father Costello starting down the aisle, still checking his notes. Neil sat back down.

Father Costello seemed to notice the strange music about halfway down the carpet and resignedly hung his head. He picked up the pace and practically sprinted up to the altar.

As soon as he reached it, he turned and waved frantically for Emily to stop. She gave him an impish grin and slammed her fingers down, forcing one more gigantic blast from the pipes. The echo reverberated throughout the church.

Neil wiped the remains of some plaster cherub off the shoulder of his suit and watched as Father Costello got back to his feet and made his way to the pulpit. He adjusted his glasses.

"Um, hello everyone. And . . . hey, whatzzzzz happenin'."

Father coughed. Clearly his mouth had never formed these words before, and the stunned silence radiating from the pews suggested they were not formed well now. "I'm just reading what Larry has asked me to read today," he said sheepishly. He gave another little cough and continued.

"We are here to remember Larry Flambé, who died at too young an age in a horrible accident."

There were sniffles and sobs from the crowd. Father Costello looked to the skies before turning to the meat of the eulogy.

"Larry Flambé was a <u>mystical</u> <u>hammer</u> <u>fish book</u>." Silence returned . . . for a moment. "Yes. His <u>noisy nose</u> and <u>greasy</u> sense of humor gave the entire <u>parrot</u> a <u>foggy</u> chance to laugh along with this <u>rancid</u> young man of the <u>peanut</u>."

There were now murmurs as people realized why they'd been asked for all those strange words as they made their way into the church.

"His <u>baseball</u>-shaped <u>interface</u> was always <u>smelly</u> with an <u>ugly joke</u> and a cheerful <u>mongrel</u>. Yes, he <u>ate</u> his friends and declared them <u>horrible</u>."

Neil found he was rather enjoying the service, and couldn't help but chuckle. Isabella shushed him again but had a smile on her face as well.

"His <u>orange</u> <u>swimming</u> friends all knew him as the <u>purple</u> <u>lizard</u>. He will <u>happily</u> miss all the <u>gargantuan</u> <u>whisks</u> that he and his <u>electronic</u> cousin Neil used to <u>slice</u> inside a <u>paper volcano</u>. Neil, known to his friends as <u>turkeylips</u>, never <u>exploded</u> without <u>instant coffee</u>. . . ."

Now Isabella was giggling, holding her me-shirt (which read, oddly, I'D RATHER BE SNOWBOARDING) up to her face to suppress the sound. By the end of the eulogy—which finished on the line "Larry is now <u>puking</u> with the other <u>moldy</u> angels in the great <u>toilet</u> in the sky"—the entire church was rolling with laughter. People even began calling out "MORE MORE!", offering new nouns, adjectives and verbs such as "farting," "loopy," and "antidisestablishmentarianism."

Father Costello, to his credit, ignored the pleas for an encore and did his best to make the service stick as closely as possible to Larry's instructions.

"May he rest in pizza," Father Costello finally said, ending the service. He breathed a loud sigh of what Neil assumed was relief and then looked down once more at his notes. "Larry has asked that everyone make their way downstairs to the church lawn for a catered meal, care of Angel Jícama, and gourmet coffee."

Everyone stood up, smiling and chatting—many now wiping away tears of laughter. Sweethearts who had been sending daggers with their eyes at the start of the service were now sharing memories of Neil's scruffy, loveable cousin. Even his parents and Larry's parents were smiling and shaking hands with the mourners.

Neil was amazed for the thousandth time in his life at Larry's ability to make a dark situation practically shine with light. He smiled broadly and looked down the pew at his friends. "Now time for my news. Larry is a—"

He was about to say "alive" when Emily Ivy kicked in with one more explosion on the organ, followed by her rendition of the White Stripes song "Fell in Love with a Girl."

Isabella signaled that she couldn't hear him. Neil just waved his hands and pointed toward the exit.

They reached the back landing just as Emily hit the final note, loosening the lead in the stained glass windows and knocking over the flower vases on the altar.

A nagging question had occurred to Neil as they'd marched up the aisle. "Hey, wait a minute," he said indignantly. "*Angel* is catering the meal? Why not me?"

Father Costello walked up behind him and laid an arm on his shoulder. "Larry was worried that without him to stop you, you'd try to serve seafood."

Chapter Nine

Vitamin See

You're very shaken up, Neil. Maybe you're imagining things?" Nakamura said, stuffing another of Angel's amazing goat cheese canapés into his mouth. "These are so good they should be illegal!" Nakamura said.

"They probably are," Jones muttered.

"I'm telling you there were POMEGRANATES!" yelled Neil. Everyone turned toward him. He lowered his voice to the level of a small outboard motor. "I'm not deluded! Larry sent me a clue. He's alive!"

A few of the mourners next to them shook their heads and walked away from Neil and his friends.

Neil heard one of them whisper, "Poor boy, so sad."

Neil hung his head and sighed.

Isabella patted his hand gently. "Let's maybe talk about this later, Neil. Let people, let his parents, say good-bye to Larry today."

"What I'm saying is that they don't *have* to. I just need to figure out the simplest way to tell them," Neil said. He was about to continue when he looked up and caught the look in Isabella's eye. It was her *think for a second before you talk* look. Why was she giving him that look? What was he missing?

He closed his mouth and thought. If Larry were alive, why didn't he just call? Why hide a clue? Was Neil deluded? He kept his mouth shut and tried to think of an answer while Larry's strange wake continued all around them.

Isabella, Jones, Nakamura, and Neil were standing by the statue of St. Lawrence. The craziness had continued as they'd all left the church. Everyone was given a me-shirt with a picture of Larry on the inside, over the heart. Except for Neil. His picture of Larry was over his stomach. "He said it seemed more appropriate," Father Costello had explained.

Larry's motorcycle buddies had been waiting on the street and greeted everyone leaving the church with a twenty-one-muffler salute. Once the cloud of exhaust dissipated, Angel had lifted the veil on tables of amazing food—all of it favorites of Larry, including French fries, lamb burgers, stuffed pasta, stuffed olives, and stuffed pies. Soon, everyone was stuffed. Then there was dessert, a cake in the shape of a coffee mug . . . and lots of coffee. Anyone walking by was invited and soon the party was spilling down the entire block.

Neil had

wondered why Gary hadn't been at the service, but it turned out that Angel had asked him to help out with the food. Neil would occasionally see him biking through the crowd with a tray of hors d'oeuvres balanced on his handlebars.

Neil leaned in close to his friends and whispered, "I'm not deluded! I'm telling you that the clue is one only Larry and I would recognize."

"Why hide a clue? Why make everyone think he's dead?" Jones said. "Seems kind of cruel. Larry's an idiot—was an idiot—but he wasn't cruel." Neil had to admit Jones had a point (and he certainly knew all about cruel).

"I don't know for sure," Neil said, thinking while tapping his fingers against the statue. "He's alive . . . but maybe there's some reason why he can't contact us directly. I just have to figure out what that reason is."

"We want to believe you," Isabella said quietly. "We all want Larry to be alive."

Nakamura signaled for Gary to deliver more Thai chicken spring rolls. "Maybe he left instructions for Hiro's sister to change The Chef on the day of his funeral. You know, as a kind of a final gift to you." Gary arrived and Nakamura grabbed a plateful of food. "Neil, you okay?"

Nakamura's suggestion made Neil's head swim. He hadn't thought of that possibility. His mind raced to deal with it. No. Nakamura had to be wrong. But why? It was like being in the kitchen and needing one unknown ingredient for a perfect stew . . . searching your brain to figure out the perfect combination that would make the dish make sense. And then, just like that, Neil had his answer.

"No. Wait a minute. Larry left the instructions for this funeral service ages ago, in case he died sometime. If he'd left instructions for Koko to change the website . . . then he would have known ahead of time he was going to die in Japan. He didn't know he was going to die. They were only going sightseeing, for crying out loud." Neil was convinced he was right. Whether he'd convinced the others was another question.

The skeptical look on Nakamura's face suggested he hadn't, at least not one hundred percent.

"Okay. Listen, Nose. I'll check it out, okay? I promise. If the police find any evidence that Larry is alive, I'll let you know."

Neil shook his head, his mind still whirling. "No. Bad idea. You can't contact the police, at least not in Japan."

"What? Why not?"

"Larry sent a clue that only I would recognize. If he'd wanted to tip off the police, he'd have sent them a message. That means secrecy, for some reason, is important. We can't risk tipping anybody off. If the police start asking questions . . ."

"I find it interesting that any idea that might disprove your theory is a bad idea," Jones said. Nakamura nodded.

"Fine. But I have an idea on how I can perfectly test my theory," Neil said, the ideas now coming fast and furious. "I'll investigate myself. Larry sent me a clue because he wants *me* to look for him."

"Oh, so it's okay if *you* ask questions but not the

police? Nothing suspicious about a teenage redheaded chef poking his nose around," Nakamura said sarcastically. But the fact that he was willing to use that tone of voice suggested to Neil that Nakamura was starting to take him seriously. "Do you mind telling me just how you plan to investigate?"

"I'm going to Japan," Neil said firmly.

"Neil, you can't be serious," Isabella said.

Neil narrowed his eyes and stared across the church lawn to where Angel and Gary were serving dessert. "I'm absolutely serious." He left his friends and marched over to the food table, pushing through crowds of black-clad mourners and leather-clad motorcyclists.

Isabella caught up with him after a few steps. "Neil. How can you go to Japan? If you start looking for Larry, you'll be tipping people off just as much as the police."

Neil kept walking. "If I were going to look for him you'd be right," he said. "I'm going to arrange a four-star cover story."

"What does that mean?"

"Let's find out."

Neil reached the food table. Angel was standing on the other side, chopping some fresh broccoli into bite-size pieces.

Neil placed both hands on top of the table, leaned across, and spoke in a low voice.

"Angel. I need your help."

"What kind of help?" Angel asked, eyeing Neil suspiciously.

"I think Larry is still alive. He sent me a clue."

Angel nodded. He knew Neil, and he knew when Neil was convinced of something. "I can see you are serious."

"Yes. Bottom line . . . I need to go to Japan."

"Okay . . ." Angel cocked his head and looked at Neil even more suspiciously.

"But it's going to be expensive. I need a reason to go there that doesn't raise too many suspicions, and I need somebody wealthy to foot the bill."

Angel's eyes opened wide. "Neil, turn right back around and start walking away."

"Why?" Isabella asked. "What's going on?"

Neil leaned forward and whispered. "I'm not leaving. I need you to get in touch with Matsumoro Nori."

Angel turned his back to Neil and began flipping chicken skewers onto a red-hot hibachi. "No. This is a stupid plan, even for you. I will not help."

Neil leaned farther across the table, his tie dipping into a dish of satay sauce. "Angel. First of all, you've put way too much cilantro in this satay, and second, I *am* going to Japan. You know that Nori has always wanted to have me battle. I have always said no."

"Is this Nori a chef?" Isabella asked. Neil didn't need to see her to know she had her hands on her hips and an angry look on her face. Neil had promised repeatedly never to fight another kitchen duel. He seemed to find just as many excuses to break that promise.

"He's not a chef," Neil scoffed. "He's a multimillionaire."

"Billionaire," Angel corrected. "Not one cent of it made honestly. He's also a psychopath."

Neil cringed. Isabella wasn't going to like that word. "He's obsessed with food. And he's Angel's former business partner."

Isabella looked from Neil to Angel, whose shoulders sagged. "That was a long time ago. It was a mistake then and you are making a big mistake now."

"Angel. You know me. I wouldn't ask this if it weren't serious. Larry needs me to look for him. I know it. But I need a cover story for being in Japan." Neil was almost pleading now, his voice rising. He took a deep breath. "I promise I'll quit if things get dangerous."

Angel flipped the skewers one more time, flames licking their sides as the sauce began to drip into the red-hot coals. He gave an almost imperceptible nod. "I will consider this, but I promise nothing. You must also promise to tell your parents."

"I promise." Neil didn't smile, but he pushed his hands off the table and stood up straight. "Thank you, Angel. I'll go pack." He started walking toward his bike but stopped and turned around. "Oh. And could you help Gary around the restaurant while I'm gone?"

Angel looked back over his shoulder and scowled. Neil turned back around, and found himself face-to-face with Isabella.

Isabella poked a finger into his chest and frowned. "Okay, Mr. *stupido*. Why did Angel say 'psychopath'?"

"Um," Neil fumbled. "It's a long story."

Isabella tapped her foot. "I have plenty of time. Get started."

Chapter Ten

The Psycho's Path

Matsumoro Nori stared at the undulating ocean. The white peaks of the waves stabbed fiercely at the horizon. Off in the distance he spied what appeared to be a small boat capsizing under a giant swell. Ah well, probably police spying on him as he sat moored in the private lagoon of his private island. No need to send them any help.

He sipped from his glass of *sake* and placed it back on his end table, fashioned from the head of a Siberian tiger. He watched the rice wine settle. In a moment it was perfectly still. Not a ripple. He smiled contentedly. His private yacht was as large as an island and just as stable, even with huge waves smashing against the sides. It was good to be rich.

"Time for some golf," he said, standing up. A butler silently appeared at his side with a bucket full of jewels. Nori waved him away and then reached down for one of the shining baubles. He held it up to the light, where it reflected the sunlight with a red glow.

"Rubies today. Very nice."

He gently rested the ruby on top of a plastic tee and held out his hand. The butler slinked up next to him and placed a club in Nori's hand. A boat with a floating golf green on its deck appeared out of nowhere and did its best to fight the waves about two hundred yards away.

With a fluid motion, Nori took his stance and with an arching swing he sent the ruby flying into the air. It gave a tiny splash a short distance away from the green and sank. He dipped his hand back in and lifted another, soon launching it a touch farther into the ocean.

"I feel like I'm improving," he said.

The butler nodded. "Yes, well played, sir."

After launching a few more rubies into the water, and one or two onto the green, Nori threw the club overboard. "Never use the same club twice, I always say." The butler nodded.

Nori clapped his hands and a table and chairs rose from the deck. "Time for lunch," he said, sitting down. His rear end had barely touched his seat when four waiters appeared at his side, looking nervous. One was practically sweating and was doing his best to suppress a nervous twitch.

"What has our wonderful chef and his crew prepared for us today, hmm?" One of the waiters stepped forward and lifted the lid off a silver serving tray. A rush of steam lifted an incredible aroma into the air. The cloud cleared

and Nori smiled. A giant sea turtle bisque sat before him, the head floating in the middle.

He dipped his spoon into the broth and lifted it to his nose. "Ahhh, cooked with beluga whale fat. Endangered and therefore even more delicious." This was the sort of meal he could enjoy only on his private yacht. These foods were banned back in Tokyo and almost everywhere else in the world.

He lifted the spoon up and turned it away from himself. The nervous waiter stepped forward and shook as he sucked some of the broth through his lips.

"Now swallow," Nori ordered.

The man gave a loud gulp and then stepped back in line. Sweat beaded on his lips and forehead. He closed his eyes and appeared to pray.

Nori watched him closely for any sign of impending death. There was always a chance that one of Nori's enemies would try to poison him. There was an equal chance that his chef would try the same thing, and an even bigger chance that one of his sous-chefs might make a mistake and grab some of the toxic ingredients Nori stocked in the kitchen. It was always better to double-check.

The waiter collapsed in a heap.

Nori stood up. "Is he dead? I'll KILL that chef!"

The waiter next to the fallen man leaned over and checked his pulse. "He's just fainted," he said.

Nori relaxed and shrugged. "Throw him overboard. I don't need any weaklings in my employ. At least I can eat my lunch in peace." The other waiters exchanged glances.

"But he's our brother," one of them said nervously.

"Then you can all jump overboard together! Never mind, you're all fired! GO!" Then he turned his attention back to the soup, which he lapped up greedily.

The waiters shuffled away behind him, carrying their unconscious sibling. Their escape was interrupted by the arrival of yet another servant, carrying a carved ivory cell phone. He had a look of panic in his eyes as he slowly shuffled toward Nori, who was now holding the bowl to his lips and drinking the soup with loud slurps.

"Um, ex-ex-excuse me, sir . . . there, there is a ph-ph-ph-phone call f-f-f-f-for you." He closed his eyes and held the phone out, standing as far away as he could from the table.

Nori suspended the bowl in mid-sip. "What? A phone call in the MIDDLE OF MY LUNCH!" He stood up so quickly the table shook. "NEVER DISTURB ME WHEN I'M EATING!" In a rage he took the rest of the meal and threw it overboard. A pack of sharks suddenly appeared and angrily battled over the gourmet leftovers.

Nori threw himself at the servant, choking him. The

man began to turn blue. As he fought to release himself, he lifted the hand with the phone to Nori's ear.

"Nori, Nori. It's Angel Jícama."

Nori's eyes darted to the phone. "Angel Jícama?" he said slowly. He scowled. "How's the underground catering business, Angel? Oh, I forgot, you're too good for that now."

"Matsumoto, I didn't call to reopen old wounds. I've got Neil Flambé here. He wants to speak to you."

Nori's lips curled into a huge evil grin. He released his grip on the servant, who fell backward gasping for air. Nori reached down and snatched the phone from his hands.

"Neil Flambé. I knew you'd call me eventually," he said, taking his seat again and resting his feet on his servant's stomach.

"Stuff it, Nori," Neil said. "I need money. Lots of it. Does your offer still stand?"

Nori paused and sighed. "You know, Master Flambé, I'm not very happy with some of the things you said about me in that interview about fishing."

"All I said was that you were killing the oceans single-handedly. Was that inaccurate?"

"The ocean is a source of fish. People eat fish. I catch fish."

"With a net the size of a small country. Then you throw the ones you don't like overboard."

"I keep the ones people will pay for. The sharks get the rest. I'm just a businessman, Neil. Like my good friend Jeanne Valette."

Neil gave a sharp intake of breath.

Nori smiled. "Ah, yes, I believe that she recently caused you some . . . discomfort. Thanks to you she's behind bars. I should like to offer you my appreciation for that. She's a friend, but it's always nice to have less competition."

"Speaking of competition . . ." Neil said.

Nori leaned forward, digging his heels into the servant's chest. He gritted his teeth. "Why now, Flambé? You have turned down repeated offers to battle my personal chef."

"You mentioned Valette. Perhaps you saw the damage she inflicted on my restaurant?"

"Ah, yes. It was very creative."

"And very expensive. The bank has given me a week to pay them back or I lose Chez Flambé."

"Then what are we waiting for? So we have a deal. The Ultimate Battle—how long I've waited for it."

"We fight the duel here, in Vancouver," Neil said firmly. "I need to keep the restaurant open."

Nori sat back again. The servant gave a relieved groan. "No, I'm afraid that won't do. You see, there are a few people who would love it if I left my yacht at the present moment. The duel will be held here in Japan."

"I can't leave my restaurant. And . . . and Japan is not a happy place for me right now."

Nori considered. "Ah, yes, your dead cousin. I don't care about that, but I do understand your concern about the restaurant."

"Gee, thanks," Neil said.

"But you must come to Japan. I so desperately want to see you lose in person. So let's say we make this worth both our whiles. You risk losing the restaurant, but if you win I will pay you so much money that you can open a new restaurant *chain*."

"And if I lose?"

"Then you won't need a restaurant. You'll become my personal chef's personal assistant and the only chain you'll have then will be tying you to my kitchen." Nori chuckled.

There was a long silence on the line.

"Agreed," Neil said finally.

Nori practically leaped out of his chair. "Perfect. A jet will be there to pick you up tonight!"

Neil's only response was a click as he closed his phone.

Nori gave out a loud whoop and began dancing a jig. Unfortunately for his servant, Nori was still standing on his chest.

"Neil Flambé! Coming here to battle. My goodness, how I have waited for this moment. Humiliation for that brat, and revenge on Angel Jícama! Priceless!"

He bent down and stared straight into the servant's eyes. "Tell chef I'd like to see him."

The servant nodded and gave a grunt as Nori stepped off him.

In a few moments he returned with an enormous man in a chef's outfit. He looked like a sumo wrestler who'd accidentally stumbled into a kitchen.

"You want to see me, boss?" said the mountain.

"Ah, Kong. Yes. I have something to tell you."

"Didn't like the soup?"

"What? Soup. Oh, yes, the turtle . . . it was sublime. I'm distracted by a bigger fish, shall we say."

"Turtle's not a fish."

"I know that. I was being descriptive."

"Description was wrong," Kong said.

Nori smacked his face with the palm of his hand. "Look, it's not important. What IS important is that you are about to face the biggest challenge of your life. I ate at his restaurant only once, but I knew instantly that I needed to have him here to battle you . . . and to add to our kitchen staff. I offered him money then, but he refused. That meddling Angel Jícama must have told him about me."

"Who is this chef?"

"Neil Flambé. A boy. And perhaps the greatest chef in the world."

Kong shrugged. "I am a man and I am the greatest chef in the world."

Nori smiled. "That's exactly what I want to hear. Now you have one more chance to prove that."

"If I lose?"

Nori laid a hand on Kong's shoulder. "Let's just say the sharks will enjoy more than leftover turtle soup."

Kong gave a shudder. A small ripple splashed in Nori's glass of *sake*.

Chapter Eleven

Girding His Tenderloin

Neil clicked his phone shut. "He bought it," he said. "There's a jet coming for me tonight."

Neil was in his kitchen, surrounded by his friends. He'd shown them the pomegranates in *The Chef*. Jones said he couldn't see how Neil could notice the difference in such a tiny drawing. Neil reminded him which of the two was a chef and which was a human retaining wall. Jones was about to remind him of the same thing, with his knuckles, when Nakamura coughed and shook his head.

Isabella had been distracted by the skimpy outfit on the heroine and had muttered something like, "If Larry isn't dead, he'll soon wish he were." Angel, on the other hand, had seen a glimmer of truth in Neil's assessment and dialed Nori from Neil's cell phone.

Neil smirked. "He seemed pretty confident that I wasn't going to be coming back here. I guess I'd better pack more than my knives."

Angel gave a loud sigh. "This is not good."

Isabella and Jones nodded in agreement.

Neil ran his fingers through his hair. "I don't have time to think of a better plan. And this is going to work: Nori believes that I don't want to go, and he's willing to pay. That's the important thing." Well, maybe there were some other important things too. No matter. He had a ten-hour flight ahead of him to figure them out.

Angel folded his arms. "I've helped you because I knew I couldn't change your mind. But Nori is a criminal, a very dangerous criminal. He has his hands in almost every illegal transaction in the culinary world. Olive oil imports, endangered species, tuna smuggling, underground duels. You must be careful."

Nakamura snapped his fingers. "I've got a good idea. Stop looking so skeptical, Nose. I'll go undercover as your translator. That way you've got some protection and maybe I can help look for Larry if you're tied up. That's a figure of speech."

"You're a police officer. Won't that be suspicious?" Isabella asked.

"As Neil may remember from the thirty or so undercover assignments we've done together, I can wear a disguise pretty well."

Neil had to admit this was true. Nakamura had also given him advice on staying incognito on their recent trip to Mexico City.

"I'll ditch the cop clothes, especially the comfortable shoes, shave my mustache . . ."

There was a gasp from everyone.

"That would be . . . amazing," Neil said, grateful and

a little shocked. Nakamura without facial hair was a bit like a curry with no ginger.

"I'll go pack as well, and I'll get one of my, er, traveling passports. I'll see you at the airport . . . boss." He left through the dining room. "When I get there, call me Hachikō."

Neil had always suspected there was a shadier side to Nakamura's police work than he let on; he resolved to ask him more about it later.

Gary arrived at the back door, carrying his bike on his shoulder. "That was the best funeral I've ever been to! Leave it to Larry to throw a posthumous party! More of my friends should croak!"

Neil walked up to Gary. "He's not dead."

Gary smiled and winked. "I know that. He's in the sky, looking down on us."

"No, I mean he's really not dead. I'm going to look for him for a while. Don't tell anyone. I need you to help Angel run the restaurant while I'm away. Try not to go broke, okay? We're about one bad night away from missing a bank payment."

Gary nodded slowly. "If he's not dead, do you think he'll mind that I was hitting on that organist with the cool hair? Cause she and I hit it off really well. We're going to a concert tomorrow, actually."

Neil rubbed his temples. Gary had somehow missed the point. He was eerily like Larry. "Gary, I honestly think he'd be angrier if you were using his coffeemaker."

"Whew. Excellent. Now, what was the bit about the restaurant?"

"Don't let it go bankrupt."

Gary laughed. "Is that a joke? I mean, thanks for the confidence, but have you seen me with money? I'll probably run the place into the ground by the weekend! Me, run a restaurant?" Gary started laughing so hard he doubled over, grabbing his ribs.

This was not the response Neil was looking for. *Great,* he thought, *now I really need to win this stupid duel.*

"Angel will cook the other entrees and the twins will handle the money, then," Neil said, his eyes shut and his temples throbbing. "Just make sure you're here for work and keep bringing in those great fish."

Gary managed to give a thumbs-up while now sliding onto the floor. Neil just shook his head sadly. "I need to get ready and I need to tell my parents I'm leaving." He hugged everyone and then walked out back and rode away on his bike.

Isabella sat at her worktable, staring blankly at the rows and rows of test tubes and beakers. She'd been using orchid and cherry blossom extract for her latest series of flower-inspired perfumes. But all the combinations and oils she'd been able to buy smelled too

bland. Isabella's reputation was based on subtlety, not invisibility.

It wasn't the wasted money that was bothering her now—it was Neil's crazy trip to Japan to look for his cousin. "Why does he keep taking off on these *stupido* adventures?" Isabella said, sitting back in her chair and folding her arms.

"Because he's an idiot, from a long line of idiots," Jones said, not taking his eyes off his wilderness survival magazine.

"And a duel!" she huffed. Isabella hated duels. Her father had died in one. "Neil promised to avoid them and here he goes to fight another!"

Jones sighed and put down the magazine. Clearly Isabella felt like talking. "Has it occurred to you that Neil *likes* duels? He seems to find an excuse to break his promise to you at the drop of a chef's hat."

"Are all men stupid thrill seekers?" she said, glaring at the cover of his magazine, which showed a group of hikers jumping off the side of a cliff to escape a pack of wolves.

"Yes," Jones said calmly. "We are."

Isabella huffed. "What do we know about this Nori anyway? I'm sure you've done a background check."

Jones nodded. "Angel told us some of the broad strokes. He's a crook for sure. He owns a fleet of illegal whaling ships. He also owns a series of restaurants that sell illegally caught fish. He bought a frozen woolly mammoth last month and has been selling it for top dollar at one of his Tokyo clubs as 'aged *wagyu* beef'."

"Stupid."

"Once a year he even holds a big dinner where the richest men in the world get to catch and eat their own endangered species."

"Disgusting," Isabella said.

"It's a thrill seeker's delight because sometimes the species catch and eat the hunter. That's why Panko Pharmaceuticals needed a new president last year."

"Sick," Isabella added.

Jones nodded. "Angel and he used to run a series of underground duels. This was before Nori developed his taste for giant panda, but that duel that claimed your dad was bankrolled by Nori and his friends in the Italian mob."

Isabella's eyes narrowed and she pursed her lips so tightly they turned white. "I hate this man."

Jones nodded. "Join the club."

Isabella sat up so suddenly she almost spilled a beaker

of perfume. "You say this horrible man, this *brutto*, fishes illegally?"

"Yes," Jones said, looking a little worried by Isabella's anger. "Why?"

Isabella smacked her forehead. "*Idiota*. I have been so stupid. This Nori is Larry's killer!"

"What, why . . . what? I thought Larry wasn't dead?"

"Dead or not, his ship was sunk. What if he and Hiro were not going sightseeing but were going to protest illegal fishing. Their boat was bombed, or rammed, just like his parents' boat . . . and this Nori gave the order. This was all designed to lure Neil to Japan. And Neil is walking right into his clutches!"

"Slow down. I didn't see any evidence of any of that," Jones said, holding up his hands in the universal sign for *whoa*.

Isabella was now pacing up and down the floor of her lab. "We have to warn him. No, he is too pigheaded to turn back now." She stopped in the middle of the floor and turned to face Jones. "It is simple. We must go to Japan. I will help look for Larry. You will help look after Neil."

Jones started to interrupt, but Isabella raced on. "You're right. We will not tell Neil. I have the perfect excuse to go there." She reached for a vial of scented oil and poured it on the floor. "I am in desperate need of better ingredients. Do you think we can get plane tickets for tomorrow morning?"

Jones now lifted his hands in the equally universal sign for *I surrender*.

"I take it that's not a real question?" he asked, knowing his wasn't a real question either.

Isabella smiled. "And don't forget to book us a nice hotel in Tokyo. We'll figure out how to make our paths cross with Neil once we get there." Then she walked out the door.

"Now who's the thrill seeker?" Jones mumbled under his breath as he typed in the number for his travel agent.

Chapter Twelve

Into the Eye of the Storm

Neil flipped open his laptop and was happy, but not surprised, to see that there was wireless connection on Nori's private jet. He was just as certain that Nori would be tracking everything he typed in and every site he searched. He'd be careful and wouldn't check the site for *The Chef*, no matter how much he wanted to see if Larry had sent any more clues.

Nakamura, clean-shaven and dressed in jeans, sat across from Neil, reveling in the amenities of the luxury jet.

"This food is amazing!" he said. "It's so hard to find real *udon* noodles in Vancouver. And the fish in this *dashi* aren't frozen, they're fresh!" Nakamura was also on his third Godzilla movie, in Japanese. "This is so much better without those horrible voice-overs." He was giddier than Neil had ever seen him, and without his mustache he seemed years younger.

"You relive your childhood, Nak . . . I mean Hachikō. I've got work to do."

Nakamura waved to the flight attendant for more popcorn shrimp and settled in with his headset. Neil heard him laughing and cheering for Godzilla as the jet smoothly made its way over the ocean. Neil spent his time searching websites on Japanese cooking techniques. He wasn't even sure what the rules were for the duel but he suspected he'd need to bone up on his knife work.

As if on cue there was a *ping* and Neil saw an e-mail from Nori titled "RULES FOR THE ULTIMATE BATTLE."

He certainly has a flare for the dramatic, Neil thought. Then he opened the e-mail and realized Nori wasn't exaggerating. As Neil had already known, the duel wouldn't be just one day, winner take all. No, part of Nori's pitch had always been that there would be five separate duels over a week.

But apparently nothing about these matches would be straightforward. Each duel would have a different theme, and Neil would receive a clue the day before that he would have to figure out to be ready for the battle.

Neil tapped on Nakamura's shoulder and showed him the e-mail.

"So you've got a week," Nakamura whispered across the aisle.

"What? Check your math. I've got four days."

Nakamura looked confused. "Four?"

"I'll win the duel three to zero, so it'll be over after just four days," Neil said matter-of-factly.

Nakamura just rolled his eyes and turned up the volume on the TV.

Neil sat back and his laptop pinged again. There was a new e-mail—"Battle #1," it said.

"That was quick." Neil opened it. *The first duel will take place in two days on my yacht. You will receive a shopping list tomorrow, on your arrival in Tokyo. Until then, enjoy the flight.*

Neil didn't like the idea of being stuck on a boat when he really needed to be following leads in Larry's disappearance. Tokyo was a good place to start, but he needed to do more than just drop in.

Neil started typing a response: *I get seasick. Can we change the venue to Tokyo?* He hit send.

Almost immediately there was a response. *Land is risky for me, especially Tokyo. I assure you my boat is very solid but let no one accuse me of being unfair. If we can battle on land we will try. It will take time to secure my safe passage. Stay tuned. Also, you can stay in Tokyo and we will arrange transport for the duels.*

Neil considered. This was better than nothing. He had no leads at all yet so he'd use his free time to look for some. Tokyo seemed a likely starting ground. Nakamura could stay behind during the duels to keep up the work. Neil wouldn't need him on board the ship.

He typed, *Okay, agreed.* Then he hit send and closed the laptop. He was still hours away from Tokyo and felt a sudden wave of exhaustion. He turned off his overhead light and fell asleep to the sound of Nakamura chanting, "Godzilla, Godzilla."

Chapter Thirteen

Tokyo

Neil had never been to Tokyo. He stepped out of the airport shuttle train onto the streets of Japan's capital city and stood still in shocked silence. It was a mind-blowing experience. Skyscrapers rose up and filled every available nook and cranny of street and sky. Despite the glare of the sun, neon lights twirled and blinked, sending rainbows of electric light everywhere.

Space that wasn't filled with concrete or glass was filled up with cars, bikes, and a seemingly endless moving crowd of people. Neil had been in big cities before many times, but he'd never seen so *much* city crammed into such a small place. It was like a normal sized city had been compressed into one block, squeezing everything together and up . . . except Tokyo went on like that for blocks and blocks and blocks.

Nakamura finally brought him back to reality with a nudge on the shoulder. "I think we should find our hotel."

Neil nodded dumbly and leaned down to grab his luggage. He couldn't take his eyes off this strange new place.

Nakamura hailed a cab and had to drag Neil into the seat beside him. "Okay, Nose. Let's drop off our bags and then we'll lose ourselves in the throng and do a little digging. Nori probably has a car here to pick us up, but I think we should take our own cab."

Neil stared at the constantly moving streetscape. Lots of people stared back. The site of a gangly redheaded chef was just as odd to them as their city was to Neil.

The cab barely moved in the traffic and soon Nakamura was sound asleep. Neil went back to gazing at all the people and shops.

A tapping noise jolted Neil from his thoughts. It was coming from the rear window. Neil turned around. There was a bike courier right behind them. He waved at Neil to roll down his window, then pulled up along-side, squeezing himself into an almost impossible space between the gridlocked cars. Neil thought for a bizarre moment that Gary had followed them to Tokyo.

Neil rolled down his window, just a bit, and the courier slipped an envelope through the slit. Then he made an abrupt left turn and disappeared.

Neil examined the envelope. *Instructions for Round #1* was written on the front. He was tempted to wake Nakamura, if only to tell him that Nori didn't need a driver to know how to find them, but decided to let him sleep.

He opened the envelope and read the instructions.

To solve the first clue,
seven days, but you have one
red hair as your guide

(PS: Be at the docks tomorrow at four
p.m. Look to the skies.)

"Oh brother, a haiku? You've got to be kidding me."
Neil stared at the clue again, his mind drawing a complete blank. It was like being in English class all over
again. "What the heck does this even mean?" The references were completely lost on him. Red hair? Was the
secret ingredient his hair? He scanned his memory for
any reference to hair in Japanese cuisine. Other than a
bad joke Larry had once told him about a waiter and
dandruff, he drew a blank.

This was going to take forever to figure out. How the
heck could he search for Larry while he was looking for
some stupid ingredient?

Nakamura blinked awake. He saw the look on Neil's
face and immediately knew something was up. "What's
the deal?" he said.

Neil handed him the letter. A huge smile spread
across Nakamura's face. "Too easy," he scoffed. "We'll
even have hours left over to look for that 'other' ingredient." Now that they were in Tokyo "ingredient" was
their code name for Larry.

Neil was dumbfounded.

Then without another word of explanation,
Nakamura closed his eyes and went back to sleep.

"You're telling me this clue is so easy a child could figure
it out?" Neil said angrily. He and Nakamura had checked
into their hotel and now were strolling down a series of
increasingly seedy-looking alleyways. The narrow paths

were made even more constricted by rows of makeshift stalls selling everything from sweet-smelling drinks to homemade reed mats.

"A Japanese child could, for sure." Nakamura smiled. He was clearly enjoying having the upper hand on Neil and had no intention of letting him in on the secret.

"Will you at least tell me where we're heading?" Neil could tell they were getting closer and closer to some seriously potent food shops. His nose had picked up that aroma, among others that were less appetizing, as soon as they'd turned the last corner. The dirtier and more cramped the alleys, the more savory the aroma. This was a part of Tokyo he hadn't seen from the cab window.

"I know a place where we can get the stuff for your so-called secret ingredient, and then start our investigating."

Neil noticed Nakamura hadn't stopped anyone to ask for directions or even slowed down to read street signs.

"How do you know where to go? You haven't been here in years."

"You don't forget a place like this," Nakamura said, making a right turn. "Almost there."

Now the smells were coming at Neil in waves—and they were glorious. Wherever they were heading, he was starting to look forward to the arrival.

"How do you know this place is still open?"

"I highly doubt it's going to close after a thousand years. Besides, I think Suzu has been running the place since the beginning; he isn't going to let it go out of business now," Nakamura said with a chuckle.

"Suzu? Who's Suzu?"

Nakamura stopped in the middle of the alley and pointed straight ahead. "He is."

Neil saw an old man with an incredibly long beard and white hair sitting in front of what looked like a wooden shack. Silk banners hung down from the sides, darkened with age and tattered.

"You're taking me to a pawn shop?" Neil asked.

Nakamura rolled his eyes. "Please. I know that your nose picked up the scent of this place ages ago, so can the cheap shots. This is Suzu's Emporium, the best spice shop in Japan, maybe the world." He stepped forward. "You can get almost anything."

Suzu's eyes were almost completely covered with thick white eyebrows but Neil saw him look up as Nakamura approached. "Sean Nakamura," he said with a raspy voice, in perfect English. "It's been a while. You look so much like your father."

Nakamura nodded sadly. "He first brought me here when I was just a little boy," he explained to Neil. "This was his secret location for great ingredients when he was a chef." He turned back to Suzu and told him the clue. "Do you happen to have seven spices that a redheaded chef might use?"

Suzu laughed, a kind of wheezing cough really. He heaved so much Neil was worried he was going to fall over and break something. Suzu stood up, still chuckling, and beckoned for them to follow him inside.

Neil passed through the silk curtain and let out a long low whistle. He felt like an explorer who had just walked into a cave of golden statues. Each possible bit of space on the shelves was filled with jars of spices, dried mushrooms, and glistening oils. The colors were glorious. The smells were profound.

Neil knelt down by open bags of rice and was blown away by their freshness. He was soon running from shelf to shelf, sniffing everything like a dog in a new home.

"I see your young friend has a deep appreciation of quality." Suzu smiled. He handed Neil a sliver of smoked eel. Neil ate it, and the flavors exploded on his tongue.

"I want to buy it all, the whole store," Neil said.

"Hold on there, Nose," Nakamura said. "Remember the riddle. Any seven spices stick out for a ginger like you?"

Neil finally figured it out. "Of course. *Shichimi tōgarashi*," he said sheepishly. "The seven great spices." Nakamura and Suzu nodded. Japanese chefs had used the mixture for centuries. You could even buy over-the-counter premixed versions in almost every corner store. No wonder Nakamura had said it was a simple clue. But he knew his young chef friend better than to think he'd be interested in supermarket spices. Premixed was not a word in Neil Flambé's vocabulary.

Bringing him here was a gift. "Thanks, faithful servant," he said, smiling at Nakamura.

"Go crazy," Nakamura said. "I'll see if there's any information available here to go with the spices."

Neil walked to the shelves and picked out red chili pepper, Sichuan

pepper, orange peel, and ginger. He used his nose to choose the best and freshest. *All red, like my hair, and spicy and amazing,* he thought. Then he rounded out the spice mixture with white and black sesame seeds and the seaweed known as *aonori*.

He still wasn't sure what type of duel he'd be fighting. The seven-spice mixture was the base of so many Japanese dishes. Neil was sure of one thing—no matter what Nori threw his way, Neil had the best *shichimi tōgarashi* possible.

Neil laid a nice pile of money on the front table. Nakamura was standing next to Suzu, nodding as Suzu told him something in Japanese. Neil walked over.

Nakamura had a wistful look on his face.

"Suzu was just telling me how my father would pick a very similar mixture, but with slightly less ginger."

Suzu nodded and looked at Neil. "The spices you are using are very powerful. Be careful not to use too much or you will overpower your dish."

Neil was not always the most grateful recipient of cooking advice, but he knew Suzu was right. He just bowed and said, "I promise to do my best to honor your wonderful spices."

Suzu smiled. "Good luck. Now I must close up for the evening. Sean Nakamura, your father is proud of you."

Nakamura just bowed silently.

Neil and Nakamura walked back out into the alleyway. Neil couldn't help but turn around to see the spices one more time. To his surprise, the front of the spice tent looked completely different. There was a wall of videocassettes and iron woks on display, but no sign of Suzu or the spices. Neil could still smell them, but where had they gone?

"What the—?" Neil said. He looked at Nakamura for an answer, but he seemed lost in thought.

Neil just shook his head. *Tokyo's a weird place*, he thought.

They turned a corner and Nakamura finally spoke. "Now that you have your spices, I think the best place to start looking for leads would be Hiro's memorial ceremony."

"When is the ceremony? Can we make it?"

"Yes. It's tomorrow morning."

"Where? I need to be at the docks tomorrow afternoon."

Nakamura smiled. "Down the street from our hotel. That's why I booked us in there. Now let's find a safe Wi-Fi spot and see if Larry's sent us any other clues."

Neil nodded. He somehow felt that Larry was close, and (he hoped) no longer in danger.

Chapter Fourteen

Morning Mourning

Hiro's funeral was about as far away from Larry's crazy service as Neil could imagine. There were no laughs, Mad Libs, me-shirts, or snacks—just a lot of sad family members gathered around a spare altar. Bells rang deep low notes to call the mourners into the temple. A wooden tablet sat where Hiro's coffin should have been. Incense burned in an urn, filling the temple with a sweet smoky aroma.

Pictures of Hiro fishing, at art school, with his family, and in traditional dress adorned the front of the room. A priest chanted some words and Neil did his best to mimic the actions of Hiro's family and Nakamura who was kneeling next to him on the temple floor.

"I'm trying to fit in," he whispered to Nakamura, as they bowed together at the priest's words.

Nakamura looked at Neil's gangly body, pale skin, and flaming red hair. "Good luck," he said.

Neil's mood didn't totally match the funeral. He was actually anxious and excited. There had indeed been another clue hidden in the final panel of The Chef.

Vegemight's ship was anchored on a port outside the Chef's cave. The port didn't have a name before, but when Neil checked this morning the name "Oshima" was clearly written on a sign in tiny letters. It was yet another detail that a normal reader would certainly miss. But Neil was sure that Larry was leaving more hidden signposts.

"It's a volcanic island a little ways south of here," Nakamura said when Neil had shown him the picture. "There are some spas and even a small airport. It's apparently a good spot for scuba diving."

"Sounds lovely."

"If I find out Larry's been updating his manga from some lounge chair in a Japanese spa, I'll throw him into the volcano," Nakamura said.

The image of Larry sitting in shorts and sunglasses with a laptop actually made them both chuckle, but also seemed sadly unlikely.

Neil nodded. "Okay, as a clue, it doesn't have much meaning yet. But it is another sign that Larry is alive and is trying to tell me something. Maybe I'll request that one of the Ultimate Battles take place at Oshima. Nori wouldn't even have to leave his precious yacht."

But Neil was feeling somber as well. Larry might be alive, but there was no indication that Hiro was. After all, Hiro was the artist—but only Larry knew the significance of replacing avocado with pomegranates. As far as anyone knew, this was a real funeral for a missing young man. Neil had no words of encouragement for Hiro's family. He was also feeling anxious about the leads he might find there.

Everyone bowed again and Neil spied a young woman at the front, giving her offering of incense. She was, there was no other word for it, cute. Koko Takoyaki, exactly as Larry had described her. She had short hair and dark serious eyes which were presently glued to the wooden tablet. She seemed to be wishing her brother back from the dead. She added her incense to the smoking urn and returned to kneel on the floor.

Now Neil couldn't take his eyes off her. Somehow Neil needed to ask her some difficult questions, and he needed to ask them without a roomful of people listening.

The funeral ended. Nakamura explained that normally the family would head to the crematorium, but with no body to cremate they mingled around the temple receiving wishes and gifts from the mourners. They'd take these and Hiro's personal belongings to the crematorium later to burn in his place.

Neil did his best to stay on the fringes of the crowd, waiting for a chance to catch Koko alone. Then he felt a tap on his shoulder and swung around to find himself staring into Koko's eyes.

"You must be Larry's cousin, the chef?"

Neil was caught off guard. He'd had a whole speech rehearsed in his head to try to bring up the question of the website and the accident without raising any suspicion. The way she stared at him with those intense deep dark eyes rendered him speechless. Nakamura finally elbowed him in the ribs, and Neil fumbled out a few clumsy words.

"I, uh, I, umm, I'm, uh, very sorry for your loss."

Koko looked down and Neil felt his face go red. "I know the time is not very . . . good, but I have some questions about . . . about what happened."

She looked back up and the spell was recast. "Why are you here?" she asked in a voice as enticing as her eyes.

"Um, well . . . I don't really want to be here at all. I was just in town and heard about the ceremony, so I thought I'd drop in and offer my condolences."

"Just in town? You just happened to be in Tokyo?"

She raised an eyebrow and stared at him. Why was she picking up the sketchiest parts of his story?

"Um, yeah. Well, not really, no. I'm just here for a cooking . . . thing." He tried to wave his hands nonchalantly.

"A duel." She nodded. "Your cousin said you did those. And what do you want to know? How they died?"

Neil just nodded. Koko had expertly put herself in the role of the grand inquisitor in this conversation.

"They went out boating. A storm came up. You must have heard that. You don't believe it?"

Neil started to say he didn't know, but Koko continued. "Neither do I. They were not going sightseeing at all. They were going out to confront a ship, a whaling ship, an illegal ship. They didn't tell me this, but I know it is true. I am a marine biologist; did you know that?"

Neil nodded, completely rattled.

She continued. "I hate these fishermen. I think they rammed my brother's boat. But the police say there was no such ship on the ocean that day."

"You think the police got it wrong?" Neil said.

"No. I think they are being paid off." She clenched her fist and slammed it down on the back of a chair. Neil noticed with concern that she had actually split the wood completely in half. "I also know there was no freak storm. But they are both dead. That I do know." Her eyes fell again.

Neil was about to tell her about Larry's clue, but something told him to tread cautiously and not give away any information. That something was Nakamura whispering in his ear, "Tread cautiously. Never give away information."

Neil chose his words carefully. "Can I ask you a question about the manga?"

She stared at him intently. "Yes, what?"

Neil took a deep breath and continued, trying to sound offhand. "Did Larry leave any instructions about the website? Any changes in case he didn't come back from the trip?" He expected an easy "no."

"Yes," Koko said. "He did."

Neil was dumbfounded. He realized with a jolt that a "no" would have confirmed that his theory was right. Larry was alive and changing the manga. "Yes" meant the opposite. He felt his knees buckle and he watched as Koko reached into her purse and pulled out an envelope.

"After his death, I found this in his room, under his pillow." She handed it to Neil, who took it with shaking hands. He opened the envelope and slid out a thick sheet of writing paper. It was a note, in Larry's handwriting, dated the morning of their fishing trip. The note asked Koko to change the avocados to pomegranates and a few days later to change the name of the port to Oshima Island. The room began to spin. Neil took a deep breath and steadied himself on Nakamura's shoulders.

"I am so sorry," she said. There was movement at the altar. The priest had returned and was summoning the family to head to the crematorium. "I have to go." She walked out of the temple, leaving Neil staring at the floor.

Nakamura watched them all leave and then put a hand on Neil's shoulder, steadying him. "Oh, boy. Darn it. Hey, Nose . . . you knew this was a possibility. I told you back at the restaurant. I'm sorry."

Neil lifted his head. He was smiling.

"She's wrong," Neil said. "He's alive."

Nakamura shook his head. "Neil, you've got to give it up. We've come halfway around the world. He's gone, okay? Maybe this was just wishful thinking . . ."

"I'm still not nuts, bonehead." Neil looked around to make sure they were now alone. "I know that this was left *after* Larry supposedly died."

"How?" Nakamura said.

Neil lifted the letter to his nose and took a long, slow sniff. "Fish. Larry smeared fish on the paper before he sealed it in the envelope."

"That's . . . gross."

"But also intentional. Any chance Larry, who hates seafood, would actually be near fish by choice?"

Nakamura had seen Larry's reaction to fish many times. "Not likely, no."

"So he wanted me to know that he left his note on purpose. But why?" Neil sat down in a chair, thinking.

Nakamura tapped his upper lip and then said. "How do we know Koko didn't have fish for dinner and rub it on the paper herself?"

Neil sniffed the envelope again. "It's only on the letter, not the envelope. . . . Well, there's some on the inside of the envelope, but it's only residue from the letter. She's handled both and kept them together. They'd have the same smell if the fish smell were coming from her hands."

"Nose, your nose is something else. Don't ever get plastic surgery."

"Agreed. So the letter is not fishy by accident, which means Larry meant for me to smell it." Neil took another sniff. "I've got it."

"What?"

Neil stood up and started pacing the floor. "Koko did make the changes to *The Chef*."

"So Larry left the note before he went out, sensing he might be killed."

Neil smiled. "No. He wrote the note after the accident, and left it for Koko to find—but needed her to believe it was written before his boating trip, so she wouldn't suspect anything, and would make the changes to the manga."

"Okay, but how do you know it wasn't before the boating trip?"

"Let's suppose Larry made a fishy mess of some kind. If that were the case, then the envelope and the letter would smell the same. He made sure to purposely rub fish on the letter."

"I repeat, gross. Why?"

"He knew that the changes in the manga would lure me here to look for him. He also knew I'd eventually find out Koko had made the changes, so he smeared fish on the note so I'd know he asked for the changes after his trip with Hiro. He left enough scent for Koko to miss it but for me to know he was still alive."

Nakamura considered this. "Wait a minute. Why go through the ruse of leaving a letter in his room at all?"

Neil thought for a second. "Maybe he doesn't want anyone to know he's alive, so this was another way to notify me without revealing himself. He knew I'd come to Japan after seeing the pomegranates, so he knew I'd eventually find this note."

"Why not reveal himself to Koko? Let her tell you he's alive?"

Neil thought of her eyes. She would have mesmerized Larry, he was sure of that. "To protect her. This way, she's not implicated because she's just carrying out his last wishes. As far as Koko knows, Larry is dead, like her brother."

"Okay. Larry is alive again. The guy has more lives than a cat! So what next?"

Neil checked his watch. "I have a duel to get ready for."

Nakamura nodded. "I'll keep looking for clues here in Tokyo."

Neil nodded and a chilling thought occurred to him. "If Koko thinks they were killed by an illegal whaling boat, then I might be heading for exactly the right place: Nori's ship."

Chapter Fifteen

Begin the Ultimate Battle

Neil stared out the helicopter window. The ocean was spread out below him like a gray steel sheet. They had been flying for what seemed like hours, and Neil wasn't sure where they were heading. A small green dot appeared and grew, and as they approached, Neil could see it was an island. There was a wide bay, and moored inside that was the largest boat Neil had ever seen. It was basically a skyscraper that had decided to go for a swim.

As the helicopter began to land, Neil tried to prep for the battle. He found it a little hard to focus. His mind kept skipping back to a few hours before, when he had decided it would be a good idea to check in back home to see if Gary and Angel were having any trouble running the restaurant. The call did not go well.

"Cool, everything's cool. We're losing a little bit of money, but nothing too serious. You know, a lot of people see that you're not here so they duck out, no pun intended. Angel doesn't want it public knowledge that he's here, something about avoiding the culinary spotlight, so people see me. . . . Maybe I should shave. Didn't have time today, though. Oh, and I lost the key and had to jimmy the back door lock."

Neil had stared blankly at his phone. He was about to start a patented ear-splitting tirade when Gary continued.

"Whoa, that's a lot of smoke. Love to talk more but I've gotta go help the twins with that fire. Say hi to Isabella for me." Then the line went dead.

"Fire? Say hi to Isabella? LOSING MONEY!?!" He'd tried calling back but no one had answered. Neil's forehead was still smarting from where he'd repeatedly banged the cell phone.

The helicopter landed. Once the rotors stopped, an immaculately dressed butler opened the door and silently beckoned for Neil to follow him. Neil grabbed his bag, containing his knives, chef's outfit, and seven-spice mixture. He stepped onto the deck of the ship. The sunlight reflected off the smooth, clean surface and temporarily blinded him.

He shielded his eyes with his hands and could just make out a dark shape rising up before him. The sun was momentarily blocked out, like an eclipse.

"Neil Flambé, welcome to my yacht." Nori's voice

seemed to be coming from somewhere in the middle of the shape.

"I don't think you've ever met my personal chef. Kong, say hello to your next victim."

The shadow leaned over and bowed. It was a person? Neil's eyes finally adjusted and he found himself staring at an enormous scowling giant in a chef's outfit. He made Jones look like a hobbit.

The mountain said something in Japanese and Nori, who came up to his belly button, chuckled.

"What's so funny?" Neil said.

"He says there is no way an infant can match a grown man in the kitchen."

Neil clenched his teeth and stood up straight. That was exactly the wrong thing to say to Neil Flambé to put him off his guard. "He's certainly a grown man. What do you feed that guy, fertilizer?"

Nori translated and Kong's scowl scowled even more.

"Enough of this pleasant chitchat. Let the battle begin." Nori clapped his hands and Neil struggled to stay on his feet as their section of the deck suddenly began to sink. They were in a glass cylinder, and the floor was passing down through the ship.

Neil watched out of the sides as they passed through floor after floor. There were several women who might have been supermodels lounging by a swimming pool, followed by a cinema, bowling alley, and what Neil assumed was an art gallery. He thought he recognized a few of the paintings from newspaper reports of museum thefts, but they were going so quickly that he couldn't be sure. Then they passed a zoo, packed with animals in tiny cages.

Finally, the elevator stopped in the midst of a gleaming stainless steel kitchen. Neil had never seen such a beautiful arrangement of unsurpassed stoves, fridges, blenders, sinks, ovens, steamers. . . . It went on for what seemed like a city block. The door opened with a rush of air. Neil walked over to the kitchen and ran his hands over the countertops. Smooth and brand-new. He went to open the oven door and was temporarily blinded by a sparkling light. The control knobs were encrusted with diamonds.

For a moment Neil thought he'd died and gone to heaven. Then he remembered they'd gone *down* a dozen flights. He shook his head to regain his senses. "All right, Nori. I got the clue. Now what's the battle?" he said.

Nori laughed with delight. "You're so eager to lose. It's like watching a gladiator right before the emperor releases the lions!" He was practically singing as he clapped again. The lights went up, revealing a whole arena full of spectators. They were all dressed in incredible amounts of jewelry and tailored suits. *Nori's millionaire buddies*, Neil thought, shaking his head. Sure enough, the crowd was speckled with large men and women in dark suits, dark sunglasses, radio headsets, and telling bulges in their jackets. Neil was sure that

Nakamura would have recognized many of them from the Interpol most wanted list.

An enormous cheer went up as Kong made his way to his stove and raised a fist in the air. A spotlight focused on Neil and the crowd booed. Neil frowned. *Nice home-field advantage*, he thought.

Neil saw five people sitting at a low desk in front of the crowd who didn't cheer or boo. *Must be the judges*, he thought. They sat with their hands in front of them, fingers intertwined, waiting, stone-faced.

Nori walked over to an enormous stainless steel box. "If you read my clue correctly, then you have arrived with the seven-spice blend known as *shichimi tōgarashi*." Neil nodded. Kong scowled. Neil wondered if his mouth muscles were frozen in that position.

Nori opened the box. "Today you will need those spices or else your dish will suffer and these five judges will suffer. Your challenge today is to make an udon noodle soup with"—he paused for effect before lifting the lid, revealing a large clear glass tank packed with— "LOBSTER!"

The crowd went crazy, chanting, "Kong, Kong! Lobster! Lobster!"

Neil stared at the crowd and back to Nori and then Kong. "Lobster soup? Seriously. That's the challenge? Am I missing something?"

Nori grinned smugly. "Let's hope not. You see, half of these lobsters have been injected with a rather lethal strain of a neurotoxin, developed by my friends in Nikita Labs." He gave a nod to a serious-looking woman in the third row, who responded with a smile of golden teeth.

Neil noticed her necklace was made of bullets. Nice.

Nori continued. "And you need to make sure you avoid them."

Neil remembered what Angel had said about Nori's fascination with food, especially dangerous food. "Wait. You're asking us to risk cooking a poisoned lobster?"

"Yes. The challenges in my kitchen duels seem simple, but the consequences are deadly."

"Don't the judges have anything to say about this? They could be killed!" Neil said, shocked.

One of the judges looked straight at Neil, her face twisting in a bizarre scowl. "Yes, I have something to say, young man. START COOKING!"

Kong ambled up to the tank and stared at the swimming crustaceans. He seemed to be looking for something specific as he stared at each lobster intently. Sensing imminent death, or simply scared, they seemed to cower in a bunch at the back of the tank. Neil walked over as well, still a little dazed. The lobsters looked identical in every respect, especially crowded together.

"You go first, Flambé. That leaves you with better statistical odds and nothing to complain about when you lose," Nori said. Neil grabbed the first lobster in the line. As he pulled it out he took a deep sniff, doing his best to hide this maneuver from the others. His lobster was clean. He felt his shoulders relax.

"Your turn, Mount Foodji," Neil said. Kong reached in and began fishing around for a suitable lobster. He was about to grab one, but paused. Whatever he was looking for still eluded him. Neil thought he saw him steal a worried glance at Nori, who gave a quick shrug. So, Neil thought, there was some sort of hint on the lobster that Kong was supposed to look for—probably a mark of some kind. Neil had beaten cheaters before and wasn't surprised he'd have to do it again.

Kong closed his eyes and grabbed the first lobster he could lay his fingers on, almost crushing it in the process.

He pulled it out then held it up to Neil's face, taunting him. Neil caught the unmistakable aroma of a lethal lobster. He was about say something, but realized in a flash that he couldn't. How would he explain that he could smell the poison? His secret weapon, his nose, was powerful because it was a secret. He'd have to come up with another plan.

"That lobster looks a little small," Neil said, hoping Kong would take the bait. But the chef just scoffed and walked over to his stove, where a boiling pot of water was bubbling away. With a smile he threw the lobster inside and slammed down the lid.

Neil walked over to his stove and filled a pot with cold salted water. Then he placed a brick on the bottom and gently placed the lobster on top. He lit the burner and slowly brought the pot to a boil.

Kong said something in Japanese. Nori laughed and translated. "He says you are a little child; you are afraid to hear the lobster cry."

"My way *is* more humane, but it's also tastier," Neil

said. Nori stopped laughing and said something to Kong that Neil didn't need translated. He knew a threat when he heard one. Kong actually seemed to cower a bit as Nori glared at him. For the first time Neil saw Kong as a chef under pressure—and human. He felt a twinge of sympathy.

Nori started to speak to the crowd in Japanese as Neil and Kong began furiously preparing their meals.

"*Psssssttt*," Neil said, doing his best to get Kong's attention. "Hey, big guy. Over here?"

Kong finally looked at him, angrily. Neil pointed to the pot with the lobster and made a face like he was grossed out. "Bad. Bad lobster," he said. Kong stared back at his pot, then scowled back at Neil. Kong waved his hand at him, sending a breeze in Neil's direction. The smell of the poison was still there. Neil didn't know what to do, so he went back to preparing his soup. The lobster was almost done, and he needed to have the miso base ready at precisely the right time.

He pulled out his seven-spice mixture and opened the package. The aroma filled the kitchen as he added the spices to the boiling fish broth.

Kong's head snapped over. Even he could tell that Neil's spice mixture was amazing. He stared down at his own mixture . . . looking a bit lost. Neil took a discreet sniff and could tell Kong's spices were adequate but not stellar. He allowed himself a smile. This challenge was a guaranteed win.

Nori marched over to Neil. "Where did you get these spices?" he asked angrily.

"Didn't I guess the hai-clue correctly?" Neil said,

feigning surprise while stirring the broth. "I'm afraid the location of my supplier is a secret."

"You won't tell me where?"

"No," Neil said. "Not that it would matter. You could have each of these spices and still not mix them together as perfectly as I can."

Nori grinned. "I could make it worth your while. I have lots of money. Perhaps you've noticed?"

Neil could imagine what Nori would do with a place like Suzu's spice store. He'd either swoop in and grab everything or burn it down to the ground so no one else could use the wonderful spices.

"Not in a million years and not for a million dollars. Now if you'll excuse me, I have a duel to win."

Nori stormed away, shooting more verbal darts at Kong, who hung his head and tried to concentrate on his noodles.

Neil grabbed his lobster from the pot. It was also perfect. He grabbed his knife and began expertly chopping it up, squeezing every last bit of liquid and meat from the shell. He added the thick succulent pieces of lobster to his broth of the spices, mushrooms, and noodles. He hadn't forgotten about the ticking time bomb Kong continued to prepare. As Neil cut into the claws, an idea occurred to him. He'd studied lobster anatomy in school. It had been one of the few classes he'd paid attention to, and had even scored extra credit by bringing in a plateful of his delicious lobster thermidor.

He needed to watch Kong carefully to see where he used the meat from the head. The concentration of the poison would be highest there. Neil added the final touches to his lobster noodle concoction, then artfully ladled out five bowls. A tiny garnish of deep-fried and salted seaweed, and he was finished.

"Time is up!" Nori yelled from the judges' table. "Now we feast and perhaps die." Ten waiters scurried to the countertops and grabbed a bowl each. Neil walked over as if to shake Kong's hand. He stuck out his foot and tried to trip the last waiter, whose bowl contained three full chunks of toxic lobster.

The waiter, unfortunately, having become expert at avoiding blows and kicks from his boss, kept his balance perfectly, not spilling a drop.

"What are you trying to do, cheat?" Nori yelled. He ran up and grabbed the bowl, practically slamming it down before one of the judges. Neil started to move toward the judge's table but Kong grabbed him from behind and spun him around. Being lifted by a giant chef was not an experience Neil enjoyed. He tried to yell a warning to the judges, but Kong was squeezing his lungs too hard. Kong lifted Neil's face to his own and growled. Neil could feel his body being squeezed like an orange. He tried to make some facial expression that Kong would recognize as a warning about the poison, but Kong didn't seem to understand or didn't care.

By the time he dropped Neil back on the ground the judges had eaten all of the soup. Neil had to kneel on the ground to catch his breath. His ribs hurt.

Nori was marching up and down in front of their table, looking agitated.

"Well? Well?" he said. The judges each flipped a

small card in front of them, each adorned with the name Neil Flambé. It was unanimous. But Neil didn't feel exhilarated. He was watching the judge on the far right, the one who'd eaten the soup from the waiter Neil had tried to trip. For one thing, he was wearing an amazingly ugly Bermuda shirt, a kind of neon green. But something else was wrong.

He was grabbing at his throat, his face turning an odd succession of greens and blues—almost perfectly matching the shirt. He stood up and fell over the judge's table. Neil thought he was still breathing, but couldn't be sure. Nori had said the strain of toxin was lethal, and it appeared he wasn't exaggerating.

Nori seemed furious, as if the judge had personally insulted him. He waved for his servants to come take the man. They laid him out on a stretcher and began walking away.

"I hope you're taking him to the sick bay," Neil gasped, the air still lost from his lungs.

Nori just laughed.

The surviving judges laughed as well. The woman who'd ordered Neil to start cooking stood up. "Sick bay? He's off to Tokyo Bay more likely!"

Neil assumed for a moment she was laughing from relief. He was wrong.

"We knew the risks, young man. We *paid* to be here," she told him smugly.

"What?" Neil said, trying to get to his feet.

"Yes, paid." She smiled, her eyes growing wider and wilder. "We paid thousands to be here for the food *and* for the thrill."

"Why?"

"Boredom. Boredom with the boring, stupid world."

Neil just stared at her as she continued her crazed rant.

"That man in the green shirt had climbed every mountain in the world, naked. This man to my right has flown airplanes through thunderstorms, wearing metal suits."

The man lifted off his toupee, revealing a scarred and blackened scalp. The others at the table exposed various scars, glass eyes, burns, and skin grafts.

Neil took a closer look at the woman. She was missing her legs below the knees. "And me? I have surfed on lava flows. What thrill is left that can compare with that?" She looked demented as she leaned forward and yelled, "Facing death, young man, that's what!" She laughed maniacally.

"You people are sick," Neil said, trying to shuffle away.

"Well, *he* certainly is." She pointed at the retreating man on the stretcher. "Or was." She laughed even harder. The whole crowd laughed as well.

"ENOUGH!" Nori yelled, slamming his fist down on the table. "Round one goes to Neil Flambé," he spat. The floor began to rise back up, carrying Neil and one of the waiters on top. Nori stayed below and the last Neil saw, he was throwing utensils at Kong and screaming in Japanese.

Neil passed back by the hot tub and the zoo. He also caught a glimpse of a second kitchen on the same floor as the animals. He'd passed it on the way down, but the door had been closed. A dozen or so chefs, looking extremely haggard, were busy chopping and prepping onions, garlic, and various meats. A few looked familiar, but Neil couldn't place them. Neil wasn't sure but it also looked like they were chained to the workstations.

They reached the top deck. The waiter walked over to the railing and threw the remaining bits of food over.

Neil heard a loud splashing sound and walked over to see what was making the noise. A dozen or more enormous sharks were fighting over the scraps of lobster shell, thrashing and biting at one another.

"Yeesh! I'll never complain about my cats again," Neil said with a gulp.

He thought he also saw what looked like an electric green shirt floating in among the bubbles and foam.

Neil hadn't found any concrete evidence that Nori was behind the boating accident that "killed" Larry, but he was sure of one thing: Nori was capable of just about anything.

Chapter Sixteen

Putting the Tea in Team

The helicopter ride back to Tokyo seemed much faster, despite all the questions that were swimming in Neil's mind. He pulled out his cell phone and called Nakamura. "Just checking in, faithful manservant," Neil said.

"Sir, I've got some interesting information on spices. I'll meet you for tea. And we'll have some friends joining us as well. I'll e-mail you the map."

Friends? What friends, exactly? Neil thought but didn't risk saying it out loud. "Okay, see you later."

The helicopter landed and Neil walked out onto the port's wooden planks. The setting sun reflected off the waves, bathing all the crates and ropes in an eerie glow. Neil had the distinct impression that the whole dock was waving and moving, but maybe it was just him finding his legs again after all that flying.

The copter took off, blowing Neil's hair in even crazier directions than usual. He ran for cover behind some crates. He was sure he saw something move in the shadows just before he arrived, but there was nothing there. A scent of something flowery lingered in the air, but with the howling air from the rotors he couldn't be sure what it was.

The copter left and Neil stood up and pulled out his phone. He opened the e-mail and was happy to see that Nakamura had chosen a tea shop not far from the dock. He'd also booked them into a nicer hotel. Good. Neil could use some tea, then a shower, then sleep.

He also took a peek at *The Chef*. He stopped mid-step. Something else had been changed—the name of the ship. It was something in Japanese. Neil was sure the name had been in English before. That wasn't in the note to Koko. Larry was still sending him clues!

Neil practically ran to the tea shop. He wasn't prepared for the sight that met him when he arrived. Nakamura had booked a private room at the back and the hostess walked him to an ornate silk curtain, then bowed and left. Neil took off his shoes and stepped inside.

"Isabella! What are you doing here?!"

"Shhhh," Isabella whispered, motioning for him to sit down. Nakamura was sitting on her other side, pouring everyone tea.

Neil heard a sound behind him and turned around. Jones had been standing flat against the wall—just in case someone had followed Neil, Neil presumed. Jones closed the curtain and then walked over to join everyone at the low table.

Neil sat next to Isabella,

shocked by her unexpected appearance, but happy.

"I am here on a scent-buying excursion," she said as she poured Neil some tea. He could smell that it was *sencha* green tea, incredibly rich and almost sweet. "But really we are here to offer you some help and protection. Speaking of that, how was your first duel?"

"Well, I won, obviously," Neil said. He filled them in on the rest of the details, including the battle, the stolen art, and the chained chefs.

"You must not go back," Isabella said. "This man is insane."

Neil nodded. "No kidding. But if I quit this battle, I have a feeling he'll be using me as shark bait. There are a lot of people paying him a lot of money to watch and I can guarantee there's a lot of money riding on the outcome. Now that I'm in, there's no getting out. Besides, if he's a suspect, then it doesn't hurt to have me stick around. Maybe he'll let something slip?"

"Like his trigger finger," Jones said flatly.

"Thanks for the cheery words. There's a chef I'd like you to meet. I think you'd hit it off," Neil said.

Jones just stared at him until Neil turned his head away.

Nakamura sipped his tea and nodded. "That guy is a piece of work, but Isabella and Jones have been doing some digging around. There are no records of any ship, Nori's or otherwise, being in that area of the ocean that day."

"Doesn't mean that they would have been registered. They are *illegally* fishing, you know."

"I never said we were checking with the *legal* authorities," Nakamura said.

"What, the perfume trade is crawling with informants?" Neil said sarcastically.

Nakamura coughed.

Neil glanced at Isabella who avoided his eyes. Jones, it turns out, was still staring at him. Neil felt an uncomfortable silence.

Isabella jumped in. "But we've also been working on a way to let Larry know that we're here and looking for him."

"How?" Neil said.

Nakamura chuckled. "They suggest we think like Larry."

"That is a scary thought," Neil said.

Isabella smacked his arm and continued. "What we mean is that if Larry has been using *The Chef* to contact you, you should use *The Chef* to contact him. Use clues only you and he will understand."

Neil smacked himself on the head and pulled his phone out of his bag. "I was so excited to see you I totally forgot. Larry's changed the site again. What does this name mean?" He held the phone up to Nakamura.

"It looks like Hiro's name, Takoyaki, in Japanese . . . but an old form of Japanese. Maybe Koko added it as a kind of honor to her brother."

Neil pursed his lips and stared at the image. "Maybe it's a sign that Larry thinks Hiro is still alive, on a boat somewhere? Maybe Nori's got him held up somewhere on that floating country he calls a yacht."

"You said there were chefs . . . in chains?" Isabella said. "Maybe he keeps prisoners?"

Neil shuddered. "I have a feeling that's what Nori

has planned for me if I lose. But I'll see if I can do any searching around at tomorrow's duel. Meanwhile, back to thinking like Larry." Neil shuddered again.

"I'm actually on record thinking this is a stupid plan," Jones said, staying as still as a statue. Neil realized he wasn't glaring at him anymore—he was keeping an eye on the curtain, like a cat waiting for a mouse to poke its head out of a hole in the wall. Jones creeped Neil out sometimes . . . no, all the time.

"Jones has a point," Neil said. "I can't change the site." He pulled out his phone and scrolled *The Chef* for any sign of a contact us or feedback button but didn't see any. "I think Larry said he got rid of those because he was getting too many readers asking him out on dates."

Isabella scoffed. "Now I *know* he writes fiction."

"Speaking of fiction, this is interesting," Neil said. "There is a link on the bottom of the page to another site." Neil clicked and was taken to a fan fiction site. There were letters of condolences in English and Japanese for Hiro and Larry, and one creepy request for a date beyond the grave from a medium named Minerva in Portland. There was also a whole collection of stories that fans had written in about *The Chef*. Almost all were illustrated, some with good and many with horrible manga-style pictures.

They gathered around Neil's phone . . . except for Jones, who continued to stare intently at the curtain.

"Okay, excellent," Nakamura said. "So how do we leave a message that only Larry will understand?"

"Easy." Isabella smiled. "Coffee!"

Neil smiled as well. "Jacu bird coffee."

An hour later, after a wonderful meal of rice, soup, fried fish, and grilled vegetables, they had a story.

Neil ran the details over again to make sure they'd hidden enough clues. "The Chef is called on to battle a flock of electronic birds. They are stealing prime coffee beans from the farms of some poor laborers."

"Sort of evil versions of those birds that poop out the coffee beans Larry likes," Isabella said.

Neil nodded. "He'll get that reference and start looking for some details. The Chef defeats them by catching them with his hat and then ripping out their circuit boards."

"And that's where Zoe's picture comes in?" Isabella asked.

"Yes. We'll hide the clue in there."

Neil called Zoe and asked her to draw the Chef crushing the circuit board of one of the birds. The circuit boards would have numbers on them. To a casual reader, they'd just look like the kind of serial numbers you'd see on any electronic device. But these would be the time and coordinates for a meeting. Zoe happily whipped off the manga doodle—"The rougher it looks the better," Neil said—and sent it back within minutes.

Neil added the file to the story and posted both to the website. "Now we wait and hope," he said.

"I think it's time we all got some sleep," Isabella said.

Neil agreed. He started to get up and saw that Jones was already standing, fists clenched, staring intently at the curtain.

"Did you see something?" Nakamura whispered, sidling up next to him.

"Didn't see. Heard. Breathing."

Jones crept silently to the curtain and ripped it open. Despite the shocked look on the faces of the other tea drinkers, there was no one else there. Jones looked down. An envelope was lying on the ground. It was addressed: *Neil Flambé—Instructions for Round #2.*

Chapter Seventeen

Going Fishing

The second clue was also a mystery to Neil, at first. It was another haiku. Neil was no poetry expert, but he thought the writing was even clunkier than the first.

> ON THE ISLAND SHORE
> YELLOW TAILS AND RIVER PIGS
> WILL YOU TAKE THE BAIT?
> (PS: A BOAT WILL MEET YOU AT THE HARUMI
> PIER AT 2.)

"It's clearly about a fish of some kind," Neil said as he and Nakamura sat in their hotel lobby. Jones and Isabella were actually at a conference on perfume and were also staying at another hotel. "And they've given me the morning to find it. Any chance Suzu stocks fish?"

"Sorry. Not fresh fish, anyway. Just spices and dried goods."

"Okay, then where do I go for the best fish market in town?"

Nakamura smiled. "Follow your nose, my friend.

There's only one place in Tokyo and it's the biggest in the world." Nakamura led Neil out the front door and pointed him north. "It's also near the Harumi pier. And the wind is coming in exactly the right direction."

Neil lifted his nose in the air and caught exactly what Nakamura thought he would—fish. Neil's feet started walking. "I'll come with you," Nakamura said. "You won't need a translator to know what you're looking for, but you'll need one not to get ripped off."

Neil gave a thumbs-up and kept walking and sniffing. It wasn't far and there was no missing it—not just because of the smell but also because of the sheer size. An entire city block was packed with row upon row of giant warehouses, gleaming glass and steel, spread out in a sweeping series of semicircles.

"Nose, welcome to Tsukiji Market, otherwise known as fish-lovers' heaven," Nakamura said. They walked inside.

The first thing Neil saw were hundreds, possibly thousands, of stalls offering everything from prepared sushi to knives to woks and utensils. The noise was

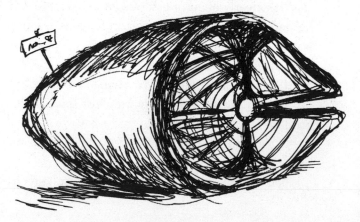

deafening as customers pointed and bought and haggled. Neil immediately thought of a thousand dishes he could prepare and began walking up to a stall.

"Not yet. Wait until we hit the inner market," Nakamura said, gently pushing Neil on. They walked through a series of enormous metal doors and into an even bigger series of buildings. Workers unloaded fish off freight cars that pulled right up to the tables. Giant slabs of frozen tuna sat next to a huge band saw, waiting to be sliced into steaks. Buckets of rich caviar sat in ice. Row upon row of snapper, grouper, sardines, and even fish that Neil had only read about in exotic cookbooks, were laid out on wooden mats on the market floor.

The entire ocean sat waiting for Neil. Now he just had to make sure he picked the right fish. All the fish also made him think of his cousin. "He would hate this place," Neil said.

"Well, let's find your fish and then I'll go to the rendezvous point and wait. Let's hope he got the message."

Neil found it hard to concentrate on the haiku while also worrying about Larry. He and Nakamura walked from aisle to aisle. "From what you've told me about Nori, I can only imagine you're supposed to get something tasty, exotic, and probably dangerous."

Neil groaned. "Oh, I could kick myself."

"I'll always volunteer to help you with that," Nakamura said with a smile. "Why?"

"The haiku says 'river pig.' What's river pig in Japanese?"

"Ah. Fugu. Yeah, you should be kicking yourself."

"River pig, aka puffer fish, aka fugu," Neil said, shaking his head at his own stupidity. "What an idiot. Nori said the dishes were simple."

"Makes sense," Nakamura said. "Great-tasting fish that can kill you if you don't make it right. Sounds like Nori's MO."

Neil smelled the air and made his way over to one of the large tables. A handful of the fish were on display. Neil frowned. "These aren't the best I've ever seen."

"I wonder why Nori would have you look for puffer fish here in Tokyo."

"I know. The best fugu comes from the south."

"Shimonoseki is the best place to get the fish. It's even nicknamed Fugu City. Maybe part of the challenge is to find a good one here?"

Neil sniffed the puffer fish. They were passable. He needed to make sure he got the best of the bunch. He lifted one and had Nakamura ask the price. The fishmonger said something in Japanese. "About a hundred dollars," Nakamura translated. Neil looked at the fish skeptically and put it back.

"Something's not right," Neil said, tapping his fingers.

"Smells fishy, you mean?" Nakamura joked.

Neil ignored him. "Nori likes the best of the best. These fugu are okay, but not the best. I'm missing something." He pulled out the note again.

"You'd better hurry. That boat is coming in about thirty minutes."

"The clue starts, *'On the island shore.'* The market is on the shore of the city. *'Yellow tails and river pigs.'* We've been through that . . . so what's the bait he's referring to? Worms?"

Nakamura pondered for a second. "What does the yellow tails thing mean?"

Neil held up the fugu. "See the tails? Yellow."

"But the poem says yellow tails AND river pigs, not ON river pigs."

Neil stared in the distance, considering. Finally he spoke. "You still willing to kick me?"

"Consider it a standing offer."

"Yellowtail. Japanese amberjack. Heard of it?"

"Yeah. Hamachi. My dad used to use it a lot in his sushi. It's not very dangerous though, just tasty."

"The bait I was supposed to take was buying fugu. It is going to be on the menu tonight, but Nori's going to supply it and I bet it will be better than these." He flopped the fugu back down on the pile with disdain. The fishmonger scowled at Neil and reached for his large fish hook.

"I'm supposed to come with a companion dish. Ask this guy if he's got any hamachi, at reasonable prices," Neil said.

"Um, I think we should try another stall," Nakamura

said, leading Neil away as the man smacked the back of the hook against the palm of his hand. "You really have to work on those people skills."

"Oh, *I'm* the bad guy? But when he tries to charge a hundred bucks for a glorified minnow, he's just haggling?"

"You're a little rattled. Now, smell us out a good hamachi and then go catch that boat."

Chapter Eighteen

Fugu Flambé

The speedboat slashed over and through the waves like a honed steel fillet knife through trout. That was how it struck Neil as he gripped his seat with one hand and held the foam cooler pack to his chest with the other. A knife through tofu would have been smoother, Neil thought. Butter would have been even better. Neil stopped thinking about food. He was feeling too seasick.

For some reason he'd been expecting a much bigger, slower boat to pick him up. Instead, he found himself sitting in a modified Formula One race car on water. The howling in his ears was a few decibels above a hurricane.

Neil leaned forward, his cheeks pushed back by the g-forces. "Are we there yet?" he yelled over the noise. The woman who'd been piloting the boat turned around and pointed to the left. Neil saw Nori's yacht, out in open water. *I guess he decided it was safe to leave the island,* Neil thought. He leaned back.

The boats seemed to be on a collision course, until the bow of the yacht opened up. The pilot lowered the throttle and expertly steered the craft into the hull of the yacht. Dozens of boats floated lazily against their own private moorings: catamarans, sailboats, small yachts, big yachts, and solid-gold gondolas.

"Is that a submarine?" Neil asked, seeing a long zucchini-shaped vessel sitting half submerged against one side of the lake. The pilot nodded and parked the boat against a small wooden float. Neil stepped out. Nori himself was there to greet him this time.

"As you can see, we were forced to pull up anchor and leave my island for a bit."

"Storm?" Neil asked, feeling his legs shaking beneath him.

"In a manner of speaking. No matter. We're now in international waters. The point being that we are a little early for today's battle. So I can give you a quick tour." Nori led him up a small wooden staircase, with gargoyles carved into the sides. Neil remembered seeing something exactly like it in a medieval cathedral in Paris. He vaguely remembered hearing that the same cathedral had been broken into a few months back.

"Do you take these kinds of excursions away from the island often?" Neil asked, looking around at the stained

glass windows that lined the stairway. They also looked familiar and, Neil thought, stolen. "Maybe whale fishing?" Nori's yacht was certainly large enough to crush a fishing trawler without suffering a dent.

"Interesting thought. We're not actually equipped for whaling, although that's a great idea. And we haven't left the island for months," Nori said, sounding increasingly angry. "But there was this SWAT team and some arrest warrants. It's all taken care of, but we just needed to 'leave the scene,' so to speak. I don't know when we can go back." Suddenly Nori smashed his fist into the side of the railing, cracking a balustrade.

Neil wasn't quite sure how to respond. Nori turned back around and spotted the cooler pack that Neil was still clutching to his chest.

"Your knuckles look a little white, young man. Are you sure you're feeling up to a kitchen battle?"

"Yes, I'm ready. It was just an interesting ride getting here."

Nori smiled. "Would you like me to store that fugu in the fridge while we continue the tour?"

Neil had a momentary fear that he'd misread the clue, but something in Nori's grin suggested he hadn't.

"The fish in this cooler has a yellow tail, but no poison, and no puffer," Neil said, holding the package even closer.

"You mean you didn't buy fugu?" Nori's face set into a grimace.

"I didn't take the bait, no."

"Tour is over," Nori barked. "Follow me. We start the battle now."

Suddenly, a door opened in the side of the wall and the top step of the staircase detached, moved sideways, and then slid along the floor. Neil realized they were on a kind of moving sidewalk, speeding toward the middle of the ship. He did his best to take in everything they passed, in case there were any evidence or clues. There was a wine cellar stocked a story high and hundreds of rows wide. There was an aviary with birds flying around in cages. In another room, Neil thought he saw a man with a chainsaw and what looked like a charging rhinoceros but the sidewalk was traveling too quickly now to be sure.

They sped straight toward a stainless steel wall, which swung open at the last second, sending Neil and Nori flying into the kitchen. The floor stopped so suddenly that Neil almost lost his balance. He was just able to keep the cooler, and its precious fish cargo, from flying out of his arms and across the room.

The crowd cheered loudly, stamping their feet. Neil made his way to his station as Nori walked up to the judge's table. A new judge had joined the panel, with an eye patch and a kind of metal jacket that seemed to be keeping his arms attached to his shoulders. In fact, his left arm appeared to be *all* metal. He was sitting in the fifth and final chair.

Kong was already at his station with a gorgeous fugu and an equally beautiful yellowtail laid out before him. Neil wasn't going to have an advantage with his ingredients today. Kong didn't scowl at Neil, or even look at him. He seemed to be hunched over a bit and Neil noticed a slight limp as he walked over and grabbed his sushi knives. Nori was clearly not a boss to disappoint.

Neil wanted to ask Kong, *Why do you work for this bozo?* when he remembered Kong's English matched Neil's Japanese—zippo.

Neil felt more resolve to wrap up this battle soon and get away from this ship. But what would Nori do to Kong then? Neil was still considering this when Nori started his rant. "Today we eat fugu!" The crowd went wild. "But the challenge is not just to safely prepare this traditional dish but to make a dish that perfectly complements the fugu . . . but is NOT traditional! It must be as new and as experimental as possible!"

Neil saw Kong give a little confused start. This was apparently a last-second change on Nori's part— thrown together in haste after he'd seen Neil with his package. Nori must have been surprised that Neil hadn't taken the bait. Kong cast aside the seaweed wrap and rice he'd already prepared. Neil knew right away that Kong had been planning a side dish of hamachi sushi—but now had to search for some other inspiration. Of course, Neil had to come up with something else as well.

"BEGIN!" Nori yelled. "You have thirty minutes!"

"Thirty? What happened to an hour?" Neil yelled. He didn't have anything prepped and his fish was still sitting in ice.

Nori just smiled and pointed at the clock above the kitchen. The seconds ticked away as Neil whipped out his knives and began furiously preparing his fugu. He had to be careful to cut out the liver and separate the skin—not an operation he could rush. The slightest contamination could render the flesh poisonous—and Neil didn't see any backup fugu on the countertop in case he messed up with this one.

Neil stole a peek at Kong, who was already plating his incredibly thin slices of fugu, laid out in a flower pattern. The fish slices were so thin that Neil could see the pattern on the dish showing through. Neil was impressed. He'd be doing exactly the same thing, and possibly no better. Nori had said traditional fugu, and

that's what the judges were going to get.

So the key to victory would be the hamachi. Neil took a surreptitious sniff of the air as Kong began to cut up his hamachi. It was a good fish, but Neil was certain his own was slightly sweeter. It would have been hard for him to explain exactly how he sensed this—but something in the aroma of the two fish suggested that his own had perhaps eaten slightly better food, or had been less traumatized when caught.

But how to bring that out? How to make it perfect? Neil looked at his fish, waiting for inspiration. Instead, he got it from stealing another glance at Kong.

Kong was busy cutting his fish into rectangular slices. Then he placed the fish on cubes of rice, with a small bit of hot green wasabi sandwiched in between. And not the fake green horseradish that all the cheap sushi stands were passing off, but *real* wasabi root.

Kong was still making sushi? Neil was confused. That was about as traditional as you could get. Then Kong uncovered a steel bucket. What looked liked steam poured *down* the sides. *Liquid nitrogen! He's going to make frozen sushi!* Neil thought. *Wow.* But it gave Neil an even more revolutionary idea.

Neil glanced at the clock. Ten minutes left. There was just enough time. He quickly sliced the yellowtail fish into thin slices. He set some aside, soaking in a tempura batter. He threw the rest in a food processor along with some sugar, egg yolks, and heavy cream. Then he sliced some limes and squeezed the juice into a small bowl.

Five minutes left. Kong was making a kind of

whipped-cream style foam from fish stock, and was making decorative flowers on the side of his sushi platters with fish scales. *Fancy-looking, but not as tasty as he'd like,* Neil thought with a smile.

Neil threw his fish chips into a deep fryer. With a minute left he pulled them out and tossed them with a coating of sugar and spices. Then he crossed his arms and watched as the clock struck zero.

"Time is up!" Nori yelled. "The judges will sample Kong's food first." Nori walked over and examined the plates Neil and Kong had prepared. Both chefs were serving gossamer-like slices of fugu. Kong's side dish of frozen sushi and caviar foam flowers sat on bamboo plates, wisps of nitrogen still floating off the pieces.

Neil's side plates were practically empty, with just a few of his sugared fish chips arranged in a fan pattern on the corners. A blender filled with a creamy liquid sat next to the dishes.

Nori laughed. "But your dish isn't even finished. I guess thirty minutes wasn't enough."

Neil reached down and lifted up his own thermos of liquid nitrogen and placed it on the counter. "My dish needs to be finished *à la table*. If I make it now it will turn to soup before the judges get to taste it . . . that is, if they survive your gorilla's puffer fish. Show a little patience."

Nori frowned at Neil and added a menacing scowl as he waved for the waiters to collect Kong's plates. The judges oohed with delight as the fugu and frozen sushi were presented to them. The oohs soon gave way to satisfied silence as the judges devoured the dishes.

Nori clapped his hands as the judges pronounced their comments.

"Sublime."

"Fantastic."

"Delicious."

Neil noticed not one of them said "revolutionary" but he also noticed they were all still alive. This was going to be close.

Kong bowed to the judges and the waiters began to serve Neil's fugu. Neil walked behind them with his thermos and blender.

"This second dish needs to be prepared at the table, or else it will fail," Neil said, putting on his goggles and gloves with what he hoped was a dramatic flourish.

"You're not serving them together?" the judge with the eye patch said.

"No. Please enjoy your fugu. While you're doing that, I'll be making dessert." Neil turned on his blender and began to stir the lime juice into the cream mixture. The judges clearly enjoyed the fugu but were just as interested in what Neil was doing with the thermos. Neil poured the cream mixture into a stainless steel bowl, then unscrewed the top of the thermos and began pouring the liquid nitrogen over the top. Mist poured out of the bowl and across the tabletop. Neil looked more like a crazed scientist than a chef as he poured the nitrogen and stirred the mixture with a wooden spoon. Bit by bit the cream mixture thickened.

The judges finished their fugu, some even licking their plates. Neil gripped the sides of the metal bowl with his gloved hands and lifted his head slowly, smiling.

"Now, be prepared for something you have never experienced before." He pulled an ice-cream scoop from his back pocket and scooped a perfect orb onto each plate, nestling the dessert next to the chips.

"Hamachi . . . ice cream?" Nori chuckled. "Impossible!" But the judges were greedily scooping up the velvety smooth creation with spoons and the sweet fish chips.

"This shouldn't work . . . but it's amazing!" said the lava-surfer.

"I can't believe my own taste buds," said the man with the toupee.

"Revolutionary," said the man with the patch.

Nori clenched his fists so hard his knuckles turned white.

Neil knew he'd won. Kong clearly knew it too, because Neil heard the saucepan lid he fired at Neil's head just in time to duck. The lid smacked straight into the new judge, severing the metal rods  that kept his left arm attached to his body. "Ahhhhhh!" the judge yelled. "How wonderful! The glorious pain!" He fell over and writhed on the ground, smiling like a madman.

Neil spun around just in time to deflect another lid with his thermos. Kong threw one more lid, this time headed straight for Nori. Neil threw the thermos, deflecting the lid at the last second. It skipped away harmlessly across the floor.

"Ask your chef who's acting like a baby now!" Neil yelled.

"ENOUGH!" Nori yelled. He signaled for his servants to subdue Kong. They didn't seem in a hurry to do that, but luckily for everyone Kong straightened up and let himself be led away.

"Neil Flambé leads two to nothing," Nori spat. He pushed a button on the judges' table and Neil's section of the floor began to slide back toward the boat docks. "Now go away. Round three is titled Russian Roulette and will be held here tomorrow night!"

"Tomorrow night?" Neil yelled, but his words were swallowed up by the sliding metal doors of the kitchen. The floor traveled back too fast to see any details of rhinoceroses or exotic birds. The pilot was waiting for him and signaled for him to take his seat in the speedboat. Neil's head was spinning.

As they sped back to shore, Neil spied a waiter throwing the leftover sushi overboard. The sharks returned instantly, churning the water into a foaming, bubbling mass of flesh and carnage.

Chapter Nineteen

Lost and Found and Feeling Lost

Neil stepped back out onto the pier. The pilot turned the speedboat around and shot off without even a wave. The smell of the nearby fish market hung in the air. Neil's legs were a little wobbly and his face was flushed, but it wasn't the trip back—it was his nerves. Did Larry meet up with Nakamura?

Neil had been able to distract himself from the question during the latest battle, and even during the boat ride back to Tokyo. He'd had lots to think about. Was Nori going to choose a different chef than Kong for the third battle? And what did Nori mean by "Russian Roulette"? But those questions had now evaporated.

Neil checked his watch. He was supposed to meet Nakamura in an hour. Nakamura was going to e-mail him the location. Neil flipped open his phone. There was a *ping* and Neil saw that a new e-mail had indeed arrived, but it wasn't from Nakamura. It was titled *"Instructions for Round #3"* and was another haiku.

You will rue the day
Kong awaits an Angel to
cap his victory
(PS: A car, license plate 2die4, will
meet you at 8 tomorrow night at the
Imperial Palace. DO NOT BE LATE!)

Neil smacked his head. He had completely forgotten to demand they change locations for the final battle. Not that Nori had given him much of an opportunity for conversation. And what the heck did this latest haiku mean? Before Neil could ponder the clue, there was another *ping*. This time, it was from Nakamura.

"Boss. Meet me at Shibuya Station. Signed, your faithful servant, Hachikō." There was a link to a map. Neil clicked on it, revealing a timetable for the Tokyo subway. Neil gulped. The Tokyo subway system was a mass of interconnecting lines and shapes and he'd have to navigate his way solo. He even had to switch trains. He shut his phone and started walking.

The station was worse than he'd expected. Rush hour never seemed to end, as far as he could tell. Each train was packed when it arrived and packed when it left. People jostled and pushed to get close to the open doors. Three trains passed by, so full that Neil didn't even try to look for any Neil-shaped spaces inside. Somehow the people standing next to him found ways to pry themselves into the human sardine tin.

He checked his watch. If he didn't take the leap soon he'd never meet Nakamura in time. The next train pulled into the station. Neil closed his eyes and let the crowd carry him along. He felt his ribs being squeezed together and his shoulders pushed upward. Then there was a *whoosh* and the doors closed. He was in. He opened his eyes. Most of the other passengers were lost in their electronics or manga comic books, expertly managing to read them while standing closer than Siamese twins.

Neil felt a slight sense of accomplishment. Now he just had to do the same maneuver at the transfer station and he'd make it on time. Then a number of smells assaulted Neil's nose simultaneously. There was a man next to him munching on wasabi-coated peas. The woman next to him was slurping some kind of sweet coffee soda. A few feet away someone opened a package of miso soup. Everything began to mix together—sesame seed bars, green bubble tea, chocolate covered pretzel sticks, seaweed flavored ice cream, and on and on.

Neil began to panic. It was overload. Too many different sensations packed too closely together. Neil was tempted to escape, but the thought of Larry possibly waiting for him at the other end kept him rooted to the spot.

Twenty minutes later, after changing trains successfully, Neil poured out with the crowd at Shibuya Station like steam from a soufflé. He'd made it! He caught his reflection in a storefront window. He'd been so stressed out that he'd never taken his chef's hat off. He reached up and grabbed it, chuckling at himself and deeply breathing in the slightly less congested air of the station.

Okay, Nakamura, where are you? he thought. Thousands of people scurried past him to the exits or to the other trains. Neil was blown away at how orderly it

all was. He stood up on a garbage can and scanned the building. Finally, Neil saw Nakamura standing underneath an exit sign at the far end of the terminal. He was alone. Neil's heart fell. He hurried over. Nakamura's eyes were red and damp, as if he'd been crying.

"What happened? What's wrong?" Neil said. Nakamura smelled a bit like lemons, which was odd. He also smelled a little like rotten fish. Neil was having trouble putting this all together. "Is *the ingredient* here?"

Nakamura just shook his head quietly and led Neil outside. Neil caught a glimpse of his face. He seemed to be struggling to keep his muscles under control. Nakamura led him up to a large black SUV. The windows were all tinted—the type of vehicle Jones always rented whenever he was on the road. That meant Isabella was here too. That might explain the citrus-perfume smell Neil was picking up.

Nakamura opened the door. The smell of fish grew stronger. Something was definitely wrong. "Did you meet up with him?" Neil asked with a sense of dread. "Answer me!"

Nakamura hung his head. "I'm so sorry, Neil," Nakamura said in a louder voice than Neil expected. "I'm afraid Larry really is dead."

Neil felt like he'd been punched by Jones. "What? Dead? But . . ." The entire scene began to spin and Neil had to lean against Nakamura to stop from fainting.

"I know, I know. It's the end," Nakamura was practically shouting now. Why was he shouting? He helped Neil inside. Neil dumbly took his seat. Isabella was next to him. She was leaning on the window, her head in her hands, shaking. Neil was too shocked to even cry. Nakamura climbed in next to him and closed the door, wiping his eyes with a handkerchief.

"All right, let's go," he said to Jones, who gunned the engine and pulled away from the curb. The car rumbled over a series of speed bumps and then they were on the highway.

Neil felt sick. Larry *was* dead? It didn't make any sense. Did he die on the boat a week ago? Did he die yesterday, or today? Had Neil's arrival in Japan triggered some kind of attack?

He lifted his head and for the first time noticed another figure in the car. Someone's dirty blond head was emerging above the front passenger seat, like a rising sun. The head smelled like fish. At the same moment Isabella lifted her head and laughed and Nakamura slapped Neil on the back. "The coast is clear," he said.

Neil's confusion evaporated in an instant as his cousin's beaming face turned around to meet him with a huge smile. "Hey, cuz. Miss me?"

Neil leaned forward and immediately started beating Larry over the head with his chef's hat.

"You IDIOT!" he said. "You stupid . . . IDIOT!"

"I see you didn't get any wittier since I died!"

Neil smacked him again. "Idiot, idiot, idiot!"

Larry lifted his hands to defend himself, giggling like crazy. "Hey, cuz, careful. You're not tenderizing a chicken cutlet here!"

Isabella, still laughing, grabbed Neil's shoulder. "Calm down, Neil. We're all together, finally. Smile!"

Neil sat back down with a thump. "Do you have any idea how worried we've been?"

"Yeah, Jones demonstrated that just before you got here. I think I still have some teeth left." Larry rubbed the side of his face, which looked a little red.

"Well, you deserve worse," Neil said. He felt a lump in his throat and his eyes began to water. He took a deep breath. "It's great to see you . . . but you're still an idiot."

"Well, the feeling is mutual." Larry beamed and reached back over the front seat to slap Neil on the knee.

Neil had a thousand questions swimming in his head. He turned to Nakamura. "Why the big act back at the station?"

"Sorry about that, Nose," Nakamura said. "Jones and I are still worried that someone's following us. So if anyone was close enough to see or hear us talk, then they think you just got some horrible news."

"Shooting that citrus perfume in your eyes gave it just the right look," Isabella said.

Nakamura wiped more tears away. "I apologize, but we can't let anyone know Larry is alive."

"Why not?" Neil said.

"I think Hiro is still out there somewhere, being held prisoner." Larry suddenly looked more serious than Neil had ever seen him. "If they know I'm alive, it could put him in jeopardy. It's better for now if everyone still thinks I'm dead. That's why I had to hide the clues in the comic. I knew you'd notice eventually and I knew what you'd do . . . Come look for me."

"You two are so alike," Isabella said.

"No kidding," Jones grumbled.

"You said if 'they' know you're alive. If *who* knows? What's going on, anyway?" Neil said.

"I'm not sure. All I know is that Hiro and I were going gangbusters on the manga. We decided to take a break and we went out sightseeing. I went for the sun and waves. Hiro went for the fish. Yuck. We got out to the middle of nowhere and then the crew turned on us."

"Koko told me you went out to protest a whaling ship."

"I don't know why she'd say that. Maybe she's in shock? She was with us on the docks when we left. She even gave Hiro a new tackle box. She gave me a big hug." Larry wiggled his eyebrows and smiled.

"Yeah, I've seen her eyes," Neil said. Isabella elbowed him in the ribs. Neil continued quickly. "So what happened when the crew turned on you?"

"They tied me up and then started beating Hiro."

"Why?"

"They wanted to know where the sacred scroll was. They assumed I didn't know any Japanese so they just talked away in front of me."

"Sacred scroll?" Neil shook his head. "Wait, you mean the scroll from *The Chef*? I thought you made that up."

"Welllll, yes and no," Larry said. "It does exist. It's a really old Takoyaki family heirloom."

"Is it valuable?" Isabella asked.

"I guess so, but that's only part of it. Family legend says that it contains a secret to finding a hidden treasure."

"What kind of treasure?"

Larry shrugged. "Dunno. Hiro told me he wasn't sure either. I think the guys who were smacking Hiro around had an idea. They kept talking about a map. Hiro kept saying there was no map, just a lot of recipes and family stories. He refused to tell them where it was though."

"How did you escape and he didn't?"

"Remember Lesley Sprout?"

"Who? What? Why? What? Lesley who?"

"Remember what she did for a living?"

"Believe it or not, your love life isn't half as interesting to the rest of the world as it is to you."

"I don't believe it."

Neil snapped his fingers. "Wait! Was she the one who stole all my smoked salmon, the one from that TV survival show?"

"She took the salmon on a trip to the Amazon and lived on it for a month. Pretty cool, eh?"

"Yeah, it was so *cool* to tell everyone who ordered salmon that they had to have trout instead. So what happened? She showed up and rescued you?"

"No, she's still in the hospital with that weird monkey flu she caught in Borneo. What she did do was teach me how to make a raft from ship debris."

"Ship debris?" Neil rubbed his temples. Like many of Larry's stories, this one was getting as complicated as a recipe for chicken galantine, but less satisfying.

"Yeah. The crew finally figured out I was able to understand what they were talking about. I guess I was cocking my ear a little too much or something, so this big guy decked me. The next thing I knew I woke up and I was alone on the boat. I could hear something ticking

and I knew there was a bomb. I jumped in the water and *KABOOM!*"

"I guess that explains the police theory that the ship broke apart in a storm," Nakamura said.

"Almost all of it was gone. A big chunk of the deck was floating nearby so I climbed on top. I used a rough part of the wood to cut the ropes on my wrists. Then I used the rope to lash some lifejackets that were floating around to the deck, to make it more of a usable raft."

"Let me guess, then you made sails out of your own shirt." Jones sounded a bit suspicious.

"No, I mostly rowed it at that point. Oh, and the captain of the fishing boat who found me an hour later didn't hurt. Well, not really captain. Aki was more like sole crewmember. It was a small boat."

"That's a thrilling tale of survival," Jones said, scoffing. "Did you hail a cab next?"

"Ha, ha. I would have made it back eventually. It was actually a pretty sturdy raft. The fishing boat just sped things up."

Isabella leaned toward the driver's seat. "Jones, please let Larry tell his story. It's certainly more interesting than that silly camp you went to in the arctic."

"I had to outrun a polar bear, with frostbite."

"The polar bear had frostbite? Doesn't sound too hard to me," Larry said.

Jones gave a menacing growl.

"Oh, shush and keep your eye on the road," Isabella said. "Now, Larry, please continue."

"Aki and I sank the raft and then we anchored off the shore near Hiro's house. I swam ashore once it got dark."

"Why did this fisherman help you so much?" Nakamura said.

"Who said Aki was a he?" Larry smiled. "She promised not to tell anyone she'd seen me. She even told the police she'd seen the wreckage and no one had survived. I think she added the bit about a freak storm, too. What a woman," Larry sighed. "Someday I might mariner. Get it? MARRY-ner." Larry seemed pleased but everyone just

stared at him blankly. "Because she's a *mariner*."

"Your puns smell worse than your hair," Nakamura said.

"Hey, I've been telling most of my puns in Japanese lately, okay?"

Neil rolled his eyes. "And you used her fish to rub on that note you gave Koko, the one to get her to update the website?"

"That was disgusting. You know how I feel about fish. But my phone is at the bottom of the ocean somewhere and I didn't have a laptop at that point. I didn't want Koko asking any questions or looking for Hiro or me so I made sure the note looked like I wrote it before the trip. I guess Koko fell for it, because here you are!"

"So now what?" Neil said. "We go looking for this mythical scroll?"

"No need." Larry reached down and pulled out a plastic cylinder from his backpack. "I went to Oshima and got it myself."

"Oshima? Wasn't that the island you mentioned in the manga?"

"Yeah. Hiro hid the scroll there a few weeks ago. I had Koko put that in the manga in case you were able to get there before me, or if I wasn't able to get there at all. But then Aki agreed to lend me her boat. I went there, got it, and have been hiding out in the hold of her boat ever since."

"That explains the fish smell," Neil said.

"I've actually grown kind of used to it. Just imagine what the cats would do to my legs if I were back home now. Yikes."

"So how did you know to meet Nakamura?"

"Aki went out and bought me a laptop when I was at Oshima. You need to pay her back, by the way."

Neil groaned.

Larry went on. "I was still too worried to send any e-mails that could be traced. That's another reason why I left Koko that note to change the site. So I sat back and waited for you to try to send me a hidden clue. I changed one more thing on the site yesterday so you'd know I was still kicking."

"The name on the boat?"

Larry nodded. "I don't draw as well as Hiro or even Koko, so I went with characters. I figured you might try and hide some kind of hint for me in the fan site if you knew I was online. When I saw the coffee story, I knew it had to be from you guys. Nice one, by the way."

"Thank Isabella and Zoe," Neil said. "Now, why did Hiro hide this scroll there, and how did you know where to find it?"

"Hiro knew something was up. There'd been a robbery attempt just before I arrived at the house and he was sure they were after the scroll. Hiro hid the scroll in a locker at the spa there."

"He told you that?" Nakamura asked.

"Not at the time. When they were whacking him around, he looked over at me and said 'It looks like I'm going to meet Davy Jones. Say good-bye to your cousin the Chef.' The Chef's island is based on Oshima and I knew right away what he meant. Luckily the guys who were beating him up didn't get the reference. Illiterate morons."

"Wait, you searched a whole island and just happened to find the scroll in a locker?"

"When Hiro mentioned Davy Jones I knew he wanted me to look for a locker. I broke into the spa and checked for a locker with an actual lock on it. Most of them were empty so I only had to jimmy three or four . . . dozen. Then I found the scroll and high-tailed it back to the boat."

Jones was shaking his head in disbelief. "Incredible," he said.

"Yes, I am." Larry smiled.

Neil jumped in. "So if you have the scroll, why not just let 'them' know and trade it for Hiro?"

"Well, for one thing, I still don't know who 'them' are, and if I gave them the scroll, I can bet you that's the end of Hiro. He didn't give them any info, so I'm not going to either. He clearly didn't want them to get the scroll. That's why he told me where to look."

"You think he wants you to find the treasure before they do?" Neil said.

"Yes. So let's get started on this thing. But first, you all missed the biggest part of this story."

"Which is what?" Neil asked.

"I haven't had a coffee in a week!"

They all stared at him, speechless.

Larry slapped Jones on the shoulder. "So, big guy. Let's say we stop for some takeout?"

Jones ignored him, but the side of his mouth went up in an almost grin.

"We've got a better plan," Nakamura said with a smile.

Chapter Twenty

Scrolls and California Rolls

Jones pulled up next to a narrow glass building. They'd been driving for a while, backing up and retracing their route, and even making sudden turns the wrong way down alleyways and streets. Neil had no idea where they were but was pretty certain no one else did either. Larry was still feeling coffee-deprived, although they did stop to pick up some take-away veggie sushi from a vending machine.

"It won't taste too good, but there's no waiter to recognize us later and say which way we headed," Nakamura explained. Larry had devoured the food in seconds.

They got out of the SUV and walked over to the front door, keeping an eye out for anyone who might have been able to follow their tracks. The closer they got, the stranger the building looked. Row upon row of stacked cubes lined the walls from floor to ceiling. Each had a window in the front like a front-loading washing machine. Ladders led up to the top row. The windows were all dark, and only a few bulbs in the ceiling cast a soft blue glow over the glass and metal boxes.

"What is this place, a Laundromat?" Neil asked.

"It's a hotel for business travelers," Nakamura said. "Most don't need anything more than a bed for the night, so they crash here. Each cube has a bed, a small TV, even a tiny sink and toilet. It's cheap, and more importantly for keeping Larry hidden . . . it's out of the way."

Nakamura took out a key and unlocked the front door. "It's also owned by a cousin of mine, who has very kindly 'closed for renovations' for the week."

They walked inside and Nakamura flicked on more lights. He flipped another switch and blinds covered the front windows.

"Am I supposed to stay in one of those boxes?" Larry asked as they walked down the corridor. "The cargo hold of Aki's boat was bigger."

"Which reminds me, you are in need of a long shower," Isabella said.

Larry looked around. "Where *is* the shower, hidden in the light fixtures?"

"Never underestimate Japanese ingenuity," Nakamura said, smiling. He took another key and opened a panel on the wall behind the front desk. He flicked a switch and an entire bank of cubes began to hum.

They all stood amazed as the floors of the cubes

began to lower and stack together, one on top of the other. The beds from each floor slipped together to make one king-sized bed.

As the floors fell, the walls started to rise. They slipped one inside the next, and then disappeared into the ceiling. By the time all the different pieces came together, they were staring at a fully furnished bedroom, living room, kitchenette, and dining area. Two final sections of wall slid back down to encase the toilet, sink, and shower.

"The family plan," Nakamura said. "The rooms can also shrink during the busy season to accommodate more travelers."

"That was AWESOME!" Larry yelled, running up and jumping on the bed, which was so springy he immediately bounced against the wall. He slid down headfirst. "Ouch," he mumbled.

"Never dated a gymnast, I guess," Nakamura said.

"The shower appears to be in the bathroom, over there." Neil pointed.

Larry rolled over and stood up. He spied the French press coffeemaker and bags of beans Nakamura had picked up at Suzu's. "Okay, NOW I can get to work," he smiled, clapping his hands and walking toward the kitchen.

"SHOWER!" everyone said at once.

"COFFEE!" Larry said.

They compromised. Larry showered while they made him some fresh coffee. When he finally emerged, he still smelled like fish, but a fish that had used shampoo. Larry immediately downed one cup of coffee, then poured

another. He gave a loud sigh and then did a perfect one-handed cartwheel from the kitchen to the dining room without spilling a drop.

He landed and took a long gulp.

"Ta-da. By the way, her name was Nadia."

Jones gave a very mocking clap.

Larry bowed anyway. "Now let's see what's so important about this old piece of paper."

He unfurled the scroll carefully along the floor and began looking for some kind of pattern in the beautiful brushwork letters and delicate woodcut prints.

"The map could be a pattern in the words or maybe something hidden in the pictures," Larry said. "I've been going over it for a few days and haven't had anything jump out."

"Let's start with the stories," Nakamura said.

Nakamura and Larry started reading the text, periodically stopping to translate an obscure word.

"I guess we're not much use for this part," Neil said to Isabella. "Maybe I should figure out this latest haiku."

Jones went to stand by the door and Isabella sat down next to Neil. "You have another clue?" she asked.

Neil showed her the haiku. "It's not about fish or meat, I don't think."

"Do you think the Angel is our Angel?"

Neil checked his watch. "I've been waiting to call him to find out. He should be up by now." Neil dialed Angel's apartment. Angel picked up on the first ring.

"Neil! I'm so glad to hear from you. Have you found . . . the secret ingredient yet?"

"Yes, in fact. It was full of coffee and smelled a bit like fish."

"That's very good news!" Neil could hear Angel's beaming smile through the phone.

"But we're still missing a . . . side-dish. So we'll keep looking for that. Angel, the reason I called was—"

"I know, the leak in the basement. It wasn't Gary's fault. The pipe was already weakened by all the digging Valette's construction crew was doing."

"Ack" was the only word Neil's mouth was able to form.

"Don't worry. Every restaurant has little unexpected hiccups. Business has been good and the leak is fixed now. The bill wasn't too bad."

"The what? Leak? Bill?"

"Do you want me to send it to you or just tell you how many zeroes?" Angel asked.

"No. Yes. I mean, never mind," Neil fumbled to get the conversation back on track. He'd have to worry about Chez Flambé later.

"Angel, the real reason I called was a haiku I was given." Neil read it to him. *You will rue the day, Kong awaits an Angel to, cap his victory.*

"Hmm. I'm definitely not

heading to Japan, so Kong isn't waiting for me."

"You might be the key to the battle, though. Did you and Nori ever fight a battle with a white sauce, like a roux?

"Ah. You think 'rue the day' is a clue. It could be, but we never had battles that were so specific. The secret ingredients, yes, but not the way we had to cook them. Of course, Nori's gotten a lot crazier since then. I hope I have gone the other way. His way leads to death and destruction."

Neil was suddenly quiet. Something Angel said was ringing a bell. Neil tapped his fingers, thinking.

"Neil, are you still there?" Angel's voice surprised Neil back to reality.

"Angel, say that last bit again."

"Death and destruction?" Angel repeated slowly.

Neil smiled. It clicked. "Death caps and destroying angels. The clue wasn't about you, it's about deadly fungi, mushrooms."

"You're saying Angel isn't a fun guy?" Larry called out.

"Shhhhh!" Isabella said. Then she mimed for him to zip his mouth.

Larry gave a sheepish grin and went back to his translating.

"Nori's going to make us cook a roux with mushrooms," Neil said. "I'm sure of it. Destroying angels and death caps are the deadliest mushrooms in the world. Just one morsel can kill you."

"Poisonous mushrooms? That's insane . . . so I'm sure you're right," Angel said sadly.

"Yes, it's insane. But it also means I can win this thing."

"Keep that nose working and you'll be fine. And I promise I'll keep Gary in line back here. He's excellent with fish. Not so great with closing the freezer at night . . . Never mind."

They said good-bye and Neil gave a relieved sigh. "I'm glad I figured that stupid clue out. Now I only have to spend one more day on that crazy ship."

Larry and Isabella exchanged a look. "Um, I'm not so sure that's a good idea, *mon capitaine*."

"Do you have any idea what goes on in that place?"

"Okay. What will you do after you win this battle?" Larry asked.

"I'll, um, I guess I'll help you guys."

"One, you said there's a chance Nori might be the guy behind all this, so it certainly doesn't hurt to have someone keeping a close eye on him."

"Doesn't hurt *you*, maybe! The judges are dropping

like flies, and the way Kong throws pot lids I could be next!"

Larry continued. "Two, if you finish this duel and then stick around, especially with a restaurant leaking and burning back home, it will raise suspicions."

"But—" Neil started.

"Si. Larry is right," Isabella said. "This is very hard for me to say, but you need to keep dueling. You can help us search for Hiro and the treasure, but in between the matches."

Neil let his hands fall to his sides in surrender.

"And make sure you pick the right mushrooms," Jones said. "If it helps, I've got a field guide."

"Thanks, Jones, but so do I," Neil said, touching his nose. "But wait a minute. If I have to keep battling, then that means I have to—"

"Lose." Larry nodded. "Possibly twice."

Chapter Twenty-One

Into the Boiling Water

The sleek black car screeched to a halt outside Tokyo's Imperial Palace. Smoke poured from the red-hot tires, making Neil cough. He waved his hands to dispel the acrid cloud. The windows were too dark for Neil to see inside. He was tempted to make a run for it, when he noticed the license plate read 2die4. The passenger door swung open and Neil leaned down. Nori was behind the wheel.

"You?" Neil said, surprised. "I thought you didn't like land?"

"I needed to experience the thrill of the chase. Now hop in," Nori said, tapping the passenger seat. Neil

noticed it seemed to be made of some kind of alligator skin. He hesitated.

"It's Komodo dragon, very rare but oh so soft." Nori smiled. "Get in." Then he pulled out a gun and the last of Neil's hesitation disappeared. Neil got in and then Nori pulled the trigger, squirting the inside of the passenger side window with water. "It's glacier water. Very expensive."

Neil had the feeling Nori wanted to impress and intimidate him at the same time. "Nice," was all he said.

"You mean ice!" Nori laughed, running a series of red lights.

Neil was even more surprised a few minutes later when Nori drove off the end of a pier, laughing maniacally. They hit the water and Neil gave a horrified shriek and shut his eyes. He expected to hear the sound of air bags deploying followed by water rushing through the cracks around the windows. Instead, the car sped on.

Neil opened his eyes. They were floating and heading out to sea.

"It's a hovercraft," Nori said, happily slapping the solid gold dashboard.

"Why not just take a boat?" Neil said, shaking with a mixture of fear and anger. This was worse than riding on the back of Larry's motorcycle.

"That was the plan, but then I had to get away from those guys, so no time." Nori jerked his thumb back toward the pier, where two black-clad motorcyclists were stopped at the edge, shaking their fists.

"Are those motorcycle-driving *ninjas?*" Neil said, incredulous.

Nori shrugged. "Dressed like that but they're probably cops. They must have recognized the license plate. I'll have to get a new car. So, did you solve the clue? It was a pretty easy one this time."

Neil was suspicious. Nori seemed two thousand percent calmer than yesterday. "You seem two thousand percent calmer than yesterday," Neil said.

Nori turned to face Neil and smirked. "The answer is mushrooms, poisoned mushrooms—which I'm sure you have figured out."

"I already bought some mushrooms, and they are not poisoned."

"They are also NOT going to be used today. You were not meant to *bring* mushrooms, you are going to *pick* mushrooms. And can even the great Neil Flambé guarantee that the mushrooms he picks are safe?"

"What do you mean? I know what poisonous mushrooms look like."

"Yes. But fungi prefer the shadows, don't they? Now, let's have some opera." Nori smiled and stared out the front window. He pushed a button on the steering wheel and the stereo began blasting music from Japanese Noh theater.

Neil sat nervously back in his seat as the peculiar flutes, drums, and strange chanting filled the car. He felt a wave of relief when Nori's ship finally appeared on the horizon.

Instead of driving into the marina, Nori pulled up alongside the yacht. The entire hovercar was lifted by crane onto the deck of the ship. Then the deck, with the hovercar on top, lowered down to the kitchen. Neil stepped out to the familiar sound of jeering and stamping feet. He strode to his workstation, taking a sideways glance toward the crowd.

Yet another new judge was sitting in the cursed fifth chair, a woman dressed head to toe like a samurai warrior. She sat perfectly still and gave Neil the creeps.

Kong was standing at his kitchen station. Neil bowed, but Kong ignored him, instead staring intently at some point in space. Neil noticed that his left ankle was now attached to a chain that disappeared through a hole in the floor.

How does Nori expect him to cook with that thing on? Neil wondered. Neil also noticed with some relief that none of the pans in Kong's kitchen had lids.

Nori stepped out of the hovercar and slammed the keys down on the judge's table. The samurai still didn't move. "The first one to take a bite of today's meal can have this car." The crowd oohed and aahed.

Neil rolled his eyes. *Big deal, the police will chase anybody they see driving that thing,* Neil thought. Of course, that was probably a selling point for the thrill-seeking judges, so he kept his mouth shut.

Nori continued. "Today's battle will test everyone here. The judges must choose the winner based on taste and on their own survival. Because each of our chefs will make a sauce using mushrooms they themselves will pick."

Nori gave a wave and his car disappeared into the floor, replaced a moment later by a huge black cube.

"And to be sure they are extra careful, the chefs will eat the sauce themselves."

"What? That was not in the deal," Neil said.

"So you are okay to risk others but not yourself?"

"Sounds like you!" Neil yelled.

There was a brief laugh from one of the people in the crowd. Nori jerked his head and one of his attendants pulled a lever. Neil heard what sounded like a trapdoor giving way and a quickly fading "Aaaaaaaaaaaaa."

Nori turned back to face the chefs. His smile turned to a scowl. "Each chef will have two minutes in the cube. You must come out with one hundred mushrooms and you must cook them all. Kong will be first."

Kong finally budged and walked slowly toward the cube. He pulled on the chain as he walked and more came out of the hole in the floor. He entered the cube and the door shut behind him, the chain sticking out

from under the door. A large digital clock began to count down 2:00, 1:59, 1:58 . . . The clock hit zero and Neil saw the chain begin to retract.

Kong was pulled from the doorway, still reaching back into the room for more mushrooms. He held his apron tightly against his chest. It was brimming with mushrooms of various sizes, shapes, and colors. The door closed and Kong dejectedly walked back to his station. Nori made him dump the mushrooms out and then he counted.

"Ah, you are four mushrooms short," Nori said. "Four mushrooms will be chosen at random and you will cook these as well."

Kong said something angrily in Japanese.

"Did he say he couldn't see inside the cube?" said one of the judges.

"SILENCE!" Nori yelled.

Neil realized the danger of his situation in a flash. The shadows! That's what Nori had meant, darkness. The chefs wouldn't be able to see the mushrooms they were picking. It was guaranteed to make sure at least some of the mushrooms they chose would be poisonous. He and Kong were going to cook toxic mushrooms and they'd have to decide whether to poison everyone, themselves, or just one judge.

"It is now time for Neil Flambé to choose."

Two armed attendants walked up to Neil and cocked their guns. Neil gritted his teeth and walked into the cube. The light that slipped through the still-open door illuminated a floor covered with various kinds of mushrooms. "There's no way there are a hundred good ones left!" Neil yelled as the door slammed shut.

"Nori!" Neil yelled, banging his fists on the door. An electronic voice began counting down the time. It reminded Neil of Deep Blue Cheese, the evil super-computer he'd faced twice and beaten twice.

"Don't panic," Neil said to himself. "Think. Smell!" Neil got to his hands and knees and began lifting up mushrooms, smelling each one as best as he could before dropping it into his hat. The robotic voice continued to count down, and with ten seconds left Neil could tell he was going to be short. He'd have to pick more mush-rooms but pick them quickly.

An ear-splitting buzzer sounded inside the cube and the guards returned to grab Neil by the shoulders. In the final second of light he was able to reach out and grab what he hoped were twenty or so perfect *shitakes*. Then he was escorted to his workstation. Neil laid the mush-rooms out on his counter and Nori counted them.

"One hundred and five! My, aren't you greedy."

Neil could see that almost all of his mushrooms were safe. If he could just choose the one hundred to cook he could avoid poisoning anybody. Nori put an end to that. "Kong needs four mushrooms and you have extra. Kong can have these four here." Nori picked four completely safe mushrooms and placed them next to Kong's cutting board. Then he grabbed another and threw it back into the cube.

Neil was furious. He had one hundred mushrooms, at least a handful of which were toxic. His mind raced to find a way to cook them and not put anybody at risk. He glanced over to see how Kong was dealing with this dilemma.

Kong was staring blankly at his collection of mushrooms. Neil looked at them and saw Kong's problem. He'd crushed all his mushrooms in his apron as they'd yanked him from the box. Nori might have been able to count the stems but bits of all the caps were scattered over the counter. It was impossible to tell which bits were safe and which weren't.

Nori strode back to the judges' table. "You now have fifty minutes. Whoever cooks the best sauce wins. Of course, kill a judge, or yourself, and you are automatically the loser."

Kong looked up and asked something in Japanese. Nori responded, "Fine, if you each kill someone, then the chef who kills fewer judges wins."

Kong nodded and began chopping the mushrooms.

Neil began chopping all the good mushrooms as well as onions, some shallots, and numerous herbs. He set the bad mushrooms aside . . . for now.

Nori explained the challenge to the crowd. "Ladies and gentlemen, a roux is an extremely simple sauce. It's basically just flour and some kind of fat, usually butter, mixed together, but it can be the base for just about anything. So like our other challenges this one is simple, but deadly."

The crowd went wild.

Neil ignored them and began stirring some bacon fat and butter together. The saltiness of the bacon would perfectly match the earthiness of the mushrooms. Neil was careful to keep the destroying angels and death caps to the side.

As he stirred the roux he suddenly remembered, he

was supposed to lose. Nori had just said that killing a judge meant automatic defeat. He looked up at the five judges, all of them crazy thrill seekers who seemed to welcome death. Neil could prepare six dishes—five with normal mushrooms and one laced throughout with the killers.

Could he do it? Could he choose who lived and died? Sweat formed on his upper lip as he gazed at the judges, trying to figure out which one he considered expendable. The samurai, perhaps guessing his intention, finally moved. She turned her head slowly and gazed straight at Neil. She nodded. It was as if Neil could hear her voice in his head, saying, *do it.*

"NO!" Neil shouted out loud. Everyone turned to look at him.

"Are you feeling the pressure, little boy?" Nori mocked.

The sweat was now pouring down Neil's front, soaking his clothes. He put his head down and took a deep breath. "No," he said.

"Good. Keep cooking."

But Neil had meant, *no, I won't choose.* He was no killer. Everything about this duel was crazy. The people, the rules, the man behind it . . . and Neil was not going to join them in their insanity.

He grabbed a towel and wiped his forehead. Neil looked at

the towel. It was decorated with beautiful embroidered flowers. *Flowers*, Neil thought. He gave a discreet smile and got back to work. He used his roux as the base for a mushroom sauce, even giving himself enough time to make fresh pasta and to boil it to *al dente* perfection. Then, of course, he let it boil a minute longer, just to be sure he would lose.

"Time is UP!" Nori yelled. Kong and Neil put down their utensils and stood back. Kong had made a selection of baked mushrooms with a spicy mushroom and bread-crumb stuffing in each.

Neil could smell that it was amazing. He could also smell that one of the dishes contained enough death cap bits to make someone seriously ill, possibly dead. Neil couldn't tell, at this distance, which one it was. "One person is going to eat all the poison and the others will all be fine." Neil shivered at the thought. Had Kong done this on purpose?

Nori walked over and examined the dishes. "Very good! Now you'll see why we call this Russian *Roux*-lette. Because you don't get to choose who eats which dish. I do." Nori grinned and Kong's body seemed to quake.

Nori walked over to Neil's counter and his smile evaporated. "What is THIS?" he yelled. Neil had laid out six dishes of pasta, topping each with an edible basil flower and some pecorino cheese. But there was a seventh plate on the table. It was a centerpiece that Neil had made using lemon peels as petals. He'd charred the poisoned mushrooms, and used the blackened death caps as the button centre of a bouquet of daisies. They were beautiful, and inedible.

"That's cheating!" Nori fumed.

"You said I had to *cook* all one hundred mushrooms. You never said that I had to *serve* all one hundred," Neil said, as calmly as he could. Nori looked like a bomb about to explode.

"BAH!" Nori said at last, turning on his heels and marching toward the judges' table. "We will eat Neil Flambé's first. We'll see how good he was at picking the mushrooms." The armed attendants returned and placed Neil at a seat at the table, one of his own plates sitting in front of him. Then Nori made every-one pass his or her dish to the left. "*Roux*-lette," he said again.

The judges nodded and they all began eating. Neil could tell imme-diately that he'd made the perfect dish for this round. There were oohs and aahs but no one seemed to get sick. Even the samurai woman seemed to enjoy the meal. Nori seemed dis-appointed to see all the judges still breathing and he ordered Neil back to his place.

Neil took his place at his counter and watched as the waiters took Kong's six dishes to the table. Kong dragged his chain behind him as he walked over and took his seat. Neil still couldn't tell which dish was poisoned. He debated telling them that one of the dishes was too dan-gerous to eat, but before he could say a word they each grabbed a stuffed mushroom and popped them into their mouths.

The judges stole sideways glances at one another. Kong was so nervous or at least agitated that he looked like he was on the verge of a volcanic eruption. They all seemed fine. The judges smiled and gobbled up the rest of the mushrooms. Kong stood up and bowed to them all.

Nori seemed somewhat miffed that nobody was dead. "Now we will choose the winner!" he said with an annoyed wave of his hand. The crowd stamped their feet and cheered.

The judges turned over their scorecards, revealing a 3–2 victory for Kong.

It was the *pecorino* that cost Neil the victory. It was way too salty for the dish he'd prepared, and Neil knew it. That's why he'd added it. The judges also pointed out the mushiness of the noodles and suggested Neil's centerpiece had perhaps bent the rules a little too much.

Kong's food had been amazing, earthy and somehow nutty—with a rich, almost creamy sauce.

Nori was overjoyed. "We live to die another day!" he cheered as he slapped Kong on the back. Kong seemed unmoved by the victory. He followed his retracting chain back to the kitchen.

"We won! We won!" Nori sang, jumping up on the judge's table and dancing a bizarre jig. He pointed a finger at Neil, taunting him. "You lost! You lost!"

Neil knew that he had no choice but to lose. Still, he didn't like the feeling one bit. Nori's gloating didn't make it any easier. Neil was just as perturbed by how close he'd come to winning. If one more judge had chosen him, he would be the winner and also have blown his cover. Of course, he'd also have a lot more money, and it was sounding more and more like he was going to need it back home.

But something was still wrong. Kong had served toxic mushrooms, Neil was sure of it. So why wasn't anybody sick or dead?

"Hey Codzilla, how did you stop from killing anyone?" Neil yelled across the kitchen.

Kong didn't say a word but Neil saw him stumble. Kong was shaking and sweating. *Oh, no, he ate the poisoned dish*, Neil realized with a shock.

"Nori! Your chef looks sick! Get a doctor!" Neil hollered. Kong was gripping the edges of his steel counter so hard the metal was bending. The crowd went silent, sitting on the edges of their seats.

Nori stopped dancing and ran to his chef's side. Within seconds a thin, bearded man in a doctor's coat came rushing into the room on an escalator and was immediately checking Kong's vital signs. Kong seemed angry as the doctor attempted to open his chef's jacket, and took a swipe at him. The man expertly avoided the full thrust of the blow but was still struck in the side, sending him spinning across the floor like a top.

The doctor came to a stop and ducked as Kong threw a pot at him. "He is fine, but he is very irritating," the doctor said, jumping to his feet, his arms poised to deflect any more pots. He looked like a character in a martial arts movie.

Kong barked something at Nori. Nori breathed a sigh of relief. "The victory stands. He is just tired. Judges, you may go. Chef Flambé, loser, you will be escorted home immediately." Nori clapped.

The judges began to get up. They looked over at the fifth chair. The samurai was perfectly still. Nori's panicked look returned. He signaled for the doctor to rush over.

The doctor carefully placed a stethoscope to her chest. He felt her neck for a pulse. "She's dead," he said.

Nori clenched his fists. "But if she's been poisoned, then that means Flambé wins? It must have been Kong's roux?"

The doctor shook his head. He pointed at the centerpiece Neil had made. One of the buttons was missing from the daisies.

Nori's face broke into a relieved and twisted smile. "There's no way to determine whose dish actually poisoned her?"

"No way," the doctor said.

Nori laughed. "So the result stands! Ha, ha! It's a pity though. She was the first judge to take a bite. She would have won my hovercar! Perhaps I'll just change the plates and keep it myself. " Nori walked over and lifted the centerpiece above his head like a trophy.

Neil felt sick. The judge had eaten the poisoned mushrooms he'd so carefully kept separate. "She ate the death cap on purpose. Why would anyone do that?" he said.

The lava-surfer spoke up again. "Stop being such a weakling. The military was paying her handsomely for her research."

"Research?" Neil was having trouble following this.

"Yes, research. She was a scientist. She was working on a study . . . on how to avoid being poisoned."

"She was avoiding getting poisoned by showing up at a poisoned food duel?" Neil's head was spinning.

. The woman laughed. "Of course! She had a theory that by eating small bits of poisoned mushrooms, she could build up an immunity. She was practically dead by the time she showed up. That's why she wasn't moving. Half of her internal organs had shut down. She'd even bet me before we started that she'd survive the duel! If I survive the last two battles, I'll be even richer than I am now!" All the judges laughed and filed out of the auditorium.

Neil just shook his head. "I need to get out of here," he said.

"See you in two days," Nori said. He clapped his hands again and the floor lifted Neil up to the top deck. Neil didn't bother looking overboard to see if the sharks were there. He could hear the thrashing water.

Chapter Twenty-Two

Rice Whine

Neil was still shaking as he stepped off the helicopter and back onto the huge outdoor courtyard of the Palace. He'd been so rattled he'd almost asked the pilot to drop him off at the hotel. Luckily, he'd caught himself in time and had remembered that Nakamura was going to meet him in the park.

It was near a metro station, and Nakamura had promised he'd escort Neil on any more trains.

As the helicopter took off, Neil caught a familiar scent on the air. He'd smelled it before, on the dock, the last time he'd been dropped off by the copter. Was it something in the exhaust? That would be totally strange because it had more of a floral smell. He'd have to ask Isabella if she knew of any perfume scents that were added to jet fuel.

Neil looked around. Crowds of people were staring at him. It wasn't every day that a redhead in a chef's outfit was dropped off in a public square by a jet-black

helicopter. Neil gave a sheepish wave and walked toward a bench underneath one of the park's many cherry trees.

"Nice job staying inconspicuous," said a voice from behind the tree.

"Yes, well, it wasn't really my choice. I was hoping they'd drop me off in a car. You and the 'secret ingredient' have any luck with the 'recipe' book?"

Nakamura sat next to Neil. "We've finished working out all the recipes. The pictures are next. But nothing yet."

Neil nodded. "Well, I just had a horrible day. I'm getting sick of this whole affair."

"Losing is no fun, eh, boss?"

"It wasn't that. Well, okay, it wasn't *all* that. Those people are crazy. It's like they want to die. I just don't understand it."

Nakamura rubbed his chin. "I can't explain the world to you, Neil. All I can say is that the older you get, the stranger and more complicated everything seems . . . and that includes people."

Neil stood up. "Let's go check that recipe book and end this thing. I don't want to have to lose again."

"Okay. The trains are that way." Nakamura pointed at a glass building a short distance away.

They started walking. Neil thought he felt a breeze in the nearby cherry trees, and he smelled the same floral smell he'd smelled on the dock. He looked up but the leaves were perfectly still.

"Hachikō," Neil said in a low whisper, using Nakamura's code name. "I think we're being followed."

Nakamura nodded but kept walking. "We have been since we arrived in Japan. I'll fill you in later. Now, let's get home."

Larry sat on the floor of his room, the glass windows sending circle-shaped lights onto the walls. Each circle seemed to illuminate a different illustrated page of the scroll.

"Are you nuts?" Neil said as they walked in. "You cut up the scroll and put it on the wall?"

"Wall, nuts, walnuts! Hey, not bad," Larry said. "But no, I'm not nuts. Isabella took some high-def photos of the prints with her camera, and Jones went out and bought a photo printer. I said he could charge it to the restaurant."

Neil smacked his forehead. "Sure. Yes. Great, because we're just rolling in dough. Oh, wait, we might have been rolling in dough except that I had to lose today."

"You sound like you're losing it right now," Larry said, still staring intently at the pictures. "I put the pictures up to see if there's some kind of pattern. I figured we might want to write on them or cut them or something, so better to do that with copies."

"And . . . see anything yet?"

"So far, nothing. There are no maps, no images of treasure that I can see. But we think we know what the treasure is now. The text talks about it."

"And?" Neil said.

"Turns out Hiro's family used to be real bigwigs in the Japanese nobility. They fought for centuries for all sorts of emperors. But then they ticked off some shogun. He sent ninja assassins to 'take care of them.'"

"Is that a direct translation?" Neil joked.

"Just about. But someone tipped off the Takoyakis. They hid their family's gold and jewels before they were attacked. The ninjas wiped out a lot of them and the rest of the family were sent into exile. They lived on an island somewhere for a while. Doesn't say which one."

Nakamura walked into the room. "Speaking of

attacks, where are Jones and Isabella? I thought you were supposed to have someone with you at all times."

"I ran out of coffee. I figured that was important enough to bend the rules. Anyway, I knew you were coming back soon and I've been working on my jujitsu. I can take care of myself . . . for a few minutes anyway."

"You can barely take care of making a side salad," Neil said.

"Ha, ha."

"You know jujitsu?" Nakamura asked.

"Koko was showing me some great moves. She's quite an athlete, actually. I can't wait until we find Hiro and the treasure. I can just imagine the hug she'll give me then!" Larry pretended to attack Nakamura, who deftly flipped him over with just a flick of his wrist.

"Ouch!" Larry said, landing with a thud on the floor. "Where'd you learn that move? I dare you to try it again!"

"You got it."

Neil ignored the repeated thuds and walked up to the wall to take a closer look at the pictures. The artwork was beautiful. There were images of ancient warriors, cats patrolling around a house with a volcano in the background, and a giant wave about to swallow a fleet of fishing boats. Each was done in a slightly different style.

"These are just woodcut prints?" Neil asked.

"Yup." Larry nodded, lying flat on the floor. "It's amazing how much detail they could get into those with just a few inks and lots of patience."

"How old are they?"

"Nakamura and I think they are about a hundred

and fifty years old. The scroll says they were made by the great artist Tomisa, right before his death. The Takoyaki family commissioned a series of prints to celebrate what it calls their "impending glory." Of course, that was right around the time they were exiled, so . . . their glory was not so impending, really."

Neil was impressed. "The images are amazing. They look like watercolor paintings. Look how realistic everything is, from the waves to Mount Fuji, to the food they're eat—" Neil paused. Something about the pictures was strange.

"Neil, you okay?" Larry said, getting to his feet.

Neil peered closely at the picture of an elaborately dressed medieval warrior, sitting on the floor of his dining room. Neil stared at the table. Then he went to the next picture and the next and the next.

"Neil, what are you looking at, exactly?" Larry asked, as he walked next to Neil and stared at the pictures.

"The code name we use for this is the 'recipe book,' right?"

Larry nodded. "So?"

"Well, maybe it *is* a recipe book, sort of. Every one of these pictures has a table of food. Some of them are in the foreground, some in the background."

Larry looked at the

pictures. "You're right. How the heck did I miss that?"

"I've been solving a lot of food clues lately. You'd have figured it out after the coffee arrived."

"Can't disagree with that." Larry smiled.

"But something is weird," Neil said, moving from picture to picture again.

"What?" Larry and Nakamura asked.

"This picture of the guy in the crazy helmet is the first in the series. What year is he from?"

Nakamura walked over and pulled out his notebook. "Well, it illustrates a story about the Takoyaki family from about five hundred years ago. They rose to power in an area around Edo, the ancient name for Tokyo. The general in that picture was a samurai warrior who helped Empress Okiko suppress a rebellion. He was given land and title in exchange for his help."

Neil walked down to the last picture in the series. It showed a samurai standing in front of a cherry tree. "What year is this guy from?"

Nakamura checked his notes. "That's the last Takoyaki samurai, so about a hundred and fifty years ago."

Larry nodded. "He was the guy they sent the ninjas to whack."

Neil pointed at the table in the picture. "Then why is someone from five hundred years ago eating exactly the same fish and rice as this guy from one hundred years ago?"

"Well, the prints were done around the same time," Nakamura said. "Maybe the artist just plopped in some standard food bits, kind of like woodcut clip art?"

Neil shook his head. "Larry told us the artist was patient and careful. There's a reason for the food to be the same and it's not laziness."

Larry nodded. "Neil's right. The other stuff in each print, like the swords and the style of the houses, is consistent with the time period it's showing. Like, look at

the rooftop in the first print and compare it to the one in the last print. They're totally different styles. One is clearly Muromachi period and the other is Meiji."

Neil and Nakamura stared at Larry, waiting for an explanation.

"Jennifer Honda, expert in Japanese architecture at Emily Carr Art School and cutie. Wasn't she at my funeral? She has a big tattoo of Mount Fuji on her back?"

"Moving on," Neil said. "So if everything else is different, then why is the food the same?"

Nakamura closed his notebook and stared at the prints. "Are you sure they're eating the same food?"

"Is that a serious question?" Neil sounded annoyed. "Look, I'll explain it for you. As we've discussed, the detail is amazing. The general style of all the pictures is different, but the rice and fish are exactly the same in all the pictures."

Larry peered closely. "Cool. But rice and fish seem like pretty basic staples of Japanese cuisine."

"If you're going to write a manga about a chef who's based on *me*, you need to do way more research into food. Look at how white the rice is, and look at the size of the grains. That's not just any rice, it's koshihikari rice, I'm sure of it. It's probably from Uonuma, on the west coast. It's the best rice in the world."

"So? These guys were loaded. They could afford the best of the best," Larry said.

"Could they buy a time machine? The rice has only been around since 1956. It was developed as a hybrid."

"You know, Neil, for a guy who never does his homework, you actually know a lot of stuff."

"Only if it's about food. And don't you find it strange that a one-hundred-and-fifty-year old series of woodcuts has a picture of fifty-year-old rice?"

"Yeah. But as a clue it seems pretty straightforward. The treasure is hidden in Uonuma. Let's go get it and then use it to get Hiro back!"

Nakamura looked at Neil. "Let me guess. The fish in the pictures isn't from the west coast?"

Neil shook his head. "No. It's red snapper. That's fished mostly on the east coast. The best comes from Choshi, and I assume if the artist is showing the country's best rice, he's going to show the best fish, too."

Larry pulled out a road map and put a finger on

Uonuma and another on Choshi. "Great, so we've got four hundred kilometers of land to cover. If we start digging we should be able to find the treasure by the thirty-first century!"

"Or else the type of rice and the type of fish are important for some other reason," Neil said. "It seems pretty clear the rice and fish are the secret. It's too weird that they'd be there by accident. But a four hundred kilometer window doesn't seem like a very good clue. It's got to be something else."

"Yeah, but what?"

The three of them went from picture to picture to picture. The rice and fish appeared in each—painted in exactly the same way but in slightly different positions.

"I wonder if the food was painted on later, over something else. Maybe it's covering up something?" Nakamura suggested.

"I'll get the original," Larry said.

Larry spread the original across the tabletop. He

peered closely at the rice and fish. The only thing he could see underneath them was the texture of the paper.

"No. The rice bowl and fish weren't added later. They are both part of the original prints. But that's impossible."

Neil closed his eyes and leaned in close to the paper, taking a deep sniff. He stood up and frowned. "It's a fake," he said.

"What?" Larry and Nakamura said.

"The paper is rice paper, but it's not old. It's just made to look that way. The stains around the edges are made with tea, but not Japanese tea. It's Darjeeling, better for making things look old but not even grown in India until the 1870s. It certainly wasn't imported here before the 1920s. This has a slight metal overtone, which makes me think it's modern, machine-processed tea."

"So what does THAT tell us?" Larry said. "I could have saved the money on the printer and cut this thing up."

Their conversation was interrupted by the return of Jones and Isabella. Jones walked in carrying a fresh supply of coffee beans and a pile of what appeared to be doughnuts wrapped in plastic. "It's amazing what the

Japanese sell in vending machines," Isabella said. "Jones was like—how do you say?—a kid in a candy store."

Neil looked at Jones who bore absolutely no resemblance to a kid or anyone who might find himself in a candy

store unless he was planning to blow it up.

Larry immediately grabbed the coffee beans and snacks and disappeared into the kitchenette. The sound of grinding and brewing was instantaneous.

"This must be a very meticulous copy of the original, surely. The prints are so beautiful," Isabella said after Neil filled her in on his discovery.

"But why add the modern food to all the images? And if this is a copy, where is the original?"

Larry emerged from the kitchenette holding a huge mug of coffee and some kind of sweet bun.

"Hey, I have a great idea. What? Why does everyone always look so skeptical when I say that?"

"Tell us the idea and you'll probably find out," Jones grunted from the door.

"We should find some way to ask Koko if she knows anything. Don't let her know why, but just ask her what she knows about the scroll, the family history. Waddya think?"

"It's worth a shot," Nakamura said.

"I've talked to her before," Neil said. "I can try to find a way to bring it up. But how do I just happen to run into her and ask her about the scroll?"

"Maybe you could ask her out on a date," Jones suggested, the slightest trace of a grin on his lips. He was always hoping Isabella would see the light and dump the cocky boy chef.

Isabella gave a loud *humph*. "Or maybe it's a stupid plan. I thought you wanted to keep her out of all this. We don't want someone else we have to hide, do we?"

"Well, I already texted her from Neil's phone," Larry

said, sipping his coffee. "She should be here any minute."

"What?" Neil shot up, searching his pocket for his phone. "What did you do that for?"

Larry lost his goofy grin for a second. "It was a risk, but we don't have any time to waste. She wants to save her brother and she's the only one we know who might have a sense of where the real scroll is or what might have been in the original pics." The smile returned. "Besides, with those big dark eyes, she's gotta be trustworthy."

Nakamura didn't seem happy. "Please let us know when you plan on inviting a girlfriend over for tea, okay?"

"Coffee," Larry smiled and he took a bite of his sweet roll. He immediately began choking and gagging.

"Larry! Are you poisoned?" Neil rushed frantically over. Had parts of the dangerous fungi leaked onto his phone and been passed onto Larry?

Larry spat out the sweet bun onto the floor and took a long drink of his coffee. "I don't believe it . . . a dough-nut that tastes like shrimp!"

Jones gave a little cough that sounded a lot like a chuckle.

Chapter Twenty-Three

Fishy Smells

They heard a loud click and then an electronic bell. Someone was coming in through the front door of the hotel. The swinging door sent a tiny waft of air into Larry's room. Neil sniffed and then spun around in a panic.

"Quick, hide Larry, hide the scroll!" he hissed.

"What? Why?" Larry said, still trying to wash away the shrimp taste with one more coffee. "It's probably just Koko."

"Did you tell her you were alive?" Neil said.

"Um, not really. I just texted her from your phone saying to drop by the hotel."

"THEN HIDE AND HURRY!" Neil said as footsteps sounded on the tile floor of the hallway.

Isabella and Jones quickly grabbed the scroll and the pictures from the wall. Nakamura stuffed his notes into his forensic kit. They shoved them, and Larry, underneath the bed just as Koko walked up to the open door and knocked.

Neil took a deep breath and went to let her in. "Koko, hello. Thanks for coming so soon. Please come in."

"Thank you. I was shopping in the area," she said. Her eyes met Neil's and he smiled, but underneath he could feel the hairs on the back of his neck standing up. He heard Isabella growling in the background. Jones took a step forward and offered Koko a seat at the dining room table, gripping the chair so hard it creaked.

Neil gestured toward his friends. "This is Isabella Tortellini, the perfume maker, and her friend Jones. You've met my servant, Hachikō." They all bowed to one another.

Koko turned her eyes back to Neil. "I received your text message. You said you had information about Hiro. What is it?"

"You told me at the funeral that he and Larry were killed in a protest over whale fishing."

"Yes." Koko nodded. "They left to go stand up to a

whaling vessel that was trolling off the shore."

Larry gave out a surprised squeak from under the bed. Nakamura coughed and held his hand up to his mouth. "Sorry boss, I'm, having a bit of a reaction to that shrimp danish."

"Go take something for that, Hachikō. And make some tea for our guest while you're at it, please." Neil turned his attention back to Koko. He sat down beside her.

"Koko, the man who brought me here for the duel is Matsumoro Nori."

"The billionaire? He is an evil man," Koko said, locking her eyes onto Neil's.

Neil nodded. "He let something slip yesterday— something about Hiro. First of all, it was his ship that was fishing in that part of the ocean. That part wasn't the slip, though. He hates me. He wanted me to know that he was the one who killed my cousin. He also wants to rattle me so that I'll lose to his chef."

"Why do you stay?" Koko asked after a long pause.

"I can't just leave. There are a lot of reasons. For one, I need to win the duel. I need the money. Now I need to win for . . . revenge."

"I understand," Koko said.

"Nori also showed me something. Something he said his crew found floating in the water with the wreckage." Neil pointed at Isabella's feet. "Isabella has it next to her on the floor. She'll give it to you now."

Isabella appeared totally surprised, but she looked down and saw the canister that had contained the scroll. She knelt down, picked it up, and walked it over to

Koko. Koko's eyes were even wider as she accepted the canister.

"Nori gave you this?" she said.

"It's empty," Neil said. "But I know what was inside. It was a scroll. Nori has it now. He showed it to me."

Koko immediately locked her eyes back on Neil. "There is a family history of a scroll, passed down from son to son. It's nothing of value, just a family heirloom. Why would they have taken it fishing with them?" Koko said.

"Fishing?"

"They were pretending to go fishing. I meant protesting."

Neil was silent for a second. He looked over at Isabella, who still appeared utterly mystified. Jones was now standing as still as a statue, but Neil could see his muscles twitching under his suit. Neil continued.

"Nori said he had translated the text and it was about your family history. He seemed to think it might be valuable. But I know something he doesn't." Neil paused for emphasis. "It's a fake."

Koko seemed startled. "A fake? What do you mean?"

"I could tell by the paper. It's not old paper."

Koko appeared calm but Neil noted that she was gripping the canister so hard that her knuckles were turning white.

Neil looked straight in her eyes. "Koko. I know this is a lot to take in, but I need you to tell me what you know about the scroll."

Koko's fingers relaxed slightly and her eyes darted around Neil's face.

"The scroll must be a copy . . . not a fake, but a

copy. There was a fire, back when I was just a young girl, at our home in Tokyo. I overheard my father telling Hiro that the scroll was destroyed. He was smiling as he said it. I had always thought that he was happy because he was joking. I said the scroll was just a legend . . . but perhaps he was happy because he knew there was a copy." She looked away now, as if trying to remember.

"Why do you think it's a copy?"

"It *might* be a copy." Koko closed her eyes and thought. "You say the scroll was in this canister?"

Neil nodded.

Koko paused for a second before continuing. "I have seen this canister before. There was a man, an artist, who came to our house frequently before the fire. He and father would lock themselves in the office for hours. Then he left. I only saw him once more. It was years after the fire. Father was dead. Hiro and I, we went to his workshop and I saw him give Hiro this canister. I assumed it was some artwork my father had commissioned. It must have contained the scroll— the copy, I mean. I never saw the canister again until right now."

She stood up quickly, wiping her eyes on her sleeve. "I must go. The scroll is real? Nori killed my brother and Larry? This is all too much for me. I have to leave." She hurried to the door.

"Koko, there's one other thing you need to know," Neil said. She spun around and looked back. "I think your brother might still be alive."

Koko's eyes flashed. "My brother? Hiro? Alive!"

"I think Nori captured him when he killed my cousin. That's the part he let slip. He thinks Hiro knows something else about the scroll, something only Hiro can reveal."

"Where is Nori now?" she asked.

"On his yacht. But it moves around. I can try to help. I'll be back there tomorrow for one more battle. If I can find out more about the scroll or your brother, I'll let you know."

Her eyes locked on his once more and Neil felt a shiver. "Thank you," she said. Then she turned away and was gone.

Jones waited a moment and then grabbed his car keys and ran out the door.

Chapter Twenty-Four

The Race Is On

As soon as Jones left, Neil quickly ran to the bed. "You can come out now, but we've got to work fast. Pass me the pictures." Larry's hand slid the papers out. Neil grabbed the copies of the illustrations and taped them back up on the wall.

Larry groaned as he crawled out from under the bed and stretched. "Hey, Hachikō, I hope you're making more coffee in there."

There was no answer.

Neil tacked the last image in place. "Nakamura went out the back door. I imagine he's giving Jones some help. I have a feeling they'll need it if Koko sees them."

"Explain to me why we suddenly had to stash everything, including *me*, under the bed." Larry dramatically wiped a few imaginary dust bunnies off his shirt.

"Let's ask Isabella," Neil said. Isabella was leaning with

her back against the wall, her brows furrowed in deep thought, but she looked up when she heard Neil mention her name.

"Did you notice anything about her, Isabella?"

"Her mesmerizing eyes, perhaps," Isabella said with a sarcastic flick of her head.

"Yes, aren't they wonderful?" Neil said. "Seriously, though, how about her smell?"

Isabella pushed herself off the wall and walked over to join Neil. "She didn't smell odd, exactly. She smelled like cherry blossoms. It's a wonderful scent. I meant to ask her where she got it."

Neil nodded. "I noticed it too, as soon as she walked in the door. I've also smelled it before, at Hiro's funeral and then twice when I was being followed. I'd assumed it was from all the cherry trees here, but I noticed at the park yesterday that they aren't in bloom right now. But I didn't make the connection to Koko until she showed up here."

"I'll tell you one other thing I noticed," Isabella said. "That wasn't love in her eyes when you mentioned that her brother was alive, that was anger. I know the difference."

Larry got up. "Isabella, you are a very interesting person. A little scary sometimes, but always interesting. I'll go make us both a coffee." He walked into the kitchen as Neil continued to talk.

Neil ignored him. "Koko has been following me. She's been looking for the scroll too, and I think she's dangerous. Did you notice how hard she squeezed that canister?"

"Then why did you tell her all that stuff?" Larry called from the kitchen.

"I needed to know if she knew about the scroll. She did."

Isabella folded her arms and stared at the floor for a second, then spoke. "I think she was telling the truth about the copy. I think she knew, or at least suspected, that the original was lost in that fire. She looked like she was trying to piece it all together as she was talking."

"She was probably hoping that I'd fill in some details for her as well," Neil said. "Which means she probably believed my story about Nori and the scroll."

"Did you notice how she was always spying on people? She kept saying she 'overheard' conversations or 'saw' her father and the artist. I don't think she went *with* Hiro to get the scroll from the artist. I think she followed him."

Neil nodded. "She said the scroll was handed down from son to son. Maybe she wants it for herself?"

"Wait, wait, wait." Larry said, peeking around the corner. "Isn't it equally plausible that she's trying to find the scroll to help her family and find her brother? Maybe she's on our side, and maybe *she* doesn't trust *us*."

Just then Jones and Nakamura returned. "She got away," Nakamura said. Jones seemed too angry to say anything.

Neil continued to stare at the pictures. "Let me guess, she got on a motorcycle and drove off. You got stuck in traffic with that glorified troop carrier."

Jones growled. Neil took that as a yes.

"Koko is a motorcycle ninja, and no innocent grieving sister," Neil said, thinking out loud. "She's been trailing us for days. She's working for someone— maybe the police, maybe for herself, maybe for whoever attacked you and Hiro on that sightseeing boat. She told that same lie about you heading out on a whaling protest."

"Sorry about that surprised squeak when she said that," Larry said. "Nice recovery by Nakamura, though. And I still can't explain why she'd make that up."

Neil continued. "Maybe she's working for Nori. That whole hovercar thing could have been set up so I'd *think* she was trailing him. If she is working for Nori, then she knows I was lying about the scroll and she'll be back soon with backup. If she isn't, then Nori's in for a surprise visitor."

"If she attacks Nori and finds out that we're lying, then she'll be back with a vengeance," Larry said. He walked back in carrying the whole carafe of coffee and a straw. "So what do we do now?"

Neil began to rearrange the copies on the wall, putting them in a different order, and flipping a few upside down. He still didn't see a pattern. "We've got to crack this code and do it fast. We're going to need to find that treasure first. All our lives, including Hiro's, might depend on it."

"Sounds like a late night," Larry said. "I'd better make more coffee."

The late night turned into an early morning. The rising sun sent yellow beams of sunlight streaming into the room. Neil blinked. He had stared at the bowls of rice so often his eyes were practically swimming with visions of dancing rice grains and fish. He sat down at the table and rubbed his eyes.

Jones stood guard at the door, but so far he'd seen nothing. That was good. Nakamura was looking for anything in the text that might give a clue about what to look for in the images. "The stories are really straightforward histories. They mention riches and treasure, lots of food, but that's it. There's no pattern."

Larry was busily making more coffee for everyone, and drinking most of it himself. Only Neil and Isabella said no. Larry sipped his latest coffee and stared at the prints, which Neil had shifted around yet again. "I guess when you hide a treasure and leave a clue, you want the clue to be a tough one."

"I just feel like we're going around and around in circles," Neil said, rubbing his eyes. "Let's think about Hiro's dad for a bit. Koko said he had seen the scroll and was happy there was a copy. Is there anything about him that might be a clue?"

"The file said he was a mathematician," Isabella said, suppressing a yawn.

Larry took another sip of coffee. "It's funny you'd mention circles. He was a circle mathematician . . . in a way."

"A what?" Neil said.

"Circles are huge in Japanese math, at least old Japanese math."

"What do you mean?" Isabella said.

"It's all tied to the Zen theory of *Ensō*. It means

'circle' in Japanese, but it's also a concept." He walked over and put his coffee mug down. Then he formed a circle by touching his fingertips. "It means complete, perfect, like we'd say 'full circle.' But it also means strength and beauty, like the earth, or two hands touching."

"That's so sweet I might get a cavity," Neil said with a frown. "What about the old math?"

"Hiro's dad was a mathematician. In Japanese math the circle is also hugely important. The Takoyakis' house is full of pictures of mathematical problems with circles. I looked into it a bit. There was an ancient type of math in Japan called *wasan*, all based on circles. What ancient math scholars would do is come up with math problems, like how many circles fit inside a square. Then they'd draw the problem on a board, post the picture outside their houses, and challenge other mathematicians to solve them."

"Other mathematicians who just happened to be strolling by?" Isabella raised an eyebrow.

"Yup. Very educated townsfolk back then."

"Did you happen to solve any, genius?" Jones called from the door.

"Actually, yes. I solved five of the pictures in Hiro's house, because I'm a genius." Larry sighed proudly and picked up his coffee.

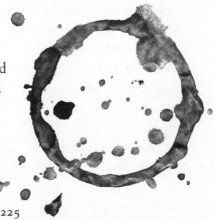

"You're a doofus!" Neil said, standing up suddenly and pointing. "You put your mug down on the scroll! It left a stain on the woodcut."

Larry, Neil, and Isabella looked. The mug had left a perfect circle impression right around one of the rice bowls. The fish on the page seemed to be swimming counterclockwise against a current of black coffee. Neil stared, cocking his head. "Hiro's dad was on the right track!"

All the words he'd been thinking merged together in Neil's brain—dancing, swimming, *ensō*, secret code. He sprinted to the copies on the wall. "It's a circle! The fish are all in different locations around the rice bowl, but it's because they're swimming in a circle around the rice bowls." He grabbed all the pages and stacked them one on top of the other, then he ran to the window and slammed them against the glass. "I knew it! Larry, bring me some tape."

Larry ran over and Neil taped one of the pictures onto the window. "Now look what happens when I match up the rice bowls, one on top of the other, and put the fish in order, counterclockwise." Neil laid them one after the other until they were stacked and taped together, each page fanning out in a different angle from the fishbowl center.

"Um, nothing happens," Larry said, looking at the resulting collage. As far as he could see, it was just all the pictures jumbled together. "Try putting the order clockwise maybe?"

Neil wasn't deterred. "No, this is it. I know it. Okay, so then maybe we have to start with a different fish on the bottom." Neil carefully tore the tape off and started putting them back together again.

Finally, on the third try, Larry's eyes grew wide. "Stop, Neil . . . wait, just turn that second one a little more to the right. Okay . . . now the top one a little bit to the left. Wow!"

They stepped back and stared. There were a number of lines in each drawing that now met, forming . . . something.

Neil squinted. "The lines in the artwork meet too neatly for it to be a mistake: what is it?"

"It's got to be a map," Larry said.

"Maybe the lines are a series of roads?"

"Or rivers?"

"It could be almost anywhere."

Neil grabbed a marker and darkened the lines. "It looks like a coastline, maybe, or a bay or something?"

Jones gave an annoyed rumble and walked over to the wall. Without taking his eyes off the trio he pulled his phone out of his pocket and held it up to the picture, clicked, and took a photo. Then he typed something into his phone and there was a *ping*.

"It's Tokyo Bay and some of the ocean. The dots down the last samurai's leg armor are islands." He held the phone up for them to look at. There were the lines from Neil's collage with a photo of Tokyo Bay superimposed.

"Hey, is that a facial recognition app, but for maps?" Larry said, amazed.

"Yeah," Jones said. "It coordinates maps with satellite images and then tells you what you're looking at. Very helpful for airplane surveillance. Also keeps me from having to listen to you spend the next five hours wondering what you were looking at." He slipped the phone back in his pocket and walked back to the door.

Now they could see the map clearly. The folds of the oldest samurai's left leg formed the eastern side of the bay. A tree limb formed the west side. And Jones was right, the dots on the samurai's leg were the islands that sat south of the bay.

"Now all we have to do is figure out whether the exact location is some dead guy's leg or a tree branch."

Neil's phone buzzed. Neil gave an audible gulp.

"Another message from Nori?" Larry asked.

"No, worse. It's from my school."

Chapter Twenty-Five

Home Work

Angel's voice, even from thousands of miles away, still sounded censorious, a word Neil was supposed to have studied for his English homework. "What did you expect? You haven't handed in more than three assignments since school started."

Neil sat in the back seat of the SUV, trying his best to stay calm. "I spent the first couple of weeks of term trying not to get killed by that maniac Valette. Now I'm trying to run a restaurant with a sous-chef who's a bike courier. How easy are YOU finding that, by the way?" Neil yelled. "And, oh yeah, I'm also looking for treasure in JAPAN! I don't have time to figure out what four times, I don't know, ten negative squared equals."

"It's zero point four," Larry said from the front seat.

"The school is not the problem," Angel said. "It's your parents.

They say they will close the restaurant if you don't get your grades back up . . . above zero. Maybe you can try to work that math out."

"Their names aren't even on the lease. Larry's is!"

"I'm dead, genius," Larry said.

Neil responded by banging his phone on his forehead. "Angel, you've got to stall them for me."

"You didn't even tell them you were leaving the country. They weren't too happy when I let that bombshell drop. You told me you'd tell them."

"I left them a note on the kitchen counter! Under the browned butter."

"Have your parents ever willingly eaten browned butter?"

"I left them a note! It's not my fault if they're too nutritionally backward to notice it," Neil sulked. "Anyway, just tell them that I AM doing my homework because I'm on a field trip with my cooking class."

"Neil. It's too late for that. The school has sent copies of all your homework to the restaurant and to your parents. It's quite a stack, actually. Your parents say you have one week to get it all done or they are going to call the bank and cancel your account."

"You could do the homework for me!" Neil said hopefully.

Angel just let out a long low grumble.

"FINE!" Neil said, frustrated. "I'll just go out and cook amazing food, save my stupid cousin, my girlfriend—"

"Girlfriend?" Isabella, Nakamura, and Larry said together.

Jones growled.

"Save me from what, exactly?" Isabella said.

"Save my friend Isabella, who's a girl," Neil said, rubbing his temples, "from eating bad food, I don't know. Now I'm also trying to find some treasure and now I have to somehow find time to research canoe making in the seventeenth century. GREAT!"

"I'm glad to hear it," Angel said calmly. "I'll let your parents know. And as for working with a bike courier, he's a lot easier on my ears than a certain teenage chef I know." Angel hung up.

Neil leaned over and put his head in his hands and let out a long, low whine. "I'm doomed," he said.

Isabella, who spent her summer working to get *ahead* on her schoolwork, showed no sympathy but turned the pages of the book she was reading for her history class. "Maybe you should try reading something other than cookbooks," she suggested.

"Yeah, listen to your *girlfriend*," Larry joked.

"I don't like anything other than cookbooks. And I'm a chef. I don't need to study anything else."

"Seriously? Maybe memory is your problem," Larry scoffed. "Hmm, let me think. Has history helped you cook any better or solve any food crimes lately?" Nakamura, who was busily eating a pork stir-fry, gave a thumbs-up. Jones tried to ignore them all and kept driving.

"I see no possible way that wood glues used by coureurs de bois are going to help me make better salmon croquettes," Neil said, staring out the window.

"You don't know it's important until it IS important. The more you know, the better prepared you are for whatever shows up," Larry said.

"You sound like Angel," Neil huffed.

"I'll take that as a compliment," Larry beamed. "If it's any consolation, I'll help you study for French and history. Isabella will help with your science. Hey! Jones can help you out in gym class."

"Leave me out of it," Jones said. "I don't take on charity cases. And anyway, we're here."

"Here" was a boat rental agency on the south end of Tokyo Bay. Larry was a little nervous about getting back on the water, but the map seemed to suggest the bay was the place to look for the treasure, so they were here posing as tourists who wanted to experience a day of sightseeing through the islands.

Larry didn't want to involve Aki anymore, "I've already put her at too much risk," he explained. So they were renting a boat.

"It's probably safer than staying at the hotel. At least we can do some searching while we look at the map for more clues," Nakamura had suggested.

Nakamura handled the negotiations while Isabella and Larry stayed in the van. Larry kept himself tucked under the dashboard. After some haggling, Nakamura secured them a boat. He'd had to pay extra for insurance, as it turned out . . . all on Neil's credit card. Neil had handed it over with so much moodiness he'd almost scuttled the deal.

"Why am I paying for everything? I'm a kid!" Neil sulked.

"Too late to try that excuse," Nakamura said. "This trip was your idea."

As he and Nakamura walked in to sign the contract, Jones signaled Isabella and she helped Larry sneak out of the van and onto the dock where he crouched behind a giant coil of rope.

"It's that boat over there," Nakamura said, pointing to a ship with the word *Izumi* in peeling paint on the back. Jones stopped at the rope just long enough for Larry to jump in front of him.

Larry read the name. "*Izumi*? Doesn't that mean 'fountain'?"

Nakamura nodded.

Larry stepped carefully aboard, grumbling. "Doesn't seem like the best name for a boat. Suggests leakiness."

"It looks a little sea-battered, but it's fine," Jones said.

"Fine, but if we sink, I'm using you as a life raft."

Neil kept sniffing the air, expecting to pick up the telltale aroma of cherry blossom, but he didn't smell anything except gasoline, fish, and sea.

Jones fired up the engine and they eased their way out into open water. As soon as they were out of eyeshot from the shore, Larry pulled out the secret map. "Maybe we should hit the islands. It would seem to make sense to hide your family wealth on an island—sort of like a pirate. And they were exiled on an island for a while."

"But there are about seven islands on the map. Are we supposed to check out each one?" Isabella wondered.

Larry shrugged. "Well, the islands make up a huge part of the map, so there must be a reason for that."

Isabella stared at the rice bowls and fish. "Why such specific types of food from such specific places?"

Neil looked as well. "Places that aren't even ON the

233

map. They don't seem to offer much help, but it's too specific to be an accident."

"I wish we had the hundred-and-fifty-year-old original," Nakamura said. "I wonder what dishes it showed? Maybe they were from someplace else. Maybe the artist changed the type to send people on an island-hopping goose chase."

Neil sat down on a bench and rubbed his temples. "There has to be another clue in the map."

"Until we figure it out, I guess we just start looking," Larry said.

Nakamura read from his guidebook. "'The islands that stretch south of Tokyo Bay are sparsely inhabited and mostly volcanic.' Seems like a good location to hide just about anything. I guess start with the farthest one, Mikurajima. It was a traditional place to send exiles from Edo. Maybe that's where the Takoyakis were sent and they took their treasure with them?"

"Even searching an island is going to take months." Larry said, nervously watching the waves. "I'm thinking this plan wasn't so great."

Jones shut off the engine. "First thing we need to do is check a better maritime map and then sync it with the GPS." He unfurled a large map on the ship's hull and pulled out his phone. He punched in a few numbers and nodded.

"The island is about fifty kilometers that way." He pointed to the southwest.

"It's funny how things have changed," Nakamura smiled. "When I went fishing as a kid, my dad used to find his way with a compass and those old dividers."

"What's a divider?" Neil asked.

"You know, they're those metal tools with two arms and one has a pencil on it. You use them in math class to measure stuff, draw circles. That is, if you ever went to math class."

Neil was up like a shot. "CIRCLES! It's still all about circles!"

"Waddya mean?" Larry said, trying to steady himself in the now rocking boat.

"The fish circled the rice bowls. That led us to the map. But maybe there are other circles hidden in the map. Maybe they're based on that wasabi math."

"*Wasan* math." Larry frowned. "You are way too food-obsessed."

"Whatever. Maybe the islands and the cities that the rice and fish come from aren't all just random. They're connected as part of a circle, or a line or . . . or *something*." For the first time in his life Neil actually regretted missing math class. He grabbed the collage and laid it down on the deck. He pulled a pen from his shirt pocket. "Let's make the two cities the centers of circles."

"Slight problem. They're not shown on the map," Larry said.

Neil stared for a moment, thinking. "Maybe the map from the scroll is just a clue itself. You need a real map to take it to the next step?" Neil grabbed Jones's maritime map. "I'll draw on this one."

"Hey! That wasn't cheap," Jones said.

"I'll pay you back. I'm spending like a crazy man on this trip anyway."

"You are crazy," Jones said.

Neil drew rough circles around Choshi and Uonuma. "If I make them the same size, then the edges of the circles meet on a city in the middle of the country called Kanuma," Neil said, pointing to the spot on Jones's map. "Maybe that's where they buried the treasure?"

Isabella shook her head. "If the treasure is on land, then why show all the islands?"

"A misdirection?" Neil suggested.

"Or maybe they are part of the solution as well. They kind of form a line . . . Not a very straight one, though," Isabella said.

"Maybe the islands are circle centers too?" Neil started drawing all sorts of different circles of different sizes on Jones's map, but couldn't figure out a way to make them meet or touch in any way that made sense.

"Nice picture. Looks like ripples in a puddle . . . during a typhoon," Larry joked.

Neil messed up his hair in frustration. "Larry, think. What kinds of mathematical problems did you see in Hiro's house?"

"Well, the *wasan* guys were all about circles and shapes like cones. They'd fit circles in cones and then try to find out how big they were."

"Why?"

"Why not? Because it was supple, beautiful? Just

because something doesn't help you cook doesn't mean it's not interesting. Oh, wait, and wouldn't now be another perfect time to lecture you on the importance of branching out."

"Fine." Neil slouched. "But let's just assume your lecture has already happened and get back to the map. Does anything look like a *wasan*-style problem to you?"

"I'll see if I can make anything out through your cute little doodles." Larry stared at the map for a few minutes. "It's funny about the islands."

"How do you mean?"

"Isabella said they aren't a straight line. But it's also strange because, in real life, the islands aren't that bunched together. They are way farther apart."

"Maybe it's like those maps of the solar system. They

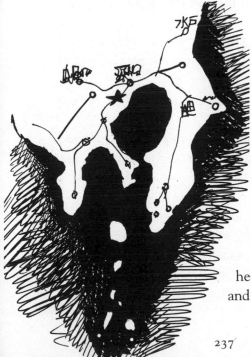

have to push things closer together than they really are so that they can fit them on a map," Isabella said.

"Maybe, but everything else in the map, including Tokyo Bay, is reproduced accurately."

"Maybe they just got the scale wrong?" Neil suggested.

Nakamura shook his head. "The Japanese were, and still are, excellent navigators. They'd have known exactly where every-thing was. So why draw the coastline perfectly and the islands out of whack? Any theories?"

Larry stared at the two maps. "Maybe Neil's right. The scroll map is just a signpost. The trick was to make people think they could find the treasure on the scroll map but you're really supposed to take the clues from this map and go to a real map. Then slot in the coordinates."

"I did that!" Neil said.

Larry looked at Jones's marked-up map. "Yeah, nice work. It looks like someone went crazy with a stencil set. I don't mean *guess* about circles. I mean that you take the coordinates that are hidden in the scroll map and then take them to a real map and then slot them in, using triangulation."

"You draw a triangle? I thought we were looking for circles."

Larry shook his head sadly. "Please, please prom-ise me you will start paying attention in geometry class when you get back."

"Please just explain what the heck you're talking about."

"Look. I'll start by drawing a line between Choshi and Uonuma. That incorporates the clues from the fish and rice. Follow?"

They all nodded.

"Then I'll draw a line from Choshi to the bottom island in the chain, then a line from that island back up to Uonuma. See, I made a triangle. In *wasan*, the key is to find the circle that then fits perfectly within this shape." Larry carefully considered the triangle and then drew a circle that touched all three lines. "And the center of this perfect *wasan* circle is smack in the middle of . . . Tokyo Bay?" Larry said. "Wait, that doesn't make any sense. It's in the middle of the water."

"They've built a lot of man-made islands in Tokyo Bay; maybe it's on one of those," Jones called from the cockpit.

"There's only one way to find out: gun the engine and turn us around!"

Jones complied, and an hour later they were back in Tokyo Bay. Jones used his GPS and the map to stop right on the coordinates that represented the center of Larry's circle. It was nothing but water.

"Well, maybe the ground has shifted. They've had a lot of earthquakes and stuff here," Neil said.

Larry did a small pirouette. "Nothing but waves. Nothing's moved *that* much." He looked down. "And nothing here but deep deep water. What'd they do, dump it all overboard? WHOA!" Larry leapt backward so fast that he fell.

"What?" Neil said.

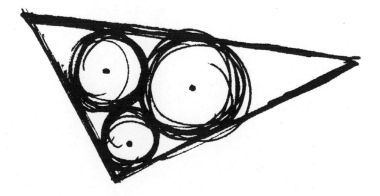

"Shark," Larry said. "A huge shark just swam under the boat. Maybe it's time we got to shore. I think he was looking at me. And if I do say so myself, I'm very tasty-looking."

"And you still smell like fish," Neil said, helping Larry to his feet. "But I think you're right. This trip was a waste of time as far as the boat is concerned. And time is something we can't afford to waste. Let's head back to shore and find another hotel and start figuring out some other options."

"We can always get another boat tomorrow," Nakamura said. "They're keeping Neil's credit card info on file."

Neil groaned. Isabella patted his back gently.

Jones steered the boat toward the dock. About halfway home Neil's phone pinged. He ignored it. He knew what it was: an e-mail from Nori with a haiku for Battle #4.

Chapter Twenty-Six

Canister Craziness

Jones and Isabella helped smuggle Larry back to the van. Nakamura went to hand in the keys. Neil stopped on the edge of the dock and checked his e-mail. He was right. The message was another clue from Nori.

> COOK AND COOK AND COOK
> YOU TRY, BUT NO VICTORY
> IT IS IN THE CAN
> (PS: DO YOU LIKE BASEBALL? I AM A BIG
> FAN.)

That's it? No details on pickup? And what does 'it is in the can' mean? I'm getting so sick of all this, Neil thought. He wondered if he should even bother figuring out the clue. After all, they were nowhere near finding the treasure, or Hiro. That meant he had to lose anyway.

Neil climbed into the SUV and sat down next to Larry.

"Why are you in the backseat this time?" Neil asked.

"Isabella called shotgun. And I think Jones actually has one under the dashboard, so I'm happier back here." He looked at Neil's e-mail.

"Bah. That one should be easy, even for a turkey brain like you."

"How so?"

"Well, 'in the can' clearly means you're going to make stuff from canned foods, so you're probably supposed to bring a lot of stuff from those weird Japanese vending machines. So all you have to do is work out a menu, buy the stuff, and get ready to cook. And BIG and baseball can only mean one thing."

"And that would be?"

"Seriously?"

"JUST EXPLAIN IT TO ME!" Neil yelled.

"Shhh. Remember Jones's shotgun, and he has very sensitive ears."

Neil rubbed his temples. "*Please* explain it to me," he whispered.

"The Giants. Tokyo's baseball team. They play downtown at the Tokyo Dome. Can't miss it, looks like a big egg."

"Hard- or soft-boiled?" Neil said.

"Ha, ha. See, you're feeling less stressed out already." Larry smiled.

"So now I know where, how about when?"

Larry grabbed Neil's phone and typed in "Tokyo Giants Home Schedule." "One o'clock tomorrow. They have a home game. Nori's probably got a private box."

"If he makes me cook hot dogs, I'll cry," Neil said.

"Neil Flambé making hot dogs. That I'd love to see." Nakamura laughed, jumping in next to Neil.

"It is NEVER going to happen." Neil slammed his fists into the seat.

"Hot dogs!" Nori said with a flourish, lifting the lid off a platinum- and diamond-encrusted serving platter.

Neil slammed his fist into the kitchen counter.

"And the canned foods you have brought must complement the taste."

"So what's the deadly health risk today?" Neil called out. "Besides the hot dogs, I mean."

Nori smiled. "I'm not going to tell you. You'll have to figure it out all by yourself . . . or not. Now you have an hour to wow the crowd with a baseball-themed dinner!"

Today's battle wasn't, oddly, on Nori's yacht. Instead he'd booked an entire section of the baseball stadium and crammed it with his cronies. They started by watching the game, with the Giants winning 3–2. It was an amazing scene, with fans banging loud drums and the entire crowd cheering and chanting from start to finish. They even released a thousand balloons into the air in the middle of an inning. Neil actually found himself enjoying the experience. Then the game ended and Nori's cronies wheeled two complete kitchens onto the field.

"I had a bit of an incident on my yacht," Nori explained vaguely. "I felt more secure here. My security staff is on-site making sure that no one gets in or out." Neil wondered if the incident was a Koko-led reconnaissance mission to the yacht. Neil also wondered if Nori had brought the sharks along in a portable swimming pool, but thought it better not to ask.

Neil examined his gleaming stack of canned goods. He'd bought the strangest collection of tuna, shrimp, even canned Kobe beef tenderloin. He had his menu all planned out. The problem was, it was going to be wonderful . . . and he needed to lose. Nori called Neil and Kong over to the edge of the outfield fence to bow to the crowd. *That's a new twist. Maybe it's some baseball tradition*, Neil thought.

The judges were seated in the front row and yet another new judge had joined the panel. This time it was a very thin man with a very pale complexion. Neil couldn't quite figure out what his risky behavior could possibly be. Breathing looked like a challenge. *Maybe he avoids sunlight*, Neil thought.

They bowed to each other and the crowd began chanting and stomping their feet. Neil looked up and noticed that he and Kong were on the giant TV screen. Animated characters were dancing around their faces. The ones dancing around his head resembled small furry cattle, or maybe demented chipmunks. They appeared to be goring him with their horns. It was unsettling.

Kong's characters looked more like smiling overripe grapefruits. They seemed to be smiling and singing a song. That was more unsettling.

Nori waved his arm back in the direction of the kitchens. "Now the clock starts. Please turn around." Neil turned and noticed with a start that all the cans had been moved and stacked into a pile, their labels ripped off.

"Hahahaha! Now you see the danger. You thought I'd let you just walk in and plan your own menu? Now you will choose ten cans each, and cook with every ingredient. Just imagine the possible combinations!"

"That's not dangerous, just annoying," Neil said.

"Except that three of the cans contain food that has been contaminated with *bacillus cereus*—a very hard bacterium to kill off. It causes immediate sickness and very often death. It's also very dangerous to handle so you'd better be careful as well. Only dishes that are cooked perfectly will be safe."

Neil counted. There were twenty-three cans in all. He didn't need to do his math homework to figure out the odds were pretty good that he'd have at least one tainted can in his dishes. Neil was always conscious about food. He could always smell when something had gone bad, but a bacterium that had been injected into the food? He couldn't be sure.

Kong seemed as impassive as ever. Neil noticed he was wearing latex gloves. *Good idea, big guy. Nice of Nori to tip you off yet again*, Neil thought.

"GO!" Nori yelled. Neil and Kong rushed to the pile of cans, grabbing ten each. They returned to their counters and began opening them. Neil was happy to see that he had chosen the beef and the shrimp. But there were two cans of water chestnuts and one of sardines. Had Kong added those to the pile, or were they the tainted ones that Nori had thrown in? They all smelled fresh. Neil exhaled a big breath. *And the cans are mostly water so I can at least drain off the liquid, in case it's infected*, he thought.

"You must also use the liquid," Nori called. He'd acquired a microphone and his voice boomed around the stadium.

So much for that plan. Neil decided his best bet was to make a kind of soup or noodle stew. At least that way he could cut the liquid with plenty of water and he could also boil it at a high temperature. He set the beef aside, planning to thinly slice it into an appetizer with rice crackers.

Then he remembered the hot dogs.

He could just serve them in buns with some ketchup and relish. No. He needed to lose but he didn't need to look like he was throwing the competition. That might get Nori asking questions. And he had his pride. So, how to cook the hot dogs and still maintain some level of self-respect?

Neil had visited the concession bar during the game. Yes, they'd had hotdogs, but hardly anyone was ordering them. More people favored the deep-fried octopus and the fried balls of mashed potatoes. Fried, Neil decided. He'd slice the hot dogs into small bits, dip them in a panko bread crumb batter, add some spices, deep-fry them, and then serve them next to the soup.

As Neil prepped his food, he saw Kong smashing his hot dogs with his huge palms. Was he frustrated, angry? Neil watched as Kong took the smashed hot dog meat and then grilled it with a sweet and sour glaze. He was making a kind of Asian-inspired steak. *Wow*, Neil thought, *this Kong guy is getting better. That's the problem with throwing two matches. Your challenger starts to get more confident and, therefore, dangerous.*

And thanks to Neil, there would be a winner-take-all final—and Kong was going to be a real competitor for it. Neil started cutting his hot dogs.

In yet another bizarre twist to the duel, the count-down for the duel wasn't shown on a clock but was represented by two mascots who raced around the base paths in slow motion. An incredibly grating electrobeat song played over the speakers. Neil watched them reach first, mesmerized, before realizing that meant they'd already been running fifteen minutes.

Neil hurried to catch up, throwing his ingredients into a pressure cooker to raise the heat even higher, hopefully killing any bacteria.

The mascots rounded third base and slid into home just as Neil finished ladling his soup into his bowls and Kong splashed wasabi-infused mustard foam on his hot dog steaks.

"SAFE!" Nori yelled, leaning over the mascots like an umpire.

"Let's hope so," Neil said under his breath.

The waiters came over and gathered the dishes. Neil knew he'd cooked his dishes long enough and hot enough to kill any *normal* bacteria, but he suspected Nori's laboratory friends had come up with a particularly tough one. He hoped everything had at least been diluted enough to maybe cause an upset stomach, but nothing worse.

Neil's dishes were served first. "Your mascot lost the race," Nori said with a shrug.

"One of those mascots was mine?" Neil said, exasperated. "That was a race?"

Neil watched in disbelief as a servant for the new judge pulled out a blender and proceeded to plop Neil's noodle soup into the container. He hit a button and

within seconds the carefully
crafted meal was reduced to
a puree.

Then the servant placed
a straw into the blender and
the judge began sipping. The
effort seemed to tax him and
he only swallowed a small
amount before leaning back
in his chair, exhausted.

The others greedily
ate up the beef, dipping it
in a hoisin sauce Neil had
prepared on the side. They
practically slurped up the
soup. Neil watched as they
finished off the deep-fried hot dogs, although the new
judge pureed that as well. Neil noted happily that no
one seemed to be feeling sick.

Kong's dishes were next, and Neil could see that the
judges preferred his take on the baseball classics much
more than Neil's. Even the emaciated judge in seat
five took not one but three sips. They confirmed Neil's
impressions a few seconds later with a unanimous win
for Kong.

Unanimous! Neil thought with a jolt. *I lost and it
was unanimous?* He looked over at Kong, who seemed to
have the tiniest hint of a smile on his lips. *Unanimous?*
Neil shook his head sadly. *Unanimous?*

Nori's voice seemed to strain the limits of the loudspeakers. "SO! We are now tied! But Kong is champion

for today!" The crowd went wild. "We meet again in two days! We have had Russian *Roux*-lette . . . now prepare for battle RUSSIAN OMELETTE!"

Neil was too deflated to wonder or even care what that meant.

Chapter Twenty-Seven

Flotsam and Then Some

The cab ride from the Tokyo Dome back to the docks seemed like the longest drive of Neil's life. Nakamura had texted him after the duel to say that Jones was taking "the ingredient" for another shopping trip for "bay leaves." Neil felt low and confused. He knew he hadn't brought his best to the baseball duel, but a unanimous loss? Was he squandering his talent, putting it at risk? Cooking excellent food was a habit, a kind of repetitive excellence. He had now cooked below his abilities twice. Kong was getting better. Could Neil kick-start himself back to his own high standards in time?

He wanted to be home, in his own kitchen, practicing dishes, practicing techniques, keeping his nose and taste buds limber. Instead, he was going to meet Isabella and Nakamura at the docks for another wild-squid chase on the water.

Neil could tell right away that something was wrong. Nakamura and Isabella were nervously pacing up and down the dock. Neil threw some money at the cabdriver and ran over. "What is it?"

"We lost radio contact with them about ten minutes ago," Isabella said.

Nakamura started walking toward the docks. "I've hired another boat to take us out to the last coordinates we have. C'mon."

Just as they stepped onto the deck of the boat, Neil smelled cherry blossoms. He looked around but didn't see any sign of Koko. He kept looking as they pulled away, and the aroma seemed to linger. It was quite breezy, though, so Neil couldn't be sure. Had Koko been on the boat before them? That was not a cheerful thought. As they pulled farther and farther into the bay, Neil did a quick search of the boat. No holes or ticking bombs that he could see. The pilot was an old man. Neil decided not to worry Nakamura or Isabella.

"We're getting close," Nakamura said. All three of them gathered up against the railing and began searching the horizon for any sign of Larry's boat.

"I don't see anything but ships and fishing trawlers," Isabella said. "And the waves from the boats are so high out here it's very hard to see anything but glimpses in between."

"I don't see anything either. Maybe they pulled up on shore somewh—" Neil was interrupted by a loud *thunk* as their boat hit something. The impact jostled Neil and he fell over the railing and into the water. He splashed to keep his head above the waves, the salt water stinging his nose. Nakamura called out and the pilot stopped the boat.

"Neil!" Isabella yelled, reaching a hand out to him. Neil caught it, and Isabella and Nakamura pulled him back inside.

"What was that, Larry's shark?" Nakamura asked.

Neil shook his head and coughed out the seawater from his lungs. "No," he croaked. "Larry's boat." He opened his hand and held out a cell phone.

"That's Jones's phone," Isabella gasped.

Neil nodded. "It was floating on top of the waves. I guess his cover is designed to protect it in case he drops it in water."

"That's not what we hit, though," Nakamura said, looking back over the edge. "We hit a big chunk of the hull." He pointed to a large section of wood that was bobbing up and down in the waves. Surrounding it were floating bits of wood, cloth, and shirts and jeans.

"They're not dead," Neil said, pointing to the ratty-looking jeans.

"How do you know?" Isabella said, tears welling up in her eyes.

"I don't. But part of the debris is made up of their clothes. Jones and Larry probably weren't hanging out on the boat naked, which means they took off their clothes after the boat sank."

"Why?" Isabella asked.

"So they could swim," Neil said. He sheltered his eyes and scanned the horizon. "But where did they go?"

Nakamura pointed to a trail of more clothing that seemed to be heading back toward shore. "That way, I'll bet," he said.

"*Andiamo!* Let's hurry and start looking!" Isabella yelled.

Nakamura called out to the captain and the boat took off, cutting through the waves and following the debris path.

"It was a good thing we pulled you back in when we did," Isabella said. "I'm sure I saw that shark swimming around down there."

I hope it didn't show up until after Larry and Jones got away, Neil thought, but he kept it to himself and just said, "Thanks."

The boat soon passed the last bits of floating wood, some of it still smoking. "An explosion for sure," Nakamura said. "Let's hope Larry and Jones are close."

"How are we going to find anyone in this water?" Isabella cried.

Just then the breeze shifted. "Turn that way!" Neil yelled above the engine, grabbing Nakamura's shoulder and pointing toward their right.

Nakamura yelled and the driver made a quick turn. Neil ran to the bow of the boat and stuck his nose in the air. Every few seconds he would point in a slightly different direction, and finally he turned around and held his hands up. "Stop!" he called.

Nakamura noticed that he was smiling.

"Larry, you are a genius!" Neil called over the bow. Nakamura and Isabella ran to join Neil. Larry and Jones were floating in the water. Larry was taking sips from a giant thermos of coffee and spitting the liquid high into the air. The hot liquid hitting the cool air created little clouds of mist—coffee-scented mist.

Larry smiled. "I figured it was worth a shot, although what a waste of really good coffee. Now could you get us on board? We're freezing!"

"And your cousin hasn't shut up since we started swimming!" Jones snarled.

Both of the men were dressed in only underwear

and lifejackets. "It was way easier to swim away from the fire this way," Larry explained as Neil and Isabella wrapped him and Jones in towels and handed them some hot tea.

"I hate tea," Larry said shivering. "But in this case I'll make an exception."

Neil waited until they'd warmed up, then started asking questions. "Was it another explosion? I'm sure I smelled Koko on the dock and I suspect that tackle box she gave her brother was what sank your boat last time. I think it had a bomb hidden inside."

Larry sipped his tea and shook his head. "It might have been, but this time there was no warning, ticking, nothing like that. Something hit us from *outside*. At first I thought it was a big fish or a log. But then another one hit us and we started burning and sinking fast."

"Armor-piercing torpedoes," Jones said, staring straight ahead.

"Torpedoes?" Nakamura said, incredulous. "You're kidding me."

Jones shook his head slowly. "If not torpedoes, then something pretty close. They hit the hull and we started sinking."

Larry smiled. "Yeah, but they didn't sink *us*. I'll tell you one other thing; this makes me absolutely sure that the treasure isn't on an island or anywhere in Tokyo."

"What do you mean?" Neil said.

Larry sipped his tea and looked up, grinning. "Our map coordinates are perfect. The treasure *is* under-water. We were right over the coordinates when we got attacked."

"Great. So then we've got a zero percent chance of getting to it first," Nakamura said. "Unless you know how to swim down a thousand feet."

"Well, maybe not *zero* percent," Neil said. Everyone turned to look at him. "I have an idea."

Chapter Twenty-Eight

From Zero to One Hundred

Neil's phone gave a loud *ping* as they reached the dock. He knew it was going to be the latest and last clue from Nori. He had no intention of opening the e-mail right away. He was already too rattled.

"I'll return the boat keys, and I'll explain about the missing boat," Nakamura said. Jones tied up the ropes and got the boat moored safely. Neil could hear Nakamura and the manager of the boat rental company getting into a heated discussion.

Neil sniffed the air. He didn't smell cherry blossoms anymore, but he did sense the whopping bill that was about to be placed on his credit card. Neil's head started to pound as he thought about the mounting bills and the stress of his last battle. What if he lost? Would Nori slap a chain on his leg and force him to hunt rhinos on the ship?

Neil sighed. He'd better suck it up and read the clue and try to prepare. Neil joined Larry and Isabella in the SUV and opened his e-mail.

> BOY FEELING RATTLED
> RUSSIAN OMELETS BOO HISSSS LOSE
> SHELLS SHOCK CRACKS APPEAR
> (PS: YOU KNOW WHERE THE ANIMALS ARE AND
> THEY WILL HAVE THEIR REVENGE. 11 A.M.)

"Yikes, that's some horrible poetry," Larry said.

"No kidding," Neil said, closing the e-mail and ignoring Larry's dig. "I have a feeling eggs are involved."

"Gee, with omelets? Do you think?" Larry said sarcastically.

Neil ignored him again. "Although I don't see anything that would suggest chickens or ducks or geese. Maybe he means caviar? That's fish eggs."

"Oh, my goodness," Isabella said, sitting bolt upright. "He means snake eggs!"

"Snake eggs?" Neil said.

"That's what *hissss* means."

Larry made a gagging noise. "Seriously? UGH! That's gross."

Neil ran his hands through his hair and moaned. "Snake eggs. Ohhh, can we go home now, please?"

Nakamura and Jones came back to the SUV. "Hey, what's eating the Nose?" Nakamura said as he climbed inside and spied Neil rocking back and forth with his head in his hands.

"Interesting choice of words." Larry laughed. Isabella explained the haiku.

"Good luck with that one," Nakamura said with a chuckle. "I do have some good news for you. The bill is only half of what I predicted."

Neil gave a muffled "Hooray."

Jones started to back up the car. Nakamura turned around to look out the back window. "What's dangerous about snake eggs? Are they poisonous?"

"I bet collecting them is!" Larry said.

Instantly, Neil knew that Larry had hit upon the challenge. That was the final trial. Not cooking snake eggs, although he'd have to be ready for that, but collecting eggs that were being protected by snakes. Neil was going to have to grab the eggs himself. If he refused, he would lose. If he didn't, he'd risk getting bit himself . . . and ending up dead.

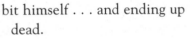

"So Nori wants me to get bitten by a poisonous snake!"

"Actually snakes are venomous, not poisonous," Larry said.

"What?"

"They're venomous. They inject venom," Larry said.

"Let me guess, you learned that in biology class?" Neil said.

Larry nodded. "Yes. *Your*

biology class. It's on page five of your homework. I peeked."

"Does page six tell me where the pickup point is?"

Nakamura jumped in. "I think I've got that figured out. 'You know' is a clue. He's referring to the Ueno Zoo. That's where they are going to pick you up tomorrow."

"Or maybe that's where the battle will take place," Isabella suggested.

"So then what's the bit about animals having their revenge? Are they going to make me battle a gorilla?" Neil thought of Kong. "Wait, I already am." Neil did not look happy.

"The Ueno Zoo is the oldest in Japan," Nakamura said. "I used to go there as a kid, with my dad. He told me wonderful and horrible stories about the animals."

"Horrible?" Isabella said.

"Just before the end of World War Two the authorities worried that the animals were going to escape. The bombs were wrecking the cages. So they poisoned all the animals rather than risk having them roam the streets. Dozens of rare and beautiful animals died. The elephants could sense the food was poisoned. They didn't eat. They died of starvation."

Everyone was quiet.

"Well, that's a cheerful bedtime story," Larry said finally. Isabella nodded.

"So what kind of 'revenge' does Nori have in mind?" Neil grimaced.

"The animals were poisoned by humans. Maybe the 'revenge' is that the humans are going to get poisoned? Seems pretty consistent with the other battles," Nakamura said.

"Well, if anyone has any experience fighting venomous snakes, I could use some advice," Neil said.

Everyone looked at Jones.

"Wear gloves," he said.

The pickup point *was* the Ueno Zoo. Neil lingered by the gate for ten minutes before a large white van drove out of the zoo and screeched to a halt next to him. The door swung open and the driver motioned vigorously for Neil to hurry up and jump in the cab. Neil heard a growling from the back of the van. He had a sneaking suspicion the cargo was some poached rare animal for Nori's floating zoo. He nervously got in, hoping the animal wasn't also on the menu.

They sped to the dock, boarded a barge, and a short trip later, they were at the yacht. Neil was relieved to be back on the familiar territory; it would make his plan easier. The crane lifted them onto the deck and then the driver practically shoved Neil out of the cab door. The van sank down into the floor and disappeared.

Neil looked around at the ship, which seemed exactly the same. If Koko had attacked, there appeared to be no visible damage. Of course, it was a big ship. The deck rose again, vanless, and Neil stepped on. The deck slipped back down into the bowels of the ship. Neil could hear the lusty cheering of the crowd, even through the glass walls of the elevator shaft.

Neil took a deep breath and slipped a glove over his right hand. It wasn't just any glove; it was one of the gloves Jones wore when he went diving in piranha-infested waters, or so he said. It resembled the chain-mail glove one might see as part of a suit of armor in a museum—but lighter and with no holes between the links for any fangs to find their way to inject poison—or venom—into a person's circulatory system.

He reached the kitchen. Neil saw Nori parading around a series of glass boxes, periodically smacking the sides with a stick. The resounding *thwack* did nothing to settle down the dangerous and angry-looking snakes that lay inside, coiled and ready to strike. Neil was pretty sure that was the point. Cobras spat venom at the glass, and rattlesnakes bared their fangs.

"Today, battle venom!" Nori yelled, repeatedly smacking a glass case with a red and black snake inside. The snake looked extremely ticked off. "This is our final battle! Winner take all!"

Kong stood perfectly still. He wasn't wearing gloves. Hadn't Nori tipped him off this time? It didn't matter. Neil needed to forget the competition and worry about himself. Today he would make a true Neil Flambé meal. Everything depended on it. Neil actually felt a thrill as he thought of the challenge. He could feel the energy pulsing in his hands, and in his nose. He might lose, but . . . actually, there was no way he was going to lose.

"Today's challenge is to make the perfect omelet. Simple. We have five judges and each has asked for three eggs. How many eggs will each chef need, Chef Flambé?" Nori pointed at Neil.

"Fifteen," Neil said. Honestly, was there anyone in the world who didn't want to nag him about his homework? Neil noticed with some surprise that the emaciated judge was still alive and still seated in the fifth chair.

Nori smiled. "Yes, fifteen. You will only have five minutes to collect those eggs. These 'gentle' little reptiles are guarding them." There was an *ooooh* from the crowd. "You may choose only fifteen, and you must cook them all. But be warned . . ." He paused for effect. "Some are chicken eggs, some are actual snake eggs.

Not all are safe to eat. Can you tell the difference?"

Neil smiled. "Thank you, Jones," he whispered under his breath, quickly running through the litany of information Jones had taught him.

"Of course, if a chef gets bitten by one of these poisonous snakes, then perhaps the battle will be over before it begins. Neil Flambé, you are first! The clock starts now." He smacked the sides of the boxes one more time and then moved away.

Neil approached the snakes slowly and carefully. Jones had told him to lull the snakes into a sense of safety. Sudden movement would make the snakes move. *And they are a heck of a lot faster than you*, Jones had warned him.

There were two holes cut into each box with one-way doors. His hands could get in, but the snake couldn't get out . . . unless it bit him and then hung on as he yanked his hand back through. The first snake was some kind of small viper with a diamond-patterned skin. As Neil approached, it coiled itself and began to make a loud noise. Neil could see three eggs inside, all of them oval. "Chicken eggs," Neil said. *Snake eggs are longer and thinner*, Jones's voice came back to him again.

Neil took his armored right hand and gently slid it through a hole. The snake's hissing noise grew louder. "C'mon, closer, closer . . ." The snake struck at his gloved hand. Neil could feel the incredible pressure of the viper's jaws as it attempted to drive its fangs into Neil's hand, but the glove worked. As the snake recoiled Neil was able to reach out and take a firm grip of its neck, or at least what he assumed was its neck.

As quickly as he could, Neil shot his left hand through the other hole and grabbed the eggs. This was harder to do than he'd imagined and he was only able to grab two. He could feel the snake wriggling free. He yanked his left hand out and let go of the snake. It struck at his gloved hand again and again as he yanked it out.

"Ten minutes left!" Nori called.

Surprised, Neil checked his watch. Nori was right. Five minutes gone and Neil had two eggs! He moved onto the next cage. A giant python was inside. *Not a biter*, Jones had said. *But don't let it coil itself around you or you're a goner.* Neil couldn't see any eggs from the outside.

Neil stuck his right hand in and lifted the snake. It was slimy and heavy. Five large and long eggs were nestled together in the straw. *Python eggs!* Neil thought. He put his left hand in and gently felt the eggs. Snake eggs all have soft shells but two of the eggs were firm underneath. *Try to cook snake eggs that are hard and you'll have a live venomous snake baby on your hands, literally,* Jones had said. The other three were squishy. "Squishy means sterile, which means edible and actually pretty delicious." Neil grabbed them and got his hands out, just as the python began to tighten its grip on Neil's wrist.

"Whoa! That was close," Nori announced to the crowd. He was enjoying this way more than Neil. Neil repeated the process in four more cages, cornering a king cobra, rattling a rattlesnake, and ticking off two black mambas for good measure. But he had his fifteen eggs and no bites.

"Congratulations," Nori spat. He seemed disappointed. "Now Kong will choose his ingredients."

Neil watched as Kong strode toward the snakes. Without hesitating, he stuck his bare right hand into the first snake cage. But Neil saw he was holding something, a tiny spray bottle. Kong pushed the top and a fine mist hit the snake in the face.

Neil caught the scent. Cinnamon and cloves? He was confused. The viper recoiled as Kong sprayed the mist into its face. Then Kong reached in with his left hand and grabbed the egg Neil had left behind.

"A food-based snake repellent," Nori said to the crowd. "Only a clever chef could think of that!" He looked at Neil and winked.

Kong had twelve eggs by the time he approached the second black mamba. But Neil was certain he'd seen only two eggs left in that cage, and neither was any good. Kong stuck his hand in and apparently came to the same conclusion quickly. He yanked his hand out and went back to the python and rattlesnakes, finally getting his last three eggs just as his time ran out.

"Egg hunting is over! Now you have ten minutes left to make your dishes!" Nori hollered into the microphone.

From that moment on, it wasn't much

of a competition. Neil was an omelet expert. He cut the soft-sided python eggs with a knife, letting the soft interior spill into a large bowl. Neil knew the snake eggs would get too tough if he cooked them on their own, so he set them aside. He took his chicken eggs and separated the whites from the yolks. He whipped the whites before adding the yolks and snake eggs back in, folding them together gently.

Then he quickly set up his five plates, chopped some fresh herbs, and leaned back and waited. The best omelets were cooked right before being served, and there were still five minutes left on the clock.

Kong, on the other hand, had made the fatal mistake of starting his eggs too early. Nori became increasingly agitated as Kong struggled to keep his omelets from getting too tough and too dry. It didn't help matters that Kong had chosen more of the tougher snake eggs than Neil.

Three minutes left. Neil fired his burners on high and threw some butter in his pans. Once the butter began to foam he used a ladle to put equal amounts of his egg mixture in each. The eggs sizzled and bubbled, filling with the air pockets that Neil knew would make his omelets fluffily perfect.

With expert precision he quickly agitated each pan. He waited for exactly the right moment before adding a sprinkle of salt, pepper, and fine chopped herbs to each. Within seconds each omelet was on its own plate, awaiting the praise of the judges.

The omelets were cooked so perfectly the old man didn't even need to resort to his blender and straw. The other judges hummed contentedly as the eggs melted in their mouths.

Then it was Kong's turn. The judges practically broke their knives trying to saw through the tough skin on Kong's omelets. The old judge didn't even attempt to eat it, merely asking his servant to hold it to his mouth so he could smell and lick it.

It was looking like a clear victory for Neil.

Nori must have had the same impression because he ran over and began smacking Kong repeatedly with a whisk. "You will pay for this. Remember what I told you."

Kong didn't say a word but fell to the floor in a heap. Nori stood over him and yelled. "Yes. Die now. That will save me the trouble!" Nori walked away in disgust.

Neil sensed something was wrong. Nori hadn't hit Kong that hard with the whisk. Why had he collapsed? Neil ran over to the chef's side.

"What's wrong?" Neil said.

Kong held up his hand and nodded with his head for Neil to shake. It was a tender gesture that Neil hadn't expected. Neil took Kong's hand, shook it, and then noticed the bite marks from the black mamba, turning Kong's flesh purple.

"Congratulations," Kong said.

"You speak English?" Neil said, flabbergasted.

"You win. I die," Kong said. "I saw you threw the other battles. I do not know why, but I knew you would not let Kong win today. I will not give Nori the satisfaction of killing me. I have taken another way out."

"No, no, NO!" Neil yelled. He ran over to his

workstation and grabbed a towel. Rushing back he twisted it around Kong's arm until he winced in pain. Jones had also given him some first aid tips, in case he messed up with the snakes. "Now sit up. Keep this stupid wound under the level of your heart. That will keep your heart from pumping the poison, venom, whatever, through your body. C'mon, sit up!"

"Who cares about this pathetic man; he will soon be food for sharks!" Nori said. The crowd stamped their feet.

The lava woman stood up. "This man is lucky to die. His loss is his shame but his death is his reward for living a glorious life of risk! Now, let us announce the scores and make it official. There is an eruption predicted for Mount Etna tomorrow and I would like to be there early. The best lava always spews out first."

"NO!" Neil said. He needed to set his plan in action. "Before the judges announce their scores, I would like to ask for a slight change."

"Change to what?" Nori said. "The battle is over."

"A change to the grand prize," Neil said.

Nori glowered at him. This was not going to be a slam dunk. Neil would have to appeal to Nori's main personality feature—greed. Well, greed was probably in a close tie with cruelty, but Neil was banking that greed would win out this time.

Neil stood up. "I am about to be declared the winner— and you are going to owe me a *large amount* of money. I'm willing to sacrifice that for two prizes."

"What?" Nori snapped. "TWO! You're lucky I don't send you over the side to join Kong with the sharks." Nori took a step toward Neil.

"WAIT! Hear me out! You'll save the money!"

Nori stopped. "I'm listening."

"The prizes are these. One, you will NOT feed Kong to any sharks, and you will get that nasty bite on his arm looked at ASAP."

Nori didn't react. "And two?"

"I want to ride on a submarine. I want to look for my cousin's body," Neil said.

"My submarine hasn't been in the water for months." Nori stroked his chin, then shook his head. "No. I don't care about money that much. You get the money; the sharks get Kong." He started walking back toward the judges. "Now let's see the scores."

Okay, strike one, Neil thought with a bit of panic. Time to appeal to his cruelty. "I'll lose my restaurant if you agree."

Nori stopped and slowly looked back over his shoulder. "What do you mean?"

"If I don't take the prize money I'm going to lose Chez Flambé. Look, I don't want this man to die." Neil pointed at Kong.

Nori smiled. "You are stupid enough to sacrifice that for this useless dying man?"

Neil nodded. "Kong will live. I will see the ocean floor, but I will have nothing left in my life except pain and loss."

Even the judges smiled at this thought.

Nori walked over to Neil. "It's a deal. BUT, if the judges don't choose you, then you get to see the ocean floor, without a submarine, if you get my meaning."

Neil felt a shiver but nodded. "Deal."

All eyes turned to the judges.

The first two flipped over their cards. Both votes were for Neil. Neil breathed a sigh of relief. The next two flipped their cards. Both votes were for . . . KONG?

"What? That's impossible!" Neil yelled.

The judge with the toupee smirked. "We enjoyed the omelet you prepared, but where was the thrill? Kong's omelets were far more dangerous."

"They were certainly a choking hazard," Neil said.

"And unlike you, Kong didn't wear gloves," the other judge added.

Nori was thrilled. "Oh, but this is too wonderful!"

he said, dancing and pointing a finger into Neil's chest.

There was only one vote left—the emaciated fifth judge. Neil's heart started pumping faster than the motor of Nori's hovercar. The crowd was absolutely silent. Neil could hear the sound of all the eyeballs turning to watch the emaciated judge.

Neil stared at him as well. The man sat perfectly still. *Is he dead?* Neil wondered. Everyone waited for the man to flip his scorecard. The silence was broken by a low, scratching noise. It was coming from the man. Neil listened. The man was laughing!

"Oh, no," Neil thought. *He's going to destroy me!* He started looking for any kind of exit and took a step backward toward the kitchen and his knives.

The man seemed to take forever to flip the card, using a bony finger to lift it up and over the top of its board. It seemed to turn and then fall in slow motion, and as it turned everyone clearly saw the name Neil Flambé.

Neil gave the loudest *whoop!* of his life. He was so relieved that he actually jumped into the air pumping his fists.

The crowd went crazy.

Nori's face fell. He stood in shocked silence.

The two judges who'd voted for Kong shook their heads in disappointment. "Why did you pick the boy?" the lava woman said.

The man chuckled, his whole body shaking with the effort. "I liked his food better. And to be cruel, to cause the most pain, it made sense for me to pick the boy." He looked straight at Nori and began laughing harder and harder, his breath getting raspier by the second.

Nori looked at him and shook his head. "Father. How could you?"

Chapter Twenty-Nine

Dive

Dive! Dive!" Neil yelled. The submarine captain threw the engines into full gear just as Neil slammed the hatch shut. Neil could hear the *ping* of metal ninja stars ricocheting off the hull. The submarine eased out of the yacht's hold and into open water.

They'd gotten inside just in time. As Neil ran to use the periscope, he replayed the last few minutes in his head. *What the heck happened?* he thought.

Nori had begrudgingly escorted Neil down to the interior boat launch. He'd called for someone to come pilot the sub.

"You have one hour," Nori said. "If you're not done by then, the captain has orders to shoot you out of the ballast holes. You can try swimming to safety from wherever you happen to be at that moment, and I hope it's at the bottom of the sea with your cousin!"

Nori had given another wave and the giant doors of the yacht's hull had begun to swing open on their enormous hinges, letting in the sea breeze.

Neil had smelled cherry blossoms, and then everything had gone crazy.

Another ship was floating just outside the yacht with a band of people in ninja outfits standing on the deck. They stormed into the hull. Neil had noticed with shock that they seemed to actually be walking on the water and jumping from ship to ship. "How can they do that?" Neil said, but his curiosity was quickly replaced by panic as a ninja star lodged into the wooden pier by his right foot.

The captain had already climbed into the submarine and was reaching up to close the hatch. Neil rushed over and angled himself to climb in. The captain tried to pull it closed. Neil had to yank with all his might to keep him from succeeding.

There was a loud whooshing noise and a series of small arrows fell all around them. Neil's baggy chef's coat was nicked and torn but the arrowheads missed his skin. He could smell the poison. It was made from the liver of the puffer fish. It was probably just enough to knock you out, but get hit by a half dozen and you were done for.

Neil opened the hatch and started down the ladder. The captain had fallen down the hatchway, an arrow lodged in his arm. He got up and shook his head and then, seeing that Neil was blocking his exit, he rushed to the bridge and started the engine.

More arrows flew at the sub. Neil's only thought was escape and that's when he'd yelled, "Dive! Dive!"

Neil hadn't realized how large the sub was inside. It was like Dr. Who's TARDIS. He passed through sleeping quarters, a dining room, and a lounge with a pool table bolted to the floor, before finally arriving in the cockpit. The sub was almost free of the yacht now and the front window just looked out on open water.

Neil found the periscope and thrust it up. He held the arms and looked into the viewfinder, turning it to face the inside of Nori's boat.

"Ahh!" Neil yelped, falling backward in shock. There was a face!

He got back up and cautiously leaned his face toward the lens.

It was Koko. She was mouthing something into the lens. It looked to Neil like *I will get you*, or something equally threatening, judging by the look on her face. Then the submarine began to dive underwater. Neil watched as Koko jumped off the top of the sub. Then the sub submerged and all Neil could see was water and what Neil was sure were Nori's sharks, circling the open doors to the harbor.

Out of the frying pan, Neil thought.

The sub kept diving. Neil turned to tell the captain the coast was clear, but the captain was now slumped over the control panel.

And into the fire. Neil ran to the captain and tried to shake him. He wasn't dead but he was so drugged by the fugu toxins that he was practically in a coma. His breaths were deep and slow. Neil was going to have to learn to drive the sub and in a hurry. It was heading straight for the bottom.

A *crash course*, Larry would have called it.

Neil carefully laid the captain down on the floor where he began to slide toward the nose of the cockpit. Neil stared at the array of dials and buttons, and decided to ignore them. He spun the wheel and pulled it back.

The sub groaned but leveled out. "Whew," Neil said, wiping the sweat from his forehead. The sub was still going at top speed. He pulled and pushed the wheel and even tried spinning it from side to side. Each effort sent the sub lurching and reeling but none of them slowed it down. Neil could see fish scrambling to get out of the way of the careening vessel. Neil suspected he'd be heading for something a lot harder than a tuna, like the shoreline, and smashing into that was not going to end well.

Neil started pushing random buttons, and succeeded in turning off the lights, making a giant TV screen appear at the back of the room, and even lowering a glittering disco ball with the song "I Will Survive" blaring away over the loudspeakers.

"Creepy," Neil said and quickly retracted the ball and muted the music.

The sub raced on. "Okay, think, chef, think." Nori said the sub hadn't been out in months. For one thing, that eliminated the sub as the boat that had attacked Larry and Hiro.

It also meant that the captain was the first person to touch any controls in a long time. Neil leaned over and sniffed the captain's fingers. He'd eaten tuna for lunch!

Neil ran to the control board and began sniffing. At the very top, right next to the switch for the disco ball, was a small latch. The cover smelled like tuna! Neil flipped it open and inside was a tiny wheel. He spun it clockwise and the ship lurched ahead even faster. "Other

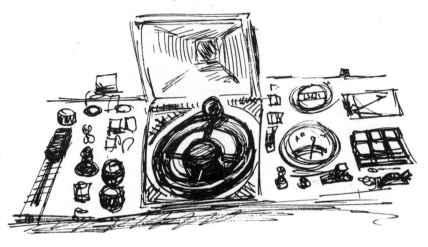

way, idiot!" he yelled, twirling the knob counterclockwise. The sub began to slow and slow. Within a minute it was gliding along with the fish. Neil slumped to the floor and sighed. "Now to find everybody else and then find the treasure."

Neil pulled back on the steering wheel and the sub slowly rose to the surface. He flicked the latch again and pushed the red button in the middle of the wheel. As he'd expected, the sub engine stopped. Neil ran to the ladder and quickly climbed it and unlocked the hatch. Neil felt the sun on his face and smiled. He pulled out his phone and dialed Jones.

"I'm on the surface. Come meet me," Neil said.

"Um, try turning around," Jones said. Neil turned and gave a start. Nakamura, Jones, Isabella, and Larry were sitting in a boat just off to the side of the floating sub. They'd arranged to meet somewhere in the water, but Neil was completely surprised at how close they were.

"Well, that was lucky." Neil smiled.

"Nice driving, leadfoot," Larry said. "You almost crashed into us! We thought you were Koko and her buddies trying to run us over."

"Yeah, I had some steering . . . difficulties. And as for Koko, she'll be here soon enough, if Nori's gang don't get her first. Let's move."

Jones anchored their fishing boat and they all clambered into the sub. Jones tied up the sub captain, as a precaution, and Nakamura and Larry carried him back to the sleeping quarters.

"It's a Ballast 2300," Jones said, spying the control panel. "An idiot could drive one of these."

"Luckily one was!" Larry called.

"Thanks," Neil said. He closed the hatch, spinning the wheel to seal it tight. "All clear," he called.

Jones reached over and plugged the coordinates into some computer screen that Neil assumed was the sub's GPS, and then they were back underwater and moving fast.

Nakamura joined Jones at the front window. He seemed to be enjoying the underwater view of his hometown.

"Hey, is there a coffee machine on this tub?" Larry

called, rummaging around in the back of the sub. "Tea! Is everything here tea?"

Neil and Isabella took a seat at the back of the bridge.

"I take it that you won today," Isabella said.

"Yes. It was horrible. I meant it when I said I don't want to duel anymore."

"I am not happy you were in a duel, but I was happy to see this sub." Isabella smiled.

"It's not any consolation, but I might have saved another chef's life."

"The chef whose life you put in danger by agreeing to the duel in the first place?"

"Um, yeah. When you put it that way, it doesn't sound so good."

"No. It doesn't."

"Although I don't think he was enjoying life as Nori's chef much. And I was a little too close to joining him." Neil suddenly felt absolutely drained. He leaned against Isabella's shoulder. She stroked his cheek and he smiled, then dozed.

About five minutes later Neil awoke with a start. Swirling dots of light were dancing before his eyes. Had he been poisoned by the arrows? Then "I Will Survive" blared over the ship's speakers.

"Larry, get away from that control panel!" Nakamura yelled.

"But that's awesome!" Larry was saying.

"Larry!" they all yelled.

"Fine, fine, let's do a *boring* treasure hunt," he said, and the ball and music disappeared.

"We're here," Jones said. Neil felt the sub slow and Jones started to steer in circles. It was getting darker and Neil could see that they were heading down.

Chapter Thirty

Treasure and Treachery

The water grew murkier. The light from the nose of the sub seemed to stop just a few feet away. Jones slowed their decent. "Naks. How far are we from bottom?"

"'Naks?'" Larry started laughing.

"Put a lid on it, Flamb-chop," Nakamura said. He was staring intently at a small screen on the side of the console. He turned a dial and a low beeping started to come out of the speakers. "The sonar is picking up lots of debris about twenty feet down."

"Let's get a better look." Jones pushed another button

and the big TV came sliding back down from the ceiling.

"Video games or movie?" Larry said.

"Neither. 3-D imaging." Jones turned on the TV and a three-dimensional image of the floor of Tokyo Bay filled the screen. "I've gotta give the Nori guy credit. He's got all the toys," Jones smiled.

"Is anyone else wondering *why* Nori has all these toys?" Isabella said.

"What do you mean?" Neil said.

"Nori lends you his submarine. Maybe he knows what you're looking for and maybe he wants you to find it? It saves him the trouble."

They all looked around the cabin suspiciously, half expecting some giant Nori face to appear, chuckling.

"Hello?" Larry called out.

Nothing.

"You're just being paranoid," Larry said.

Isabella glared at him.

Nakamura watched the screen. "It doesn't hurt to be cautious. I can't imagine the comatose captain back in the hammock was something Nori had planned."

Neil wasn't so sure. "I think it's worth taking a close look around the sub while Jones looks for something treasurey-looking on the screen there. What kind of treasure are we looking for anyway?"

They all shrugged. "Actually, I have no idea," Larry said. "I kind of imagined some big pile of coins sitting around in a box."

Suddenly, the sub slammed to a stop. They were all thrown around the cabin. The sub stared to list to the side and the engines groaned. Jones reached up from the floor and shut them off. The nose of the sub seemed to be sinking.

"What was that?" Larry asked, rubbing his forehead.

They looked out of the front of the sub. The lights shone on something large and square, covered with mollusks.

"We hit a box?" Nakamura said.

"Is that the treasure?" Neil said.

Jones looked at the GPS. "This is the place, roughly." He turned on more lights. The cube was almost completely sunk into the muck. The TV just showed a slight bump in the floor of the bay. If they hadn't hit it, they might have missed it. Fish swam around a series of bubbles that began to rise toward the surface. "Whatever it is, we just jammed the nose of our sub into it."

"I hope those bubbles are from the box and not our sub," Isabella said.

"So do I," Jones said. "With the pressure down here we'll find out soon enough if the front of the sub starts caving in."

"Hey, sad sacks, how come no one else is *excited?*" Larry said, beaming. He pointed out of the front window. "That's it. That's the treasure!"

"Maybe," Nakamura said. "It could also be a hunk of an old battleship or part of some old bridge they threw down here to be an artificial reef."

"Party pooper," Larry said. "I say it's the treasure."

"What, you have a hunch?" Nakamura said.

Larry stopped smiling and folded his arms. "First of all, the sea growth on the box is consistent with the time period of about a hundred years. It takes about that long for that crusting of mussels and also for that amount of that particular type of coral to grow. Then there are the obvious patina and oxidation levels of the iron—also consistent with about a hundred years at this depth and temperature. Much longer and the salt in the water would have eaten it all away. AND, the silt has been built up around it by the current but hasn't completely buried it . . . also consistent with—all together now—a hundred years or so underwater." Larry rested his case.

Nakamura took his finger and dramatically pushed his lower chin up to close his mouth.

Isabella applauded and Larry took a deep bow. "I must share this award with Maxine Gill, shipwreck hunter."

Jones seemed less impressed, as always. "Okay, genius, we found the treasure. Now what?"

Larry's smile didn't fade a bit. "You said Nori had all the toys. What are the chances there's some deep-sea scuba gear inside this baby?"

The first thing Larry and Neil did once they were outside the sub was to check the nose. Luckily, it wasn't damaged, but it had become entangled with a series of iron chains that were draped over the top of the iron box. Larry swam up to the front window and gave a thumbs-up while swimming in a slow circle, like a seal.

"There is an intercom, you idiot," Jones said into his

microphone. "It works if we're close to each other."

"Oh, you're no fun," Larry said. "If you lower the nose and then tilt back up, you should be able to shake free of the chains. Let me and Neil get to the other side first."

"Why should I?" Jones said, gunning the engine.

"You know your mike is still on!" Neil yelled.

"He knows," Larry said. Then Larry splashed away from the sub, singing, "I'm a little mermaid shrimp and trout. Here is my haddock, here is my . . . What kind of fish rhymes with trout?"

"Remind me again why you two idiots are handling this?" Jones barked.

"We're the only ones who fit into the suits. And you're the only one who knows how to drive that thing."

"And you and I lost to Isabella and Nakamura in rock-paper-scissors," Neil added.

"Oh, yeah, and that," Larry said.

Jones nudged the sub free and then Larry and Neil began examining the metal box. "It looks like the chains were used to lift it down. They must have had a crane on the ship."

"So they sailed out here, dumped the treasure, then sailed off?" Neil said.

"Yes and no by the looks of it," Larry said. "Yes, they dumped the treasure, but then the ship was blown up. There are fragments of wood down here, but scattered around. My guess is the crew unwillingly went down with the ship."

"No witnesses that way," Neil said.

"I bet the artist was on the boat too." Larry stared at the box for a moment, thinking. "Here's what happened,

I bet. The Takoyakis got tipped off that the emperor was about to attack, so they picked a spot to hide their treasure where nobody was going to find it, in the middle of the water. Then they commissioned the prints and told the artist to hide a map inside. Then they sent him and the crew out to dump it . . . which they did."

"Then BOOM," Neil said.

Larry nodded. "The good news is that the chains still look strong enough to use. Ramming into the box loosened it from the muck, so it shouldn't take too much more to lift it, assuming it's not *too* heavy."

"So how do you propose we do that?" Nakamura asked.

"I think we could use the hook on the chains to attach them to the sub's railing."

"And lift it to the surface? I'm not sure that's a good idea."

"No. I agree. But when we smashed into the box, we actually broke the seal on the door. Half the door is still below the muck level. So if we can just drag the thing out, we should be able to wrench the door open."

"Okay, it's worth a try," Jones said.

"Those bubbles were a good sign, actually. It means the stuff inside stayed dry and wasn't corroded. But now that we've let the seawater in, we're going to need to get the treasure out fast."

"So what do we need to do exactly?" Neil asked.

"Hook these chains onto the railing and let the sub do the hard work. Easy!" Larry said.

Neil and Larry had to strain to lift the chains while trying to swim upward in the cold water. "This is EASY?"

Neil said, breathing heavily. "I can't wait to see your plan for opening the big iron door."

"Don't waste your oxygen," Larry said. "You're going to need it."

Finally, they were able to get the hook attached to the railing. Then they swam away to a safe distance. Neil lay on the ocean floor and watched the fish swimming past his face shield. "Some of these fish would be worth a hundred dollars at market," Neil said.

"I'd pay that much to keep them in the water," Larry said.

Neil could see Jones inside the cabin of the sub, playing with the controls. He pulled back on the wheel and the sub began to rise. The chains went taut and the sub strained against the weight. Jones drove straight ahead and the box began to shift.

"Gout," Larry said, watching Jones try to fight the box.

Neil sat up and stared at his cousin. "What?"

"Gout. It rhymes with 'trout.' It's not a fish, though. Hmm, better keep thinking."

"How about lout?" Isabella said.

"Stakeout," Nakamura said.

"Out," Jones said.

Larry laughed. "I didn't peg you as a word-game kind of guy, Jones."

"I'm not. The box is out."

"Oh. Great!" Larry and Neil swam over to the box. The force of ripping it from the muck had weakened the door hinges even more. Neil and Larry undid the chains and then reattached them to the door. Jones lifted the nose of the sub and the door ripped off.

They turned up their headlights and gazed down into the box.

Neil gasped. Stacked inside were hundreds of small wooden boxes, elaborately carved and decorated. "Wood! I guess they never expected the treasure to be stuck down here for so long. If that seawater had gotten inside, wow . . . we'd be looking at a lot of rotted treasure."

"Okay, you two, start bringing those on board," Nakamura called.

"Aye, aye," Larry said, saluting. He turned to Neil. "Okay, cuz, this is going to take a while. We can't just open a hatch and start dumping them inside."

"Pressure problems. I do pay attention sometimes."

Larry smiled. "I'll open the outside hatch and then we can start loading the boxes."

Once the hatch was filled, they closed the lid and waited for pumps to drain the seawater. Then it was finally safe for Isabella to open the inside hatch. She grabbed the boxes and stacked them in the dining room. It was painstaking work.

"It feels like *Natale*, Christmas! I can't wait to open the boxes," she said.

"One more batch ought to do it," Neil called after an hour of work.

Just then something came flying at them out of the void, knocking Neil off the top of the sub.

"Sharks!" Larry yelled.

Neil reached out and caught the railing. His back slammed against the hull of the sub. Turning his head he saw: "Propellers. That's not a shark. It's another submarine."

"Koko's tracked us down!" Larry called.

Neil peered into the gloom as the sub turned around and prepared for another attack. "That's not the ship I saw Koko using! That's someone else!"

Chapter Thirty-One

Overtaken Underwater

Hurry, get up here. We've got to get into the hatch!"
Larry called. Neil pulled himself up. "Duck!" Larry
called and he flattened himself onto the deck just as the
submarine came at them one more time. It was much
smaller than Nori's sub and seemed to have mechanical
arms on the front. It looked like a deranged king crab,
Neil thought.

Neil had seen Larry watching a documentary about
raising the *Titanic* and they'd used something like that.
Of course, Neil had instantly changed the channel to a
Gordon Ramsay Christmas special, so he wasn't exactly
sure what they did. On the flip side, he did know how to
swear at a stuffed goose.

Larry crawled over and banged on the hatch door.
"Open up!"

"The pressure isn't equalized yet. I can't open it until the pressure is the same," Jones called.

The mini-sub made another turn and headed back toward them. "Hold on TIGHT!" Jones yelled. Neil and Larry grabbed the railing with their legs and arms as Jones went full speed ahead. They shot forward and the mini-sub narrowly missed smashing into the tail. The remaining boxes of treasure slid off the deck and fell into the darkness below. Larry turned back and saw one of them crash into the front window of the mini-sub, sending sparkling golden coins flying into the darkness.

He also noticed that the mini-sub was following them and was gaining on them. "How are they gaining on us?" Larry yelled.

"You never took that chain off!" Jones said. "We're still dragging that stupid door."

Neil tried to pull himself forward to loosen the hook but realized it was useless. He looked back just in time to see the mini-sub's arm reach for his leg. He pulled it back but the arm moved closer and grabbed him around the waist. The other arm reached over and grabbed Larry, who tried in vain to kick himself free.

Just then the old iron chains finally snapped and the large sub shot forward.

"Neil, let go!" Larry yelled.

Neil could feel his arm sockets being pulled apart. He let go with a loud yell.

He heard Isabella's voice yelling "Neil!" Then he blacked out.

* * *

"Neil, wake up. It's me, Larry, wake up." Neil blinked. The lights were blindingly bright and every part of him ached. He turned over toward Larry's voice and yowled. His left arm felt like someone was stabbing it with a thousand needles. He flinched and grabbed it with his right, which also shot with pain.

Neil's eyes adjusted to the light and he saw Larry sitting next to him on a wooden bench. They appeared to be in a . . . sauna?

"Are we in a sauna?" Neil asked.

"Yeah, pretty weird but I think it's because there are no windows and it's small. We're on a boat, though. I can feel it rocking, which means we're on the waves, not under them."

"How did we get here? The last thing I remember hearing was Isabella yelling my name."

"I told you to let go. Jones and the others got away. Two guys with harpoons came out of the mini-sub and dragged us inside. Good thing too. I think those mechanical arms were cracking our oxygen tanks. I hear rapid decompression is a horrible way to die."

"So who's got us?"

"I don't know. They blindfolded me and then stuck something in my arm. Next thing I knew I woke up here and you were talking in your sleep. I figured I'd better wake you before you said anything stupid."

"Whereas you do that when you're awake," Neil said.

"Jokes are a good sign." Larry smiled. "Not funny jokes, but you're trying and that's a good sign."

The door to the sauna opened and two men dressed

head to toe in black clothes motioned for Larry and Neil to stand.

"Are those outfits really necessary?" Larry said. "I mean, something more modern possibly? Ninjas are so fifteenth century."

The closest ninja grabbed the hilt of his sword and took a step inside. Larry stopped talking and stood up. "I guess we'd better go," Neil said. The ninjas nodded.

Neil and Larry found themselves side by side walking down a long hallway, with a ninja behind and in front. The sides of the hallway were metal and painted white. They passed a series of barred windows and Neil could see that they were indeed on a boat, but weren't out at sea. They were anchored on the shore of an island. The island appeared to be covered with derelict and abandoned buildings. Neil even saw a huge section of one break off and crash to the ground.

"What is this place?" Neil whispered.

"Hashima Island," Larry whispered back.

"Did they blow it up in the war or something?"

Larry shook his head. "The whole island was a mine, and hundreds of people used to live and work here. The mine closed in the 1970s and everyone left. Then it started falling apart. The wind and sea air don't help."

The ninja behind smacked Larry on the back of the head. "Silence!" he yelled.

Neil looked outside again and saw more bits of buildings flaking off in the wind.

The hallway ended at two bamboo and paper doors. They were decorated with a beautiful brush

and ink painting of a cherry tree in full bloom. The guards stood on either side, and Larry and Neil stood, waiting.

"Koko," Larry said, looking at the cherry tree.

Neil didn't say anything. He sniffed the air but didn't smell cherry blossoms. "Paper and bamboo doesn't seem like a great security system," Neil said.

"Not as bad as you'd think. Those kind of doors are known as shoji," Larry said. "The light is coming from behind us, which means the people inside can see our shadows but we can't see them."

The doors slid open, revealing an incredibly ornate room. Golden walls were decorated with elaborate paintings of peacocks, trees, and ninja warriors attacking wooden forts.

The guards motioned for Neil and Larry to step inside. They stepped onto the matted floor. The doors slid closed behind them and they were alone in the room.

Neil looked up. The ceiling was also made of gold leaf and lacquered wood. Daylight streamed in from their left, but it was filtered through more colored paper, enhancing the opulent yellow glow of the room.

"This looks like another of Nori's boats," Neil whispered.

"You're both wrong," said a voice. It was coming from behind a set of shoji doors ahead of them, the ones decorated with the ninjas. The doors slid open and a man walked into the room. He was wearing a dark blue suit and golden tie. His face was covered with cuts and bruises.

"Hiro!" Larry yelled.

Chapter Thirty-Two

Anti-Hiro

Hiro, you're alive!" Larry said. He rushed forward to hug his friend, but Hiro slammed his palm into Larry's chest, sending him flying back onto the floor.

"Of course I'm alive," Hiro said. "I was never in any danger of NOT being alive."

Neil ran over to help Larry, who was struggling to regain his breath.

"What did you do that for?" Neil yelled. "We've been trying to help find you!"

"Don't be an idiot. I didn't need any help . . . Well, not any help being found. I did need help finding the treasure and you two did a wonderful job. *Arigatō*." He bowed.

"You were the mastermind behind this whole operation," Neil said.

Hiro grinned. He snapped his fingers and two ninjas rushed in with mats and a low table, followed by a tray of tea. Hiro waved for Neil and Larry to join him.

"It's not a request," Hiro said. "I have some questions to ask you and custom dictates that I show you hospitality first."

Neil could smell that the tea was wonderful, and not drugged by anything he could detect.

"It's not poisoned," Hiro said, sitting down and taking a sip. "That's more your friend Nori's territory. Thank you, by the way, for not mentioning the treasure to him. It would have complicated things. Now please, come to the table or I'm afraid my guards will have to force you to come, and that will not be quite as . . . comfortable."

Neil helped Larry crawl to the table. Hiro poured them some tea. They sipped in silence for a few moments.

"Good, now that the custom has been fulfilled, the questions. First, where is the treasure now?" Hiro picked a piece of imaginary lint off his suit coat.

Larry seemed too shocked or winded to say anything. Neil turned to Hiro angrily. "It's at the bottom of the bay, you idiot. It was on the deck of our submarine when your sub attacked us. It slipped off and floated away. Good luck finding it now."

Hiro frowned. Clearly he didn't like this answer. He lifted his hand and summoned one of his guards over and began speaking to him in Japanese. Then he saw that Larry was listening. "Ah, I forgot that my good friend understands us." He stood up. "I will return in a few moments." He bowed and disappeared behind the screen.

"What did he say?" Neil asked.

"He wants to see the submarine pilot. I don't think it was to offer him a pay raise."

Neil looked around the room. "We've got to get out of here. I don't see any exits."

Just then they heard a muffled yell, followed by a splash, coming through the rice paper windows. Hiro walked back in a few seconds later, wiping his hands on a towel.

"Yes, well, it turns out that part of what you say is true. Some of the treasure was lost. This is unfortunate. My *new* submarine captain"— Hiro nodded toward the guard who had opened the door—"will go searching for the treasure that fell into the bay. But my former captain insists—sorry, *insisted*—that most of the treasure had been transferred to your submarine. It seems he arrived a bit too late. Now, tell me where the treasure is."

Larry rubbed his chest. "I thought we were friends."

"Be careful whom you trust on the Internet," Hiro said, sitting down and sipping his tea. "We'd only met once, you may remember, at the comic convention in Seattle."

"That's when we worked out the idea for *The Chef*. Koko was there too," Larry said.

"Yes, Koko always seems to be there." Hiro frowned. "And *The Chef* was the perfect start of my plan."

"Plan? It was just a manga, for crying out loud!" Larry said.

Hiro chuckled. "It was, first of all, a manga about food. For years I had pored over the secrets of the scroll, at least the copy I was able to finally track down. I knew the key had to do with food but could never figure out how."

"How did you know it was about food?" Neil asked.

Hiro paused, thinking. "I had seen the original scroll only once. There were turtles in each print."

"Turtles?" Neil asked.

"Yes, there were turtles on the original prints, not rice or fish. Very odd, don't you think?"

"Yes, you are," Larry said.

Hiro ignored him. "Why turtles? I always wondered, and why replace them with food? I thought about this a lot. It was actually my sister who gave me a clue. She was inspired by my mother to become a marine biologist, and one day she was telling me that Japan's turtles were dying off."

"Killed by loonies like Nori," Neil said.

Hiro nodded. "Koko said that Japan once boasted hundreds of species of turtles, each with a different name depending on where it lived. Then it struck me. The turtles in the original prints were tied to specific places in Japan. But as the turtles vanished so did any hope of figuring out the secret. My father suspected the geography was important, without knowing why exactly, so he had a copy made without the turtles."

"So future generations of nutbars like you could try to discover the secret?" Neil asked.

"I will ignore that for now." Hiro smiled. "I thought I might *persuade* Koko to help me determine the location of the turtles, so one night, I tried to see the original again. I triggered a trap my father had set. The fire destroyed the original and then our home." Hiro sipped his tea calmly. "I remembered the copy, and bided my time until I could discover its location. My father let it slip that the artist was from the far north, on Hokkaido. It took me years to track him down, but I did."

"Why didn't the artist use the scroll to look for the treasure?" Larry asked.

"My father chose well. The man was a monk, unconcerned with earthly things. He was very talented, as I'm sure you could tell by looking at the beauty of the copy. It was a shame to kill him, but I don't like witnesses."

"Funny that you became an artist yourself, considering how your family deals with them," Larry said under his breath.

"After I left his home, I looked at the copy he had made of the scroll. Where I had once seen turtles, there were now rice bowls. Why? I asked. Why that change? What was the geographical clue?"

"It wasn't obvious?" Larry asked. "Neil figured it out in two minutes."

"No. It wasn't obvious. I asked a number of chefs to help me break the code. None could. They paid for their failures. Then, when you told me about your cousin's incredible ability for cooking and solving mysteries, I knew I would have to lure him here. That's why I invited you here first and then used your death to lure your precious cousin. I knew he would come looking for you, or your body. I have had to be very patient, but it will soon pay off."

"Why not just *ask* me to come?" Neil asked, feeling his anger rising.

"Well, I had my reasons for setting up this charade."

"You needed your sister to think you were dead so she'd stop chasing after you," Larry said.

Hiro put down his tea. "Enough exposition. I feel like a villain in our manga! I always loved the villains. Didn't you ever notice how well drawn they were?"

"You can definitely draw. Too bad you're such a jerk," Larry said.

Hiro slammed his fist into the table, smashing the teapot. "Enough! The treasure. Where is it?"

"You know it's on the sub!" Neil yelled. "It's Nori's sub. Maybe he's got it! Then Koko can get it back for you. She's probably already taken over his yacht."

This seemed to surprise Hiro for a second, but he quickly regained his composure. "Koko was on Nori's yacht?"

"Wasn't she there working for you?" Neil asked. He instantly realized he'd drawn the wrong conclusion because Hiro gave out a long high-pitched laugh.

"Koko, working for me? You must be kidding. She has done nothing but work against me for her entire life. Always hovering around the edges, in the shadows, trying to stop me from stealing the scroll. Then she tried to stop me from killing our parents. . . ." Hiro stopped for a second as Neil and Larry gasped.

His face twisted into an evil grin. "I'll kill anyone who gets in my way. And look what the insurance money for their deaths got me." He raised his hands to indicate the golden room. "That's why I needed Koko to think I was dead. So she would stop following me! I knew she'd send her friend Aki out to search for my body. I made sure she'd find Larry alive, and Larry would find the scroll."

"How did you know I'd survive the explosion?" Larry said.

"I didn't trigger the explosion until I'd seen you jump in the water. I was in the submarine right underneath you."

Neil remembered Koko's words into the periscope. *I will get you.* Had she meant that as a threat or a promise? Would he ever find out?

Hiro gave a small snicker. "So Koko is attacking Nori. This is good, very good. It means you've somehow convinced Koko that Nori was behind all this. He'll likely wipe her out along with her little group of followers. Then I can use the treasure without risk of interference. It would be nice to be alive again. As you can see from my bruises and cuts, I've been horribly treated by my kidnappers."

"Is that what you'll tell the police?" Larry asked.

"Yes. And you two will be killed in the rescue attempt here on Hashima island where I've been held prisoner," Hiro said. "Sounds like the real final chapter for *The Chef.*"

Neil clenched his fists. "If you're so wealthy, then why do you even need the treasure?"

Hiro leaned forward. "Do you have any idea what the treasure is?"

"Coins? Statues? Gold?" Larry said.

"I expected so much more from you," Hiro said, leaning back and shaking his head. "There *are* coins and statues, of course, but the real treasure is a collection of documents—scrolls and tablets and contracts and the real history of our family and our country. The true treasure is evidence!"

"Evidence of what?"

"Evidence that my ancestor was the true husband of the Empress Okiko. Evidence that I should be Hiro, Emperor of Japan!" Hiro stood up with a crazed look in his eyes.

Just then Neil caught the faint scent of cherry blossom. A millisecond later a tremendous explosion sent them all flying across the room.

Chapter Thirty-Three

Salvaged by Scrap

Quick, follow me!" Koko yelled from the window. The explosion had shattered the bars, sending burning flakes of rice paper and bamboo all over the room. Smoke stung Neil's lungs and eyes. He saw Larry next to him, bleeding from a cut on his forehead, and together they struggled toward the window.

"Am I glad to see you, and your eyes," Larry said, squinting.

"Hiro's alive!" Neil called. "He's in here somewhere."

Koko didn't even blink as she leaped into the room and drew her sword. "Your friends are waiting for you below. Hurry, I'll protect you." A ninja star came flying at them out the haze and Koko expertly deflected it with the sword. "I SAID HURRY!"

They climbed over the railing and saw Jones and Nakamura on the dock thirty feet below. They and four gray-clad ninjas were fending off a pack of Hiro's black-ninja guards. Jones was using a bamboo staff to expertly block all the sword thrusts and knives the ninjas could throw at them. Nakamura seemed to be using a round lifesaver as a kind of shield. Neil could hear Koko deflecting more deadly metal behind them.

The ladder she used to climb up now stopped at a smoking hole in the side of the ship.

"So how are we supposed to get down there?" Neil yelled.

"Jump!" Koko said. Then Neil heard Hiro give a furious yell, followed by the sound of clashing swords.

Neil and Larry jumped, pushing themselves away from the ship with their legs. They missed the end of the dock by inches and landed in the cold water. They could see that the hole extended down the entire side of the boat, which was starting to list as it took on water.

There was another splash as Koko joined them. "Now swim!" she yelled, gasping for air. Neil looked up and could see Hiro nursing a cut on his arm and yelling something at them in Japanese. Then he and his guards disappeared back into the smoking room.

"Your brother doesn't sound happy," Larry spat out between swim strokes.

"He will be after us in a moment," Koko said. "He has just enough time to grab more troops and weapons before the boat sinks."

She led them under the pier. They could hear the battle going on above them and then Jones yelling, "Fall back! We'll join them on shore," followed by hurried footsteps on the wooden slats.

Koko, Neil, and Larry climbed up from under the pier and onto the debris-strewn shore of Hashima Island. It looked to Neil like a postapocalyptic wasteland. A stone wall separated the beach and water from the crumbling buildings.

There was an opening ahead of them and they could see Jones and Nakamura disappearing through. The wall on either side rose twenty feet high.

"Now what?" Larry yelled, as a ninja star whistled by his head and ricocheted off the wall.

"MOVE!" Koko yelled. She turned and deflected more knives as they clambered up the slope to the opening. Then she threw two smoke bombs into the gap.

"Were those avocado-shaped or pomegranate?" Larry asked as they ran past chunks of concrete and steel.

Koko just rolled her eyes and kept running.

"Where's Isabella?" Neil said, ignoring the pain in his arms as he swung them to go faster.

"She's on the far side of the island with Nori's submarine. We anchored there and then snuck through the island to attack Hiro's yacht. She's safe, but we have to get there quickly, and the fastest way is through there." Koko pointed at the crumbling buildings.

Neil watched as another huge chunk of building slid off and fell to the ground, right in the middle of the "path" Koko suggested they travel.

"The explosion must have weakened more of the buildings," Larry said.

As if on cue, an iron girder groaned and collapsed, narrowly missing Neil's feet. He leaped over it and then looked back. Hiro was leading a charge of black-clad

ninjas. The girder momentarily slowed their progress but Neil could tell they were getting closer.

Neil ran faster, sometimes catching glimpses out of the corner of his eye. Collapsed stairways led to what looked like bombed-out apartments.

He didn't want to die here. Shots rang out behind them and bits of concrete chipped off the buildings. "Turn right!" Koko yelled and they dashed down the remains of an alleyway. The buildings leaned so much they practically touched at the top, blocking out the sunlight.

"Where are we going?" Neil called. "I can barely see two feet ahead."

"We're almost there," she called. "But we needed to get away from the main road. Too much to shoot at." Neil heard a commotion behind him. Hiro certainly saw them go down the alleyway and was yelling at his own guards to hurry after them.

A thought occurred to Neil. What if this was another trick? What if Koko was working against Hiro but for herself and this was her way of getting back at Hiro while getting rid of any witnesses? "How do we know this isn't a trap?" Neil asked Larry as they struggled to keep up with Koko.

"It is," Larry said gleefully. "We passed a window back there. I saw Jones, Nakamura, and Koko's ninjas waiting. If Hiro and his cronies follow us, then they'll be sitting ducks for our guys."

As soon as Larry said this, there was a loud boom behind them. Neil stopped and looked back. A plume of smoke was quickly filling the alleyway. "Was that a bomb or is the island crashing?" Neil asked.

"Both," Nakamura said, sprinting past him. Jones and the ninjas were right on his heels. Neil and Larry turned and sped after them as the alleyway began to collapse in on itself. If Hiro was back in the alley, he was likely crushed. If he retreated in time, he'd have to look for another way around.

There was a dim light coming from up ahead. Neil could smell a sea breeze coming through. He closed his eyes and sprinted through. He could hear more of the buildings crashing down behind him and he kept running.

"STOP!" It was Isabella's voice. Neil stopped just as he was about to run over the side of a stone wall. His toes were hanging over the edge. He twirled his arms to stop from going over. Waves splashed onto jagged rocks below. He regained his balance and stepped back.

Neil looked out over the water and saw Isabella waving from the open hatch of the submarine. She pointed to Neil's left, where he saw a ladder. Larry and the others were already scrambling down to a waiting life raft. Neil looked back at Isabella, gave a thumbs-up, and rushed toward the ladder.

Just then a shot rang out. Neil saw Isabella fall down into the sub. "NOOOOO!" he yelled. Another bullet hit the ground next to his feet. He glanced back at the buildings. Hiro had climbed to a pile of rubble and was taking aim at him with a gun. Neil leaped from the wall as another shot grazed his leg.

He closed his eyes, expecting the bone-crushing

impact of his body on jagged rocks. Instead, he landed
with a much gentler jolt in someone's arms.

He opened his eyes. Jones was carrying him toward
the life raft. He jumped in and Koko fired the engine.
Jones slipped Neil into a seat and they both stared intently
at the hatchway of the sub. Another shot pierced the side
of the raft and air began to pour out. The sub was just a
few feet away. They jumped out of the sinking raft and
into the water. More shots ripped through the raft as they
climbed up the side of the sub. Jones and Neil led the
way, desperate to help Isabella.

Jones reached the hatchway first and climbed
down. Neil reached it moments later and looked down.
Jones was cradling an unmoving Isabella in his arms.
A spot on her shawl was a horrible crimson stain. Neil
rushed down the ladder. She was still breathing. Jones
carried her to the crew cabin and grabbed a first-aid kit.

Jones lifted the shawl and Neil saw with a rush of relief that the bullet had hit Isabella in the shoulder, and not the heart. Still, it was bleeding and horrible-looking. Jones quickly cleaned the wound and dressed it with gauze. Neil held Isabella's hand, caressing her fingers. Neil was suddenly struck by an odd thought. He had a scar on his shoulder from a similar bullet wound. It was something he would never want anyone else to suffer, but it was a strange bond he now had with Isabella.

Nakamura, Koko, and the rest made their way down the hatch and Neil could hear a flurry of activity as they began to fire up the sub to sail away. "Jones," Neil said, touching his arm. "You need to go help get this thing moving. I'll take care of her." Jones looked at Neil and Neil was shocked to see actual tears in his eyes. Jones nodded and stood up. He paused in the doorway. "Of course, if she even whimpers in pain, we'll see how fast a boy chef can be shot out of a torpedo tube." Then he hurried to the bridge.

"Whew, I was beginning to think he was turning into a giant teddy bear," Neil whispered to Isabella. She didn't open her eyes, but a weak smile played on her lips. Neil suddenly realized he wanted to kiss them more than anything in the world. He leaned over, just as Larry burst into the cabin.

"Jones didn't say that her lips were injured!" Larry chuckled.

Neil felt his face turn red. "I was just seeing if her breathing was okay."

"Ha! I saw the look in your eyes. It was the same

look you get when you're making roasted potatoes."

Neil noticed that the smile on Isabella's face grew larger.

"Do you have a compelling reason for being here?" Neil said.

"Just checking on you both. Jones has pulled us away from the island. We're on our way to . . . actually I'm not sure where we're heading."

Neil looked around. "Wasn't the treasure in here? What happened to it?"

"Aki," Isabella whispered. "It's on Aki's boat."

"Aki!" Larry smiled. Then he grimaced. "Great, now it's all going to smell like fish."

Koko stuck her head into the cabin. "Is everyone all right?"

Isabella winced in pain as she nodded her head.

"Good. I'm just brewing some tea. And I suppose you all have some questions. We have time now before we meet up with Nori."

"Nori!" Neil was shocked. "I knew it. You're working for that nutbar!"

Koko smiled. "Work for Nori? No. Let's just say that we have come to an arrangement. He let us keep the sub. In return we returned his captain, and we will give him a portion of the treasure. Not that Nori had much choice. Right now he's dangling over the side of his yacht, gazing at a very hungry pack of sharks. He's also covered with bacon fat, making him especially appealing."

"Who covered him in bacon fat?" Larry asked.

"Kong. He also told me how you fought Nori and helped save his life. That's when I discovered that you had demanded use of the submarine. I knew then that you were going after the treasure."

"Isn't Kong working for Nori?" Larry said.

"Kong is no friend of his boss. But he needed Nori's protection."

"From whom?" Neil asked.

"My brother. I knew Hiro was forcing chefs to help him unlock the secrets of the scroll but I never knew why. Kong was one of the chefs who failed Hiro, but he escaped before Hiro could . . . *fire* him. He'd been working for Nori ever since. But he'd always been looking for a way out."

Neil had to shake his head. "Okay. I still have about two hundred questions. First of all, why did you attack Nori's boat?"

Koko took a long pause before continuing. "Let me do my best to explain. My brother is very clever. I wasn't convinced that he was dead, but I did think that he and Larry had been attacked. I assumed it was because of the scroll."

"Why didn't you warn me about the danger?" Larry asked.

"I still thought you were working with my brother!"

Larry started to defend himself, but stopped. "I guess we *were* working on the manga together."

Koko looked back at Neil. "Then, when I visited you in the hotel you convinced me that Nori was holding Hiro, that Hiro was alive. That could only mean one of two things. Either Hiro and Nori were working together, or Nori was going to look for the treasure and would force Hiro to help him. I didn't like either option."

"Because either Hiro or Nori was about to find the treasure," Neil said.

Koko nodded. "I tried sneaking onto the boat by myself, to look for Hiro or the scroll. Some crazed woman with metal legs attacked me with a surfboard."

"Yeah, she's a real piece of work," Neil said.

"I left. I knew the only way to get inside was to attack with force. Aki agreed to sneak us up to the yacht with her boat. We waited for an opening. I had followed you that day you escaped in the hovercar and suspected there was another way inside for boats. We waited and attacked."

"And when they opened the doors to let me out, they let you all in," Neil said.

Koko nodded.

"Who is the 'us' that helped you attack Nori?" Larry asked.

"I have many friends who have helped me in my training as an expert in jujitsu. They knew my brother was evil. Some had even studied under the monk he killed. They have joined me in my fight to stop my brother from finding the treasure."

"So you knew that the treasure is some kind of historical evidence about your family?" Neil said.

"My brother has done many horrible things for money, but his pursuit of the scroll was a lifelong obsession. I always suspected the treasure was something more than wealth. Can you imagine my brother as emperor? That would be the end of everything."

"You said you expected to find me at the hotel. So you knew I was alive?" Larry said.

"The tackle box I sent along was equipped with a

homing device. When you didn't return, I sent my friend Aki out to see what had happened and she found you floating on the surface. I knew you were alive, but I also knew that meant Hiro *wanted* you alive for some reason. I didn't know why. Perhaps you were left behind as a decoy? Perhaps you were working with him? I needed to find out more."

"Why didn't Aki just search me for the scroll?" Larry said. "I might have liked that, actually."

"Aki let you borrow her boat to go to find the scroll. She should have gone with you. When you came back, you disappeared before I could confront you. Her mistake has cost us. We could have avoided so much destruction. Now that we know the truth, I will do my best to help you all. The gold and jewels can help solve lots of problems."

"What about the scrolls and stuff that Hiro is after?"

Koko stood up. "If that is inside the boxes, then they will be sent to the bottom of the ocean or destroyed. I will not allow my brother to use them to destroy our country."

Larry stood up and smiled at Koko. "I have just one more question. Does this mean I can gaze lovingly into those beautiful eyes again?"

Koko smiled and their eyes met. The tender moment was destroyed a second later when the sub gave a sudden lurch forward.

Larry was thrown to the floor. "Jones, what's going on?" he called down the hallway.

"Something smashed into us from behind!" Nakamura called back.

Koko and Larry ran up to the bridge.

"I'll be right there," Neil said. He kissed Isabella on the forehead and tucked her into her bunk. There were security ropes to make sure she wouldn't slip. Neil tied them tightly and then made his way to the front of the sub.

A ghostly image was illuminated on the TV screen, beamed from a camera on the rear of the submarine. Neil could see the bubbles from the propeller and the fish fading away from the lights. He also saw what appeared to be a glowing blob in the gloom. The blob came closer and Neil saw that it was the mini-sub. The arms had been replaced by menacing-looking drills. The mini-sub flew at them, smashing into the rear and sending them lurching forward again.

The cockpit of the mini-sub came closer to the camera and the TV screen was filled with Hiro's crazed face.

Chapter Thirty-Four

Cracked

Grab something!" Jones shouted. He turned the steering wheel all the way to his left. The submarine banked abruptly and Neil held on to the back of a chair as his feet slipped and slid across the floor. If he let go, he would certainly go flying down to the far wall.

Jones straightened out the sub and Neil looked worriedly back up the hallway. Isabella was still lying in her bunk, held tight by the straps. Neil hoped she was sleeping through the twists and turns. He was starting to feel seasick.

Neil looked at the TV screen. Jones's maneuver had momentarily shaken Hiro loose, but Neil could see the blob was still following them and was again growing closer.

Jones waited until Hiro was just on their tail and then turned to the left again. Hiro's craft was smaller and nimbler than Nori's large submarine, so each time Jones succeeded in shaking him for only a minute or so.

Neil suddenly noticed an odd sound on the hull, like a kind of constant drumming. "Is that the drills?" he said, panicked. He looked at the TV screen, but Hiro wasn't close enough to be drilling, so what was it?

"Sound waves," Larry said. "I think Hiro's trying to send us a message."

Jones reached over and flipped a switch on the console. A speaker crackled to life. Hiro's voice came across in a muddy kind of static. "If you can hear me, then turn to the right." Jones turned to the right, but then quickly spun left. Neil noticed he'd turned left way more than he'd turned right, changing their course yet again.

They saw Hiro follow them on the screen. "Good. I'll take that as a yes. Now, I think I have established that I can catch you and then I can sink you. But I'm assuming that you offloaded the treasure before coming near the island." Jones turned right and then farther left again.

"So, sinking you would be pleasurable, but not very helpful. Let me propose a plan where almost all of you live." Hiro seemed to consider for a moment. Neil noticed Jones slightly adjusted the course to the left again. *He must have completely turned us around from our original course by now*, Neil thought. Koko seemed to have the same thought. Neil saw her peek at the console. What was she looking at?

The pinging noise returned and Hiro's voice came back over the speakers. "No one will ever accuse me of being a cruel emperor. I will show mercy. Tell me where the treasure is and I'll let you go. Simple."

There was silence again for moment.

"Emperor of the idiots," Koko muttered.

Hiro's voice returned. "Oh, and I want you to jettison my sister out of the airlock."

Koko lowered her head, but nodded as she laid a hand on Jones's shoulder. "If he follows, he will only have himself to blame," she whispered. Then she walked over and took a tight hold of a steel pipe. Neil grabbed a hold of his chair but wasn't sure why. Were they going to go in reverse and ram Hiro's sub?

Hiro came back one last time. "You have one minute starting NOW!"

Jones's response was to look at Nakamura. "Ready?" he said.

Nakamura nodded. "Definitely." Then he pressed a button and the entire ballast tanks emptied, sending huge bubbles straight at Hiro's sub. Jones shoved the steering wheel forward quickly and the sub dove almost straight down, at top speed.

Neil peered at the console and saw what Koko had seen—the GPS. Jones had somehow turned them completely around and had taken them far out into the sea. What was he doing? Hiro was certainly going to try to sink them now and there was no way they could be rescued way out here.

"Jones, what are you doing?" Neil called. "Trying to get us killed? Hiro's going to come after us!"

Jones concentrated on keeping the wheel steady as the sub nose-dived toward the ocean floor.

"He's catching up!" Neil yelled.

Nakamura turned around. "That's what we're banking on."

Sure enough, Neil could see that the glowing orb had again caught up with them and was diving just behind them, following them closely.

"Wow!" Larry laughed. "Banking! That's what Jones was doing—banking so we'd be out over the ocean trench! Jones you great big, ugly, malicious . . . genius!"

"I could still jettison *you* out of the hatch," Jones said.

"It's funny how you only speak in complete sentences when you're delivering a threat."

"Yeah. Funny," Jones said.

"Banking?" Neil said.

Larry nodded. "We've moved out into open ocean and we're diving. The ocean floor is incredibly deep out here. Dangerously deep for—"

Hiro's voice came back over the speakers, cutting him off. "You FOOLS! You are all going to die! I'll track down everyone you know. I'll kill them all AND I'll get that treasure!"

They continued to dive and dive, lower and lower. Neil could feel the pressure building on the hull of the sub. The metal creaked and groaned. Neil's ears began to scream.

With an effort, Neil turned his head to look at the TV screen. Hiro had pulled close behind them again, the light just illuminating his crazed, screaming face. The drills must have been right next to the hull, spinning and getting ready to rip the propellers to shreds. Neil tried to step toward Isabella, to be with her when they were destroyed, but the descent was too steep.

Hiro continued to rage at them over the speakers. "You can't escape! I will get that treasure! I will kill you, Koko! I will kill you all, I will . . ."

Hiro's voice was interrupted by a loud *crack*. Neil

looked at the screen. Hiro's eyes were wide with horror. A giant crack appeared in the screen, but it wasn't the TV, it was the window of Hiro's cockpit. Neil could see bubbles starting to escape from the cockpit, and then the crack grew suddenly larger.

Hiro immediately pulled back on his descent, but it was too late. The glass shattered. Hiro's sub flew off into the darkness, spinning and quickly disappearing. "Ahhhhhh . . ."

Jones reached over and flicked off the speaker, then pulled back on the wheel. The sub began to rise, slowly toward the surface of the ocean. The sub stopped creaking.

No one said anything for a long time.

Koko finally let go of the pipes and slid down the wall to the floor. She sat there looking completely exhausted. "He was such a fool," she said. "But he was my brother." She gave a deep sigh.

Jones stared at the window, the last bubbles from Hiro's sub rising up beside them. "I'd seen a tiny nick when the treasure crashed into the sub's window. I knew it wouldn't hold if we dove deep enough."

Larry made his way over to Koko and hugged her. Then he sat down next to her and, for once, didn't say a thing.

Nakamura turned around. "We should be able to surface soon. We'll give Aki a call and figure out a rendezvous point. Then we'll notify the coast guard and tell them where to search for Hiro's sub."

Jones turned the wheel to his right and the sub made its gradual way back toward Tokyo. "I hope for your sake that Isabella didn't move a single inch in her bunk," Jones said, turning to look at Neil.

"Another compete sentence," Larry said. "I'd get moving, Neil."

Neil nodded, backing away from Jones and out of the room. Then he went back and checked on Isabella. She was groggy, but awake.

"What happened?" she asked. "Are we safe?"

Neil nodded. Then he sat down next to her, took her hand, and kissed it.

He heard a loud whistle and remembered that Koko had been making tea. Could that conversation really have been just a few minutes ago? Neil felt like he'd aged ten years. He took a look into the kitchen. The teakettle was bolted to the counter and hadn't spilled a drop in the battle with Hiro. *Nori does have every gadget in the world*, Neil thought.

"Would you like a cup of tea?" he asked Isabella. He untied the restraints.

Isabella nodded and sat up on her bunk. "Maybe everyone would like some?" she said softly. Her voice still sounded like music to Neil.

"I'll go ask," he said.

Neil walked to the bridge. "The water is boiling. Who could use a cup of tea?"

"I could," they all answered.

Koko got to her feet. "You know what? I'll make it," she said.

Larry stood up. "I'll help," he said.

As they walked past Neil into the kitchen, Larry whispered to him. "Do you happen to know if Nori keeps any coffee on this boat?"

Neil thought back to the last crazy few days. "I'm sure he does, but I'd be *very* careful opening the container."

Larry looked confused. "Um, cool . . . I'll take your word for it."

"You won't regret it," Neil said.

"Oh, one other thing," Larry said, popping his head back through the doorway.

"What?"

"I think Isabella hurt her lips during our dive back there. You better go take care of that. You won't regret it." Then he winked and disappeared.

Epilogue

Neil stared at the gleaming stainless steel counters. They were so clean they sparkled. "Thank you, Angel," he said to the empty room. The kitchen, *his* kitchen, had rarely looked better. Angel and Gary had done an amazing job filling in, and the customers had been very happy.

Of course, the wait list for reservations grew a lot longer once word leaked that Neil Flambé was back behind the stove.

Zoe did point out, however, that the customers weren't told it was Angel pinch-cooking for Neil. "If they had, the reservation list might actually be getting *shorter* with you back." Neil merely nodded his agreement.

Neil took a long sniff. The wonderful aroma of the glorious seafood Gary and Angel had been cooking still lingered in the kitchen. Neil smiled. "Oh, if only," he said wistfully and then walked over to the fridge. "Time to get back to some serious red meat," he said, grabbing an entire tray of organic Kobe beef steaks. He laid them out on the counter to warm.

Larry had made a personal request. For his return he wanted an entire week of seafood-free cooking. "If I never smell seafood again, it will be too soon," he'd said. "If you cook one salmon this whole week I'm booking a flight back to Kokyo—I mean Tokyo!"

Koko had held another funeral for her brother, a real one this time. Neil and the others had stayed behind to help her say good-bye. She'd given them all a generous portion of the treasure—well, not the treasure, exactly, but some of the fee she'd received from the Tokyo National Museum for the ancient scrolls, boxes, and coins.

At the airport, Larry had suddenly asked her to come to Vancouver with them. Neil had been a little surprised that his cousin had shown such . . . commitment. "Yeah, well, I probably should have been committed years ago."

Koko had hugged him and said she would see him soon. "The people at the museum are planning an exhibition," Koko explained. "I'm sure it will travel to many countries and I will travel with it. I have always wanted to see more of the world. I will see you when we come to Vancouver."

Then she'd waved good-bye to everyone, sending a cherry-scented breeze toward them as they stood in the security lineup.

They'd all sighed. Well, Jones, Larry, Nakamura, and Neil had, anyway. Isabella didn't smile until Koko was out of sight.

"I am going to miss those eyes." Larry sighed.

Neil had nodded. Luckily, he'd been standing next to Isabella's injured shoulder and she'd been unable to give him a proper shot in the ribs. Then they'd all flown home.

Things had actually wrapped up nicely, for once, Neil thought. Nakamura had talked to his friends in the military police. It turned out the military had been on to the general for some time and they agreed to waive Gary's AWOL charges in exchange for any evidence he could give them.

Neil even agreed to keep Gary on, part-time. He would join them after Larry gave them permission to serve seafood again. Neil wasn't being totally altruistic— Gary brought in the best fish Neil had ever been able to get. Gary had said that he was actually happy with the part-time arrangement.

"I miss the risky exciting life of a street-riding bike courier. Dodging traffic is a kind of a kick, you know?"

"I know a lunatic who sets up duels you might want to judge sometime," Neil had said.

"Hey, I'm up for almost anything!" Gary had said.

"Exactly," Neil had said with a smile.

Neil was shaken from the memory by the *ping* of his cell phone. He pulled it out of his back pocket and saw that he'd received an e-mail from Kong. Kong had left Japan and had taken his skills to a new city, New York City, in fact. The e-mail was titled "An Invitation" and Neil groaned when he opened it. "Another haiku."

> BIG APPLE, LOVE PIE
> YOU MUST COME AND VISIT SOON
> KONG'S AT EMPIRE STATE
> (PS: SORRY FOR HAIKU. THOUGHT IT MIGHT
> BRING SMILE. SEE YOU SOON.)

"Sorry, Big guy. Not likely," Neil said, putting the phone back. "I've got too much to do. Homework and work work."

What Neil really wanted—and needed—was a nice long uninterrupted break. He needed to lose himself in the kitchen again, find his groove, get his life back. No more crimes, international intrigue, or crazy wannabe royalty. Just cooking.

Well, cooking and school. Neil's parents were thrilled that their nephew was alive, and Neil had hoped this would end their attempt to use the restaurant as leverage. It had been a vain hope.

"Nice try," his dad had said. "But we're still your guardians and we expect better grades. . . . ANY grades would actually be nice."

A tutor was going to come by after school each day. Neil agreed to listen to the lessons while he was prepping—but NOT while he was cooking. Neil's parents had even agreed to pay the tutor extra to let Neil dictate his essays to him. It wasn't a great situation, but it was better than nothing. Besides, Neil thought, if he was lucky, his parents would hire a tutor who could be bribed with dry-rub ribs and roasted vegetables.

Neil took a deep, satisfied sigh.

Finally, Neil thought. *Things are back to normal. Time for some peace and quiet.*

BAM!

Neil jumped as Larry stormed through the back door. "Have I got news for YOU!" Larry yelled. He was carrying an ancient-looking crate.

"Or back to *ab*normal," Neil said.

"I'm fab what?"

"Skip it," Neil said, willing his heartbeat to slow down.

Larry walked over to Neil and saw the tray of steaks on the counter. "Finally, REAL FOOD! Boy, it's good to be home. Mom and Dad will be happy!" Larry and his parents had shared a tear-filled reunion at the airport. ("And for once, Dad's not lecturing me to get a real job," Larry had whispered to Neil as his dad wrapped up his fifteen-minute hug at the arrivals gate.)

"I've made sure Amber and Zoe save them the best table for dinner tonight," Neil said.

Larry beamed but his eyes quickly welled up with tears.

"Everything okay?" Neil asked.

Larry wasn't crying over his parents. He had spied his coffeemaker in the corner. "My one true love!"

he said, running over to hug and plug in the machine. He wiped a tear from his eye. "I didn't know I'd missed you so much!"

Neil groaned. Then he remembered that Larry had arrived with news. "Larry, what's in the box?"

"Oh, yeah. Well, remember my friend Penny, the one from Liverpool?"

"The one with the tattoo of the queen on her arm?"

"That's the one. Her dad is a bigwig, like royalty."

"So?" Neil asked nervously. Even the mention of "royalty" had his sensors on high alert right now.

"He's coming to town next week." Larry busied himself with the coffeemaker but didn't add any more explanation.

Neil watched him for a minute and then spoke. "Larry, I can't help feeling that there are some gaps in your story."

"Oh, yeah, the box. Lord Lane is really into gourmet food, especially preserves. He has this amazing collection of antique ingredients. Wine bottles from shipwrecks, that sort of thing. Some of it is hundreds of years old."

"So the box is full of wine bottles?"

"Um, no. It's full of bottles, but the bottles are filled with honey."

"Honey?"

"Yeah. Penny's dad owns a lot of really old buildings. They were getting ready to wreck this warehouse or factory or something from the Victorian era. Anyway, they smashed down a wall and found this old hidden room. It was filled with bottles of honey! It's a real mystery."

Neil felt his danger radar kicking into even higher gear. He had a sneaking suspicion that this was going to be leading to someplace he really *really* didn't want to go.

"Okay, this is an amazing story, but I've got to get back to work cooking your steaks." Neil quickly turned back to the counter and busied himself peeling garlic cloves.

"Yeah, but you haven't asked why I have a crate of the honey!" Larry said.

With a sense of foreboding, Neil closed his eyes and asked, "Does this have anything to do with *me?*"

"Of course! He wants us to cook a meal using this honey. He's going to pay us a lot!"

Neil relaxed. Cooking. That was something he could handle. "Next week?"

"Yeah, on Monday when we're usually closed. And don't worry, I'll help you with your homework that day," Larry said. Neil could hear him prying the lid off the box. Neil's radar started going off again.

"Boy, this honey is beautiful!" Neil looked over and Larry was holding the bottles up to the light. For some reason, Neil held his breath as Larry pulled them out one by one, gazing at each. Neil agreed, they were beautiful and he couldn't wait to break the wax seal and see what one-hundred-year-old honey tasted and smelled like.

"Hey, this last bottle is a little weird," Larry said, pulling it out. He held it up to the light.

Neil closed his eyes. "Please don't say there's a note hidden inside, please don't say—"

"Hey!" Larry called. "Waddya know. There's a note hidden inside! I can only make out the first word; it's kind of all rolled up in there."

Neil reached for a frying pan.

"It says *H-E-L-P*. Hey, that spells 'help'!"

Neil sat down and began to smack his head slowly with the pan.

Acknowledgments

This book has a special nod to my mum, who started studying Mishima when I was about twelve. Growing up in a small town, this problematic, mesmerizing guy blew my mind and started a lifelong interest in all things Japanese. Mum, you rock! (You too, Dad!)

I have to thank the old WUTV Channel 29 in Buffalo. My brothers and I grew up watching Godzilla trash Tokyo, fight Rodan, Megalon. I had an old metal hamper that sounded just like Godzilla's roar if you opened the lid just right, and the memory still sends chills down my spine.

Doug and Mike and later Tim have always been there for all the fun stuff. Mike's still watching with us up in heaven (the great Toho studio in the sky!)

We even started a letter-writing campaign when Channel 29 changed its programming and dropped Ultraman. NOOOOOOOOO! Our repeated pleas, sent with different signatures and from different addresses, failed to move the powers that were . . . sigh.

The people of Japan have put up with incredible struggles and challenges, yet they continue to create some of the most amazing art, culture, music, and food in the world. *Domo arigato*.

And to all the musicians who keep me happy as I work and rework these stories in my attic studio—Coeur de Pirate, Joel Plaskett, Juston Rutledge and especially Rich Stirfry, I mean Terfry, and the rest of the crew on CBC Radio 2—*MERCI!*

Last and never least, Emily my music bud, Erin the horrible and Lolo. Love and tempura. . . .

Kevin Sylvester

is an award-winning writer, illustrator, and broadcaster. *Neil Flambé and the Marco Polo Murders* won the 2011 Silver Birch Award for Fiction. Kevin was particularly pleased by this because the kids vote! *Neil Flambé and the Aztec Abduction* was the runner-up in 2012. His other books include *Gold Medal for Weird* (Silver Birch winner in 2009!), *Sports Hall of Weird*, *Splinters*, and *Game Day*. He spends most of his time sitting in his attic studio, drawing and writing and listening to Neil and Larry arguing over, well, everything. He also loves to cook.